BEST BLACK GAY EROTICA

BEST BLACK GAY EROTICA

Edited by

Darieck Scott

Published in the United States by Cleis Press Inc.,
P.O. Box 14697, San Francisco, California 94114.
Printed in the United States.
Cover design: Scott Idleman
Cover photograph: Photodisc
Text design: Frank Wiedemann
Logo art: Juana Alicia
First Edition.
10 9 8 7 6 5 4 3 2 1

TABLE OF CONTENTS

Acknowledgments

I would like to thank all the writers/artists who contributed their work to this anthology. Warms thanks to Don Weise for conceiving the project and shepherding it from afar. Thanks also to Ty Blair for assistance and wisdom, and to Robert Reid-Pharr for making this fun for me. And, as always, my profuse gratitude to Stephen Liacouras for boundless love and support.

This collection is dedicated to my sister Dionne, with whom I can talk about everything: the greatest gift. And to Ciro, Adib, Cameron, Luis, Thomas, Dino, Dean, et al. for inspiration.

Introduction: Black Gay Pornotopias or, When We Were Sluts

One of my favorite black gay fictional characters is the euphoniously named Billy Biasse, a gambling house owner in Claude McKay's rambunctious 1928 novel *Home to Harlem.* Biasse is nicknamed the Wolf because "he eats his own kind," and with a suitably lupine air of predatory glee he prowls the edges and the underbelly of the novel's black demimonde. A marginal presence in a world of marginalized characters, Billy the Wolf nevertheless lives large: While one character bemoans the fact that "Life ain't no country picnic with sweet flute and fiddle" as in Sunday school tales and "the sweet snooziness" of storybooks, Billy declares, "Ise a wolf all right, but I ain't a lone one... I guess Ise the happiest, well-feddest wolf in Harlem...!"

Let Billy Biasse the Wolf serve as the emblem for the rich feast of erotic imagination, the abundance at the outer rim of literature's pornographic edge, to be found here in *Best Black Gay Erotica.* Amid the profusion of erotica collections and revivals and faux-revivals of erotica classics that have earned a separate section of their own in your neighborhood multiplex bookstore, the celebration of sexual fantasies centrally involving black characters has been rather slow to materialize. We do now have, to join the compendious *Erotique Noire/Black Erotica,* which planted the early seed, such excellent collections as *Black Silk*, *Brown Sugar*, and *After Hours*, as well as Zane's various publications and a few others—but, not surprisingly, stories in which black gay men (or black MSM) are hotly desiring subjects and/or panted-after objects of desire probably occupy an even lower percentage among these black erotica works than black erotica occupies of erotica publications as a whole. The reasons for the low rates of appearance of both black erotica and black gay erotica are myriad—assuredly the publishing industry's myopia (*i.e.*, conscious or unconscious racism and heterosexism) is chief among them—but, tendentiously, I'll elaborate upon just one reason here, which has to do with the disturbance brought on by public attention to and consumption of the African American sexuality as image or idea. We might think, in this vein, of such '90s obsessions as Anita and Clarence and O.J.; and today, of Kobe, and Janet's bared breast. And though this is not the place to adduce a history of the cultural representation of black sexuality (for one such account, see Cleis Press's Lambda Award-winning *Black Like Us*), we might think of how post-Reconstruction white supremacist manipulations of the myth of the black male rapist and the black female wanton seemed to necessitate an adoption of strict Victorian prudishness on the part of African American artists and intellectuals, which then gave way to a mostly white reading public's primitivist hunger for depictions of black sexuality as the authentic antidote to the perceived bankruptcy of Western traditions during the period of the Harlem Renaissance. This then gave way to the repackaging and clever deployment of the black male rapist as a political threat and weapon (often with a misogynist and homophobic serrated blade) during the period of the Black Power and Black Arts Movements, which then—you get the picture. Suffice it to be said that on this deeply scarred discursive field of battle, the arrival of literary or semi-literary troops openly marching under the banner of a black sexuality already deemed brazen and dangerous—and likely to look all the more so when that sexuality is vociferously not heterosexual—puts the established armies in a posture of momentary disarray, or at the very least makes all assembled come to a standstill in flummoxed embarrassment.

The history of the different ways representations of black sexuality have been deployed as a cultural weapon does, like it or not, impart to collections such as these a frisson of the political, however modestly conceived with the goals of making money and making readers jack off they may be. It seems useful to briefly resurrect at this moment the assertion of our late fathers/brothers Essex Hemphill, Marlon Riggs, and Joseph Beam that "black men loving black men" is a revolutionary act—an assertion that at its simplest level may seem quaint now, even disproved, but that nevertheless suggests in its vision connections between desire, sex, intimacy, community, and justice that have not yet been thoroughly explored, or seriously taken up. I cannot claim—I will disclaim—that there is anything about this collection that should be construed as "revolutionary." But it is my intuition that these jack-off stories begin to hint at the ways that pleasure is or can be political—even if the politics aren't "correct" and maybe aren't recognizable in standard understandings of the political—and how pleasure can be found in circumstances politically defined as limited, disempowering, even degrading. In this way these stories form a tributary to a current I see running through the contemporary black gay literary enterprise (and arguably through African American literature as a whole), which, from James Baldwin to Essex and Randall Kenan, asks questions about the relationship between sex and spirituality, between sexual pleasure and the possibility of freedom. They illuminate, in ways sometimes distinctly and sometimes just minutely different from other stripes of erotica, sexuality, and sexual desire's protean quality, the way it ubiquitously flexes its tentacles throughout our concepts and our lived realities of family, community, gender roles, work, money, morality—many, if not all, of the things we need to address to achieve freedom.

Several of these stories—Thomas Glave's sensuously lyrical "The Blue Globes," James Earl Hardy's classic romantic fantasy "B-Boy Blues," Red Jordan Arobateau's '70s tale of ghetto lust "Where the Word Is No," Christopher David's broken-hearted story "Kevin," and Tip Langley's Noel Cowardesque "The Passion"—take as the setting for their pornotopias (a term Samuel R. Delany uses to speak of the imaginary space where all interactions between people are potentially sexual) various corners of the down-low world. (Brothers on the down-low, for those few who might not yet know, do not identify as gay or bisexual, are often involved in romantic and sexual relationships with women, and pursue clandestine sexual liaisons with men.) DL as social and sexual practice has somewhat deservedly acquired a bad reputation, and is the target now of AIDS prevention campaigns that have identified it as a source of the spread of HIV in African American communities. While it seems to me that the identification of this vector for the spread of the pandemic is a vitally important move, blaming DL—all too familiarly—confuses the problem as a question of moral lapse (he's lying to his girlfriend/wife, *and* spreading disease), when the rock-bottom issue is the lack of use of condoms. Glave, Hardy, Arobateau, et al., in the depiction and elaboration of their characters' hunger for sexual release and connection, bring a perspective to DL—eroticizing it—that renders it an object of intense imagination, and therefore of potential understanding. If they distort the phenomenon in one way by emphasizing the allure and appeal of secret sex, they revealingly illuminate it in another by casting aside the distortions of so-called morality.

To me, in their common interest in suborning, seducing, and indeed celebrating in the form of their ardently declared desire the B-boys, the gorgeous thugs, and the conservatively religious, in their forays through the subterranean grottoes of the down-low world, these pieces demonstrate a playful willingness to locate and describe the ways that pleasure asserts its tumultuous demand despite and *because of* the very forces of AIDS, violence, political failure, and the blindness wrought by religious fundamentalism that continually threaten to devastate black communities.

A similar interest in the restlessness and unrealized potential of the force that is erotic/sexual desire, the *fierceness* of eros, pervades the pieces that investigate in new and intelligent ways terrain more familiar in the universe of gay male imagination—bars and sex clubs—such as Delany's "The Sleepwalkers," Robert F. Reid-Pharr's "Horse Philosophy," and Giovanni's "The Pain Seeker." While Reid-Pharr explicitly raises the question of the relation of pleasure to revolution, Delany's story is an excerpt from a longer work, *The Mad Man*, that provides one of the most compelling and evocative considerations ever to appear in American literature of how to think through, experience pleasure in, and reconceive our relation to the histories of enslavement and racial subjugation of which all of us in the Americas (at least) are inheritors.

These pieces are sexy, they're often funny, and they're occasionally healing. But they are not so much an escape from the world as a momentary rearrangement or reframing of it—not unlike the euphoric disorientation of the orgasmic moment and those states of agitation and satiety immediately prior and post.

A line from *The Mad Man* that is Delany's reworking of the Beam-Hemphill-Riggs line I piously invoked earlier provides an apt conclusion to these ruminations—"a nigger pissin' on a nigger [...] A fuckin' revolutionary act!" (you'll understand once you've read "The Sleepwalkers"). Delany's act of signifying—an act of high mockery and high praise—helps ground us back in material reality: at their best, these are jack-off stories.

For those of you who, like me, only take a look at these erotica intros in order to see which stories you should read first, here, in no particular order, is the quick-and-dirty sex précis: "The Blue Globes"—worship of a heavenly ass; "B-Boy Blues"—sexy B-boy makes new conquest beg for it; "Photographic Memory"—thuggish lovelies lovingly photographed by exploitative photographer; "One for the Road"—huge and delicious dick overcomes narrator's resistance to taking it up the ass; "The Sleepwalkers"—Wet Night at the local gay bar; "The Pain Seeker"—high school boy's initiation into S/M club; "Miracle 5"—hot blow jobs demanded in high school reminiscence and in the janitor's closet of a movie theater; "Some People Wear Green"—a hooker with a cherry ass loses it in France to a transsexual and flirts with a "straight" boy; "Rude Boys"—chaotic sex party in the UK with an African prince; "The Gift"—a dying man receives the erotic help of a loving friend; "Horse Philosophy"—surprising sex club encounters; "Kevin"—an affair with a soon-to-be married man; "Where the Word Is No"—young hottie thinks he likes women, dreams of dick; "The Passion"—evangelical Christian seduced; "Stank"—smelly athlete dominates his college roommate. In addition, you'll find a couple of cartoon fantasies by the ever-magnificent Belasco.

Feast and, like Billy the Wolf, emerge from these pages well-fed.

Darieck Scott
San Francisco
October 2004

from *B-Boy Blues*

James Earl Hardy

As Sade sings, it's never as good as the first time.

To be honest, the only thing that made the first time different from any of the other sexcapades Raheim and I had is that it was just that—the first. But, there were other, important firsts that occurred that night (which we will get to later).

After six whole days of aching, craving, wishing I had him in my bed, I had him—and I couldn't control myself. I was overwhelmed, overjoyed, overwrought, just over him. My hands, lips, tongue, and teeth explored his terrain with a vengeance, leaving no nook or cranny, corner or crevice unconquered.

So, what did he smell like?

When I (finally) asked him what he was wearing as I inhaled him, he said, "I don' wear nothin'." Yup, that's just the way he smells. And the aroma is indescribably infectious. Everyone has their own body odor, and, unfortunately for some, being Sure ain't enough to suppress it. But one whiff of Raheim and my nose was opened. His scent permeated my nostrils and made me tingle all over. And it just made me want him more.

And what did he feel like?

While his physique was as solid as a rock, it was also as smooth as a baby's bottom. His clear skin didn't have a bruise, a blemish, or a blotch anywhere—not even on his big pretty feet. And the only cuts to be found were those that defined his manly muscle legs, manly muscle thighs, manly muscle arms, manly muscle hands, manly muscle abs, manly muscle chest, and manly muscle back. Uh-huh, a brick...*howse.* I had a field day giving him a massage—rubbing, prodding, and knuckling as he called, "Ooooh, Baby, yeah..."

And, what did he taste like?

Well, let's say that I finally knew what the folks meant by "the blacker the berry, the sweeter the juice." He was the flavor of, not a Hershey's bar, but a Häagen-Dazs dark-Belgian-chocolate-on-chocolate ice cream bar. (Now *that's* sweet!) He was finger-lickin' good. All natural—no additives or preservatives—*mocha chocolate ya ya.* And there was no need for dessert toppings, not even whipped cream or a cherry (although we did experiment later on), because he was, as Michelle surmised, a full-course meal plus the entire dessert tray—and did I chow down!

I had to be feasting on him for an hour when he pleaded with me to stop (I assumed he couldn't take the inspection anymore, which he did pass with flying colors). But then he pushed my head toward the one thing I was saving for last. I hadn't really gotten a good gander of it until then, and, when I saw it in all its glory, I *gagged.* His shoe size was a great indicator. No doubt thanks to my navigation, he was as long as a Charleston Chew and thick as a cucumber. It looked so yummy, I had to bite.

And it was just like M&Ms: It melted in my mouth, not in my hands.

As I licked him like a Charms lollipop, he begged me to swallow him. ("*No,* Baby, don' fuckin' *teeze* me...*suck it!"*)

And, when I did, he begged me to stop ("*No, Baby, no...*").

And, when I went all the way down on him, my nose tickled by his neatly shaved and succulent-smelling pubic hair, he began trembling uncontrollably, his teeth chattering as if he were caught in the cold, snorting and stammering like Porky Pig.

I knew he couldn't take any more when he threw me off of him (I wouldn't let go—I was greedy, what can I say?), screaming something that sounded like Pig Latin. And then he came.

And came.

And came.

I swear to God, he must have been shootin' for a good minute and a half. And I mean shootin'. Yeah, he's got a loaded weapon, an Uzi if you will, and, if you tug it the right way, it'll getcha.

And he did get me. I couldn't get out of his path. He managed to christen the comforter on the bed and my dresser drawer, which was at least three feet away from the bed. Almost all of this happened without his hand's help. That dick had a mind of its own.

I picked up the towel I had left on the night table earlier that evening and wiped him, the dresser, and the bed up. When I thought the coast was clear, I climbed in between his raised legs and lay on top of him. I kissed his face as his body continued to jerk.

"Oh, Bay-bee," he moaned, folding me in his big, strong arms. He was still shaking. His eyes were still closed.

"Yes?" I asked, getting comfortable.

"That was *so* good...I ain't neva cum like that..."

I had heard that one before, but I bought it this time. (How could I not? It was the first time I had ever seen anyone cum like that). He slobbered a kiss on my forehead. I was too happy with myself.

We took a little nap. It seemed like the natural thing to do.

We slumbered for only maybe fifteen minutes, but it seemed like hours. I didn't feel him get up. I was awakened by a familiar feeling between the cheeks below my waist.

"I wanna fuck you..." He was on top of me. He already had my legs spread.

"You do?" I asked, being rather coy.

"Hell yeah, Baby, you know I do," he exclaimed, his arms slipping under mine, locking me in that position, and poking me with his sweet sticky thing. He opened his left fist to reveal a Zulu. "An' ya know ya wan me to..."

Yeah, I knew I did. But, he was a big boy. We're talkin' *big*. Sucking that chocolate joystick was one thing; being invaded by it, I knew, would be quite a different experience. I didn't think I could take it. And the idea that he might break me in two was a big possibility. He sensed my uneasiness.

"Wha's up?" he said, somewhat concerned.

"You ain't got tha package...?" He started to ease off of me.

"No," I protested, pulling him back. "Package" is what they call AIDS on the street. "It's just that I...well...I haven't done it in a while..."

He rolled off me and onto his left side. "How long?"

I sat up on my right side. "Like six months."

"Six months? *Day-am!* I ain't neva gone that long...six days, maybe..." He paused. "So, wha'cha sayin'?" By the look on his face, I knew he thought I was going to say no.

"Yeah, I do want to do it," I said brushing his chest. "I just want you to be patient with me, that's all."

"No prob," he shrugged. "I ain't gonna hurt ya. If I do, tell me, a'right?"

"OK. But I am pretty tight."

"Ooooh, I *like* that," he grinned, pushing me on my back. "But we can get ya a little loose."

And did he ever. It was then that I knew those thick lips, which were so incredibly cotton-ball soft, weren't meant just for kissing mine. He nuzzled my neck, nibbled on my ears, grazed the arch of my back, sucked my hard nipples, grooved across my torso, searched the insides of my thighs, trailed my spine, puckered my belly button, and, the thing that really had me going, parted my cheeks, making this baby's back go whack! He enjoyed this too, saying between blows, licks, and slurps, "Shit, Baby, you so fuckin' tay-stee..."

What made all of this even more mind-boggling was that I didn't expect him to do any of it. I mean, B-boys ain't exactly known for being giving. They usually like to be taken care of. Serviced. Sexed. My experiences with Royal and Ricky convinced me of this. But, of course, I had a lot to learn.

It all made me squeal and shriek with pleasure—and beg for it. "Oh, Raheim, fuck me...please fuck me..."

"Ya sure, Baby?" he anticipated. We were right back in the position we started in.

"Yes...," I sang, throwing it at him.

His expression reminded me of how I looked when I was about to bust Ricky's cherry.

He positioned me in the middle of the bed and turned me on my back. He pushed my legs up and out. I tried to relax as he continued opening me up, this time using his long, thick, left middle finger. I was prepared for pain, but it didn't hurt at all.

I watched as he put the condom on himself in ten seconds flat.

"A'right, Baby, help me," he said. He proceeded to enter me, slowly. I braced myself again but was shocked when, a couple of minutes later, he moaned: "Ah yeah, Baby, I'm all in."

I couldn't believe it. "*What?* You, you're kidding?"

"Nah," he assured me. "An' you feel *so* fuckin' good."

I held on to his shoulders and relaxed as he began to expand, sliding in and out of me. He grew larger and larger *and larger*, and with each thrust, our groans and grunts came together, each set louder than the ones before. I *loved* it.

"Oh yes, Raheim...fill me the fuck up...," I cooed.

"Aw yeah, Bay-bee... Le'me get all up in dat bad boy... Ya like it, hunh?"

"Mmmmm-hmmmm..."

"Uh-huh...," he giggled.

He grabbed me around the waist and lifted me, so that we were sitting up. It is then that I *really* felt it. It all took me by surprise.

"Oh, Raheim!" I cried, not exactly in pain but flustered by the friction.

"Cool out, Baby, chill now...jus' work it..."

After a little maneuvering, I found the right spot—and the feeling it gave me was unlike any I ever had before. I lost all control and started to, as he advised, work it. I gyrated my hips, up and down, left to right, using reflexes and muscles I never knew I had. I locked my legs around his waist and my arms around his neck. I licked his face and his bald head. He *loved* it.

"Yeah! Work dat dick, Baby... Day-am you so fuckin' wicked...," he strained. He started whacking me on the ass. That really turned me the fuck on.

"Sssss," I hissed. "Ooooh, whip it on me, Raheim, yeah..."

"Uh-huh, Baby, I'm gon' whip dat shit... I'm gon' rock yo' ass..."

We tumbled back down. He drove his fists into the bed and proceeded to rock me, bumping and banging, grinding and galloping. I pulled my legs all the way back 'til they touched the bed. I grabbed a meaty handful of his ass, pushing him in deeper, *deeper*, inviting him to go where no man had gone before. We smacked between our sighs and cries of satisfaction.

"Uh-huh, Bay-bee, take dat dick!"

"Oh yes, Raheim..."

"Ha, ya want it, don'cha Baby?"

"Yeeeeaaaah! I want it, I want it!"

"Oh yeah, Bay-bee...ya wan' me to take it, hunh?"

"Take it, Raheim, take it, yeah!"

"Ha, don' worry, cuz I'm gon' take it...ya jus' gotta give it up...now, give dat shit *up!*"

I did.

The scene was reminiscent of *The Exorcist*. Our faces were distorted, our eyes retreating to the backs of our heads. Our words were unintelligible, our hollering horrifying. Our breathing was so hot it was like fire. The headboard of the bed was drumming its own beat on the wall. The lamp on the dresser next to the bed fell to the floor. I could feel my blood pumping through me like raging waters out of control. I saw that his was, too; his veins were bulging through his skin. My body was twisting as if I were possessed. I clawed his back, digging my nails into his skin. Uh-huh, I was Linda Blair.

But when it was all over, he growled like a tiger; I purred and scowled like Eartha Kitt.

And then we came. And came. And came.

And with all that cummin' came a couple of other firsts: being fucked so good, so right, that it alone made me climax. And, what's more, we reached it together. And it certainly wouldn't be the last time with Raheim.

I was the one having convulsions now. Not even Raheim's sweaty weight, pressed against me as he went through his own spasms, could hold me down. It was a good five minutes before I actually came down.

We were still for some time, just stirring. He then climbed off of me and out of bed without a word. I watched his big beautiful body strut out the door. The bathroom door hit the towel rack behind it. He took a leak.

I sat up and reached for the lamp, which I then remembered was on the floor, and just clapped my hands twice as the room light came on (that "clapper" gadget is a miracle). I wiped myself off, threw the comforter off the bed, and sat up. After the toilet flushed, I knew he was going to come back to the bedroom, throw on his clothes, tell me how he had such a great time, and that he'd call me (and, of course, they never do). He appeared in the doorway.

"Day-am, why ya turn on tha light, Baby?" He hit the wall switch off.

I didn't even have the chance to respond: He pounced like a panther, tickling me. When he finished, I was lying on top of him. He started spanking me.

"Stop!" I yelled.

"Huh, ya know ya like that shit, you freak," he said with glee. "Yo' ass is so fuckin' good. I'm gon' have some mo' when I wake up tomorrow."

When he wakes up...*tomorrow?* He was staying!

"Well, don't you want to get under the covers?" I asked, grinning and reaching to pull down the sheets.

"Nah," he mumbled. "'They jus' get in tha way."

No argument from me. He spread out, his hands clasped behind his head and his feet touching the corners of the bed. I placed my legs parallel to his thighs. I rested my hands on his shoulders and was about to lay my head on his chest when...

"Yo, ain'cha gonna kiss me g'nite?"

I smiled. I did.

Which brings us to the last first of that night: I went to sleep with a smile on my face.

Wouldn't you?

from *Where the Word Is No*

Red Jordan Arobateau

In the back of his mind was the chirping of mice. He reached out and touched the bedpost, as he groped his way in by the deep red light. "Would you like to see my pictures?" Mr. Lee smiled a Cheshire cat's grin, which made his chin double. A warm summery night seemed to float in from the radiator. Cozily steaming on its silver stand. You could hardly see in the red light. When he made contact with the room, he saw a tiny place, taken up by a bed spread with purple satin sheets which were washed clean but had hidden stains of cum shots from years of heavy loads of a processional of Lee's male trade. One dusty window draped, blocked the view of the street. Where outside, hustlers were on their hustle; and a streetlamp shone faintly thru the fabric. The red lights made the pictures more pornographic. Buttholes being pummeled by rigid dicks, being fucked. These pictures sent a warm glow rushing thru the boy. The red lights made the pictures even more pornographic. The inside flesh of mouths so wide open, like fish gulping for water, hungry for a hard rod to suck until its jism spurted out like raw nectar. Round male buttocks enticing, poised, butthole red-hot, ready to be fucked. He squinted over the pictures. It was hard to see.

Mr. Lee lived in the ghetto. Being childless, he had enough money to live in a better part of town; the paycheck at the warehouse where he worked was sufficient. But he chose to live here, in the worst part of the ghetto. The lowest class of the mold-race poverty class of black, brown and white people who had been climbing up the economic ladder slowly. A mass surely, slowly, straggling upward over the pain of four centuries. And his apartment here, expensive enough...neat, but even on his back porch was the chirping of mice. It was nibbling away at his mind.

Jesse heard the mice; it frightened him. In his hotel, mice had eaten a baby alive. Its face, a ruined nose, and completely eaten lips—a monstrosity. The child was still living, but had died a day later in the hospital. The vermin had attacked its windpipe, bitten thru the throat. Jess heard the chirping of mice all night long in the same room where he slept. Now, here they were, right outside of Mr. Lee's back porch, gnawing with their long yellow teeth, but he hated to mention it. He hated to ruin his comfort.

Jazz flooded the room, from the radio on his bedside stand. It made the gnawing almost imperceptible now, but his control on the scene began to explode now, in another way, as Mr. Lee began to ask for what he wanted—by showing his box of dirty pictures. Crude drawings done by a degenerate felon, another acquaintance of Mr. Lee's he'd met sailing thru the nights; art cultivated in the boredom of doing time behind jail bars. Drawings of males depicted as nude horses galloping with their big dicks in their fists like sausages. Galloping men, waving their nude meat flesh in their fists; muscles jam-packed under taut skin. Big balloon dicks. Heavy balls strained with the pressure of needing to fuck. Lee's favorite was a hand-drawn three-way between men with sailor caps, sailor shirts over muscular chests, sailor boots, and no pants. Huge organs. Rigid dicks standing up from dangling plump balls. Mr. Lee had reproduced this particular drawing by Xerox, and had hung it throughout his house—in the bedroom, bath, kitchen, spare bedroom, living room. It proved a bright-eyed conversation piece—when the mind needed stimulation. It even encouraged him thru the wake-up hours of the roaming before work.

Jesse was fast getting hip to Lee's conversation: that the man wasn't going to let him get off so easy. At first, to preserve his manhood, Jesse had scowled, interrupted Lee's sentence—changed the subject. But now the youth realized he had no choice but to admit the proposition, and deal with it with a flat NO.

The dim red room held its two occupants. One tittering as he rummaged thru his pornographic stash; eyeliner enhancing his eyes; close-cropped head pronouncing the artistic lines of his skull. Puppetlike, the two played on the edge of the bed. Words & ideas. Hands gesticulating in air emphasized cock size and described scenes from times gone by. The walls closed around them, wallpaper of a decade past. The bed had originally folded out of the wall. Lee had substituted for it one with bronze rails & posts. Decked out in velvet. Satin sheets. And he kept it that way. Secured to the floor. His clothes, suits, a row of men's shoes sat in the closet nearby. Otherwise, the room was bare. An alarm clock—the type you wound up by hand—ticked silently, under the drone of the radio. The worn carpet under the two men's feet.

They continued flipping thru the pictures. Sometimes Jesse admitted that the sight of a man's rigid cock turned him on; a hard dick going in & out of a hole—or being jacked off by a fist like a piston pumping. Sometimes man-sex turned him on, at least it did in private, thumbing thru Lee's collection of gay male erotica. Uneasy, Jesse sat beside this live human fairy on the bed next to him, while looking at a fantasy form of a naked male upon these stained satin sheets in a photograph from the past which Lee had taken of a young stud about Jesse's own age. Secretly, Jesse observed the older man; hairy legs spread, no cunthole, but a bunghole which could be entered; and a dick—the same instrument of aggression as his own. It was confusing. Screwing a male in the ass. And the oral stuff. Thinking about this man giving him some head—it sent hot chills thru his body. He could do it—if he kept his eyes closed. He wanted to do it! If only Lee had kept on his damn dress!

Jesse sat, knees spread, head hung down. Watched Lee perform in front of him, like a dancing girl. Finishing his act, Lee flicked his cat eyes, fully aware the boy was telling himself how absurd he looked—but enjoying every minute of it. He mimicked the star, a female torch singer, who had come on the radio. His mouth opened and closed. His tongue licking over his lips.

And Jesse was participating in the act as Lee's shadow flitted in the silver mirror, like a ghost, under the gaze of his own weak eyes. Jesse was jacking off—mentally—to the picture of him as a woman. Coming, Lee kneeling before him, taking all of it in. All of him. A shudder of pleasure shot down the boy's spine. The room was dark except for the red light, and the naked man brushed his thigh with his hand. A hairy Tarzan-like body with no gash, but a body like his own. Jesse sat back, elbow on the bed, too exhausted to care. And a tremor flickered down his back, as Lee's thick male hands massaged his thigh. Like a cat, then, he turned to Jesse in the darkness.

Bedbug bites. Jesse moved back a bit. Scratching his arm in a familiar place. Fingernails digging repeatedly in the same spot, enjoying it, like a junkie with one shoe off, lounging across the bed, scratching rapidly, wiggling his toes. He just couldn't get to the bottom of the bite. "Baby, baby," said

Lee. "Come here and let me suck your dick...you know you want to."

"AW!" said Jesse, not wanting to hear it. Confused. Desire coursing thru his body.

"Come on now, darling, I'll make it nice and easy for you. Just relax—I'll do all the work." Lee took him in his strong arms. Jesse jerked away, his shoulder striking the bronze bedpost. He coughed, he sputtered, clutching his chest. "I must have a bad heart! I can't breathe!" Jesse clutched his heart a moment, thru his bell-sleeved pimping-shirt. His narrow chest rose and fell. He was dismayed, pushing Lee away, that he couldn't fight. He was too thin—tuberculosis, maybe! The act of pushing the heavier man away made him cough uncontrollably. NO. He remembered it was the DOPE made him feel rubbery. "No need of fighting it!" said Lee. And indeed the dope told him to just abandon himself. Jesse kept clutching at his chest, coughing, pounding the region of his heart. Mr. Lee just looked at him, a tired look in his old yellow eyes.

The red glow on the purple sheets burned in the night Grim, Jesse thought of the streets. This was his choice. To stay here and be humiliated, or go to the streets. He wanted the sex Mr. Lee offered, but how could he put up with those degrading overtures and go thru with it, knowing it was a man? He just couldn't make it work in his mind. Instead, he hoped La-Di wouldn't insist, and keep stroking him, because he knew what his word would be. His answer. The word was NO.

The little bedside clock ticked its seconds. Lee watched him with yellow eyes, exasperated; his lips pursed. The boy was hot, and sweat stood out, cementing his shin to his back.

Although, Jesse mused absentmindedly, brain floating back into the music on a whirl of alcohol, unlike a bitch, Lee was very open. He was no holds barred. No games played. No tricks. It would be easy. He would do everything Jesse liked. Chiefly, he mused, because Lee wanted to get into *his* pants.

A thought that made his body recoil, snap his pants legs close together for a moment. Instead of him, having to do all the seducing. He felt the warm glow rush up into his loins. He tried again. Pictured someone dressed up. Quiet. This phantom lady. Quite amazing—he felt his lust pour out again. This resemblance of a woman, Mr. Lee in drag. Jesse didn't notice the catlike, wiry man before him studying the expressions on his face, as he wearily lit a cigarette. He mused. Her, sucking his dick. Outstretched legs, ass spread before him. But suddenly he caught sight of that crew-cut head. Cat-eyed, whisker-showing face of Mr. Lee.

Suddenly he flinched.

"A piece! It's as simple as that!" came the man's voice. Impatient, explaining. Put-off. Jesse responded, the veins standing out in his neck. "A PIECE! SHIT NO, MAN! I ain't gonna do that! I ain't no trick of yours, man! Shit!" The bed bounced and squeaked in its springs, with weight of two full-grown men shifting over it having a heated argument. "Naw, man, NAW!" Now, before he knew what was happening, relaxing head dizzy with drugs, Jesse suddenly found himself having to defend his manhood. The whole room focused in, and here he was, *again!*—floating in indecision & it made him mad.

It was OK for Lee to do it to him, but he sure wasn't going to suck Mr. Lee's cock, nor be rammed in his young butthole by Lee's horny old cock.

So the man explained it to him, once more, coolly. "YES, I'm propositioning you! This is life, honey! These things happen, you know! This is Life, Jesse! That's all! It ain't Science Fiction! TRADE, honey! We both wants the same thing! You gets a nut, and I gets a nut! You ain't no TRICK now, you my *friend!*"

"I ain't nothin'!" snaps Jesse.

La-Di stood up, his mouth opened big; he's angry. "Don't

be ignorant, Jesse! I got friends I've known twelve years! We do it! We buddies! I ain't no fly-by-night!"

The youth pouted, clenched his fists. His grasshopper legs twisted. "Say, man, but you said, man—'Come up here and there be some womens up here!' That's what you said, last time! Come on back, you'd have some women! You got some records, and beer. I thought we was going to have a party—you know, man! I mean, you my *Partner*, man! I know what you do, man! It don't bother ME! But...dig, you...know...dig, I just don't—"

"Oh, now, wait just a minute!" yelled Lee, hands on his hips, his eyes flashed angry.

"NIGGER! Shit! You is a big-foot nigger, a hard-head nigger jus' like me!" said Jesse wildly. He looked at La-Di. He knew he was blowing the scene. He hated to lose La-Di as a friend, and he hated him at the same time. He wanted to take his fist and smash La-Di's face, to keep him away from him. And he was afraid. Afraid that the weakness in his eyes would show. Afraid that he'd be reduced to having to hit him—to struggle. Finally he shrugged and went limp, sinking back on the bed. "Aw, you ain't propositioning ME, man. Naw!"

Stubble on La-Di's chin, beard was showing. His nostrils flared. Sweaty brown-red face smeared with the reddish light. His mouth opened wider, in rage; becoming hysterical. He pressed his angry face closer. "This is trade, honey. You do me, and I do you! Come on now, Jesse! You ain't no CHILD!"

No coins to go anywhere. The dusty room was the last stop. Jesse looked self-consciously, as if a thousand eyes were looking at him from some praying mantis up in the ceiling of La-Di's wallpapered room. He snuck a glance at himself in the mirror. Its silver showed only a shadow, unrecognizable. Jesse hurriedly pressed his coat sleeve neatly onto his face. But only his inner mind could see that tear.

Only his feet knew the holes in the bottom of his shoes,

covered with cardboard. In another few weeks he would start to look ragged. The clothes he'd brought with him cross country couldn't hold up much longer without some kind of support. And in six months like the rest of the bitter, twisted, or mentally disturbed people or just low-intelligenced people of his neighborhood, he would have the look of incredible poverty. He suspected he would not be like the hustlers of Fillmore with their whores, wicked; their strong eyes kept them hid. Them, always in some fine rags, hold onto the green dollar bills. Their diamonds not made out of glass—imitations, but like their minds, able to cut glass itself! Their schooled brains, their herd of women on the streets, whoring and boosting, under some new plastic raincoats—looking sharp.

"Let me speak!"

"You've already did all the talking, man!"

"I *intend* to! I very well intend to! I wore the goddamn dress all night—that *entitles* me to do some speaking!"

"WHY? 'Cause womens speak mo' than mens? You got it all WRONG! MEN does the talking! And I'm a MAN! You *always* running your damn mouth! You just get people around you to talk AT? You don't never listen to people's problems! My problems!"

"Listen, you crazy young boy. If you think I brang you up here to listen to your miserable little troubles, you're—"

"I ain't crazy! I'm hip to you, man! Man, you the one CRAZY! You ain't no damn woman AT ALL! You ain't no broad in any WAY, SHAPE, or FORM! You LOOKS like a man in a dress! You ACTS like a man when you ain't in no dress! I'm hip to you, dude! You catches a dude in that dress, THEN you turns into a Man! I'm hep to yo', nigger! You ain't foolin' the kid, man! Broads *listen* to people. Shit! Broads is CONSIDERATE. Man, you is just a man thru and thru. You ain't no broad. MAN! MAN! MAN! You is a Man!" Jesse talked fast. He was trying to get his say worth back for all the listening he had had to put up with. "Man, there's sissies that's Broads in men's bodies, but you ain't one of them! You is just a fake sissy! You a jiveass, fucking-ass MAN!"

Miss La-Di-Da stood up, "WHY, you SNIP! Hold me back before I knock your teeth in!"

"Ain't nobody holdin' you back, MAN!"

"Well, take off your pants, then!" Mr. Lee said, grinning foolishly, and relaxed. He sat down. He was too comfortable to fight. "...And then I *won't* be held back," he added.

"Ahhhhgggghh!" Jesse sickened. This was the final straw. The reefer had made his mood so desperately real, for a sickening moment he was actually afraid he might die. Now, after Mr. Lee had put him thru all these changes, he was actually insulting him! Now he could never explain to this man he had just come up to drink his beer. That he'd come to be near a Person. His good nature was being trod upon. Jesse saw it all clearly—trod upon by the staccato heels of this six-foot dragon.

From his mental distance, he sneered disdainfully. (More haughty than a whore.) All wrapped up inside his male pride, moving like a cat.

Mr. Lee was moody now. He reached out and began rubbing the back of Jesse's neck. Jesse shrugged the hand off. "Jesse, it feel good, don't it? Ain't nobody up here but you and me...Nobody's going to know...If any of your little friends come by, I won't let 'em in! I won't answer that phone! Or that door!...Nigger, why you so stubborn? I done HAD two of your friends! They do it! What's wrong with you! You don't want nobody fooling with you.... Ain't nobody here to tell! Men fuck each other all the time! Nobody CARES who you FUCK! It feels good, don't it?"

"Yeah? Who did you fuck? James?"

"Yes."

"God Damn! That SISSY! I thought he was funny!...I—"

"NAH. I didn't fuck James...I'm not telling which one I fucked! Oh, NO! I won't tell! Then you won't trust me! I just wanted to see if you believed I would tell! Ha-ha!"

"It don't make me no difference if you tells or not!"

"WAIT A MINUTE, THEN!—I got something else to show you," Lee said finally, in total frustration. He got up and with barefoot steps heavy with masculinity stomped across his room to get some more dirty pictures out of his top dresser drawer. His now-heavy genitals unmasked. His organ so thick now it swung heavily from side to side like a pendulum as he walked. He returned and stood before Jesse throwing another pack of photographs down on the bed—playing his trump card. He stood there. His nipples rigid on his muscular chest; stomach rippling with muscles. Jesse sat, knees spread, head hung down speechless as he stared at the photos, recognizing faces of two of his friends amid a nude jumble of cockshafts, dickheads & football-player-strong arms & legs. "See, I told you they did," Lee said, finally, enjoying every minute of it. He flicked his tongue out. He swayed; a dancing man like a dancing girl mimicking a star, the female torch singer who had come on the radio. His mouth opened and closed. His tongue licked over his full brown lips. As Lee stood before Jesse, his pectoral muscles flexed as his hand went to his dick, took his organ in his fist and pointed at the boy a moment, waving it in a hello, a smile on his face. Then, with an imperceptible swish came to sit beside him again.

They were quiet. Feeling their heads spin with liquor. Jesse felt the man's weight shift on the bed next to him—Jesse looked at him, sternly worried. Afraid that the weakness in his eyes would show, or that the man would hear his fast, panicky breathing. Afraid that he'd be reduced to having to fight, of coming out of this comfortable world for good. He held on to the golden island in the sea of night as long as he could.

Jesse moved back a bit. Lounging across the bed, wiggling his toes. Still gazing down at the sheaf of black & white photos, muttering, "I don't believe it."

As Jesse stalled, a foolish grin spread over Lee's face; he retreated into a private fantasy which lasted the better part of a minute. In this created sex drama, Jesse made his decision to enjoy every erotic moment offered to him, to savor it to the hilt. He slid his trousers down over his skinny legs, kicked them off over his shoes. His erection bursting, straining, soiling his boxer shorts with precum. Lee slid his huge brown hand down to Jesse's underpants tented up with his erection and helped remove them. His eyes gleamed luminous as a cat, and he clung to Jesse in the darkness; thick male hands massaged his thighs, working toward his cock. The boy's body was very lean. Hard as a rock. A tight, almost hairless physique, gleaming with sweat. Smooth buttocks. A thick organ in a nest of thick kinky hairs; dick pulsating with need. In his magnificent fantasy Lee worked his imagination with everything he's got. Jesse's erection swelling even more; its thick base, shaft, heavily veined. Drops of precum dribbled out of the tip. Jesse turned now to reciprocate their lust. Grabbed Lee's stiff cock in his fist, then let go. Gazed at Lee. He tried to be normal again, one more time. Pictured someone dressed up in girl's clothes. Not a queer. This phantom lady. Quite amazing—he felt his lust pour out again more strongly for the man himself, not that resemblance of a woman, that Mr. Lee in drag of an hour long past. In the dream sequence, Jesse's lips mouthed Lee's scripted words, asking nervously, "Well, do you want me to come? You gonna do it to me?" Mr. Lee's eyes gleamed; his thick lips smiled, pleased. Lee reached down and pulled Jesse's cock with his hand. It reared up, balls hanging below the shaft, swinging taut in their sack. As he grabbed his groin, his mouth went to the boy's chest, the scratchy beard stubble of his cheek against him, and sucked hard on his nipples, twisted them around with his fingertips, while the other hand continued to pull his cock. Mr. Lee's hands and mouth worked him over like a master.

Then his head slid down his body, as Jesse drew in his stomach with a sharp intake of air. His lips took in the stiff dick, sucking, the tip of his pink tongue probed into the wet slit of Jesse's pisshole. And Jesse was participating in the sex act. Grinding his hips into the man's face. Lee's shadow fluttered in the silver mirror of the bureau like a ghost, on his knees beside the bed; big hands cupping Jesse's firm round ass; head bobbling up and down on the youth's cock.

Under the gaze of his own weak sight in the dim red light, Jesse was being sucked off—mentally—there was the picture of Lee as a man, and the memory of him as a woman. Near coming. Lee kneeling before Jesse, taking all of it in. All of him. A shudder of ecstatic pleasure shot down the boy's spine. The room was dark, except for the red light. This naked man between his thighs, bruising his lips, swallowing his dick. A near hairless Tarzan body with no woman-gash, but a male body like his own. Jesse sat back, elbows on the bed, too exhausted to care. And a tremor flickered down his back.

As his hot, plump balls grew firmer, his cock got even bigger. Lee lightly chewed the meaty cockhead with tiny nibbles, then took the cock deep into his mouth and began to suck all of it. The boy felt all of him go deeper in his mouth as he penetrated Mr. Lee's throat; felt his cock swallowed into the immense pleasure of man-sex. Lee milked Jesse's cock with expert sucking as Jesse's hips ground his dick into Lee's face. His cock began to throb and emptied fresh cum into his mouth. Streams of cum discharged. His balls pumping out seeming gallons of stored-up cum. Jesse's balls shrunk up in size now for their ferocious load was spent. Then Lee got up from off his knees to join Jesse; they lay side by side on the bed. "The first one's out of the way," Lee thought victoriously. Prolonging his erotic dream scene. Jesse's long-pent-up orgasm had shot his jism out fast. But Lee knew they had the whole night. Was resting before going for the second round.

Minutes ticked by in the red-lit room. Jesse didn't notice the expectancy of the catlike, wiry man before him studying the expression on his face as he lit a cigarette wearily—one from a pack his host kept in a dish on the nightstand. He mused about it. Her-him, sucking his dick like a candy cane. For a while Lee had lain turned over on his stomach, legs outstretched, ass spread before Jesse, inviting him to butt-fuck. But that invitation didn't work: for suddenly Jesse caught sight of the crew-cut head; cat-eyed, whisker-showing face of Mr. Lee, not Miss La-Di-Da; as he tenderly, and with unmistakable gestures, finally got up and tried to turn *him* over on his stomach instead. Jesse recoiled. Lee assured him he just wanted to lick him. That was all. Firmly Lee turned Jesse over in his muscular arms. His huge hands pushed the youth's tight buttcheeks apart. Big thick pink tongue flicked into his puckered asshole, rimming, tasting its bitter acidity; began to make it wet from his licking. Soon his butt was wet with saliva. Jesse finally pulled away—nervous, tho it felt good. Fearful this rim job was a prelude to Lee trying to insert his big cock in his virgin cherry butthole. And Lee sat up on the bed, his still-heavy male sex bobbed like thick fruit between his legs, ripe, bursting with unsucked juice; fruit waiting to be picked off his sturdy male tree. The idea was that Lee wanted to get a nut, too.

In his fantasy, Lee swallowed up all the rejection the boy spewed out and turned it around into a lecher's sly conquest. In his mind he had Jesse saying again what he'd just said moments ago—worked now into his brief bittersweet fantasy. "NO, MAN! I AIN'T NO TRICK OF YOURS!"

In the dream sequence, Lee replies, yelling, "OH, NOW, WAIT JUST A MINUTE!" Hands on his hips. "YOU LOVED IT A MINUTE AGO!" Angry, his face pressing into Jesse's space. "Come on now, Jesse! You ain't stupid. You already come! And I wants the same thing—that's all it is! It's simple," he says, and adds finally, in mild desperation, "If you can't do me that way, can't suck my dick, then you just fuck me in my booty. I'll get a nut that way."

"You sure, man? You ain't gonna try to pull no shit on me! Ain't no man try to stick his dick in my ass!" Jesse's anger was resigned at Lee's assurance.

Under firm manipulation, Jesse felt his genitals swell up again—until he was ready to fuck him. Lee turned back on his stomach; felt Jesse's lean body mount him. The rise and fall of his breathing. Lee was used to penetration; his hole was ready. He pointed to a jar of Crisco on the nightstand shelf, by the cigarettes. Jesse took a gob full in one hand, greased up his shaft, then pushed his big cockhead into Lee's anus. The young man started a thrusting assault on his asshole; drove his grease-covered cock in and out of Lee's butthole like a piston; his balls slapping his ass. Lee spread himself beneath Jesse and gripped his own erection in his fist; drops of precum dribbled out as he jacked his shaft up and down; while Jesse humped his throbbing stiff cock into his butt all the way up to his balls. Sweat ran off their bodies. Jesse pushed in him deeply, hips grinding. The size of his long, thick cock stretching Lee's bunghole. With furious fuck strokes, Jesse pummeled him. The full crown of his dick would emerge; then he pushed his slimy dick back deep into Lee's hole. The older man felt Jesse's rod deep inside. Slick cock pushing in and out matched by strokes of Lee's hand on his own dick, until Lee felt his cock about to burst in ecstasy, erupting white jism into the sheets. Lee took the boy's load deep inside him, flooding his rectum, while the satin sheets received his own white spurting juices; his pulsating stiff cock squirting out gallons of creamy sperm, so it seemed, it had been so long a tantalizing, teasing wait. Jesse's cum continued to spurt in spasms; his nuts bursting forth fruit. He bucked, thrust harder, shooting his cum in thick streams. Then they were done. There was juice all over the sheets. Cum all over both of their tan-brown bodies.

And Mr. Lee's delicious fantasy was over. Because a voice had brought him back down to reality. It was the miserable young boy again—whining. Protesting. Saying all the noises that meant NO.

BANG!

Mr. Lee had thrown a pillow at the floor. It missed Jesse, and now beer was spilling over the table from a broken glass. "You been comin' up here long enough!" BANG! He threw another pillow. "What do you do, but hustle me? And you don't do nothing! What are you worth to me? You just a little sponge that come up and drink up my beer and listen to my records!"

"You invited me up. You wanted some company—you need somebody to talk to! And I know it!"

"You running up my 'lectric light bill! Turn off the lights!"

"Naw! I'm leaving."

"You won't leave!" Jesse was infuriated—he moved out of the clutter of broken glass and beer foam. But he stopped at the thought that if it came to fighting, he would, but also aware that La-Di was no delicate girl. She could fight, and maybe take him. Jesse had noticed the large powerful hands and arms, even in the doorway downstairs, under the lace and halter straps. He put the thought hastily out of his mind.

"I'm tired of playing games! It's been your show all along. I'm tired of it! You come up here, I feed you, care about you, and you don't give me a DAMN THING! LISTEN!...Now, wait a minute!" Lee sputtered. "You think I'm content just sitting here Talking to you? Playing your little con artist's games? God Damn it!"

"Man, you know...it's...*that* just ain't my shot!"

"Listen! Let's be adult about it! Two of us Adults! We'll

make a trade—I'll do something for you, and you do something for me!"

"I like Broads! Real Broads!"

"I'm a *person*, Honey! I'm a person TOO! You aren't giving me a damn thing! You ain't no KING, you know! I'm talking about *TRADE!* You do me and I do you! Ain't nobody going to lose nothing! Give me that dick!"

"Now, what DOES that mean? You cop my joint—then what I got to do for you? You mean I got to be a broad? I MEAN if I was to be interested!"

"Well, you don't expect me to do *myself!*"

"Well, hell, no. I ain't being no broad, either. Shit."

"DO IT TO ME, AND I DO IT TO YOU!"

"I ain't no girl, man! I done tol' you that three times! You don't seem to realize! I ain't no broad. I ain't playin' nobody's nigger. Get somebody else to kiss your black ass!"

"YOU KNOW I WANT YOU!"

"Man, you won't dominate me! I'm a Man! I ain't no bitch!"

"Just what do you think you are? Just Playing? PLAYING with me?" Mr. Lee had hardened his eyes, and shut off his hospitable feelings entirely.

Jesse fumbled with the brim of his hat. Tiredly. Sitting on the bed's edge, he was losing his high. He was crashing down to sober.

The red lights hung over them, glowering. "Shit...Lee... man, tell me, I don't look like no *Sissy*, do I?" Mr. Lee stood up; the towel fell away from his waist. Hands on his hips. His big joint bobbing there, naked. But his face, angry stubble of beard told it all. Jesse swallowed, embarrassed, and turned his face away.

"Oh, I see it's not your game now! NO! Not after you get up here! Now it's not your shot! Now you've stopped playing games and you be your REAL Self! Oh. I SEE. So Mr. Lee is the Mark for the night. The Chump. Go up to Mr. Lee's! Drink some beer, maybe some Girls will come along for you to lay. Hmmmmmm that's what you waitin' for.... SHIT!"

"Honey! I'll tell you. I'm just glad I stopped being a nasty little young boy and became a MAN! Because, see, I'm a *MAN*, Honey!"

"Look Here!" cried Lee, switching around in front of Jesse, who tried to avoid him. "Any man—or WOMAN—who come up here, they know what it's for! They gonna get on that bed, with they clothes off, and they gonna have a good time! With Mr. Lee! I ain't foolin' around!"

"AW, Man! Aw...Aw...You just a Dirty Old Man!" Jesse spat, his mustache quivering, his fists clenching protectively. His face had wrinkled into disgust. "You'll fuck anything that crawls, won't you!"

"SO! I'm a Dirty Old Man! AH! Yes! All right! Well, I'll tell you...*I AM!* A dirty old man! A Dirty Old Man!" Lee rushed around on the other side of Jesse, grabbing his towel vindictively. "Well, I tell you...Listen here a minute. It's better than being like some little young childish *Punk*."

"You a freak, Lee! A nigger freak! Sucking dicks. Eating cock!"

"Jesse, you a Phony! A Phony! Sayin' you one thing, then pretending you ain't that way! I know what you want! You want to come! That's all you want! I'm a man myself. You can't fool me! Then you say I'm a dirty old man! Shit! Haven't you even been around? The young girls that you SAY you want, they don't be TALKIN' about it, but they know there's a BOY, and then there's a Dirty Old Man, but THEY real! Broads Want a Dirty Old Man! There's girls come up here! That's right! Girls come up here because they WANT a Dirty Old Man!"

The two men stood like prizefighters framed by the tiny room. Red lights glared down at them, sweat dripping into their nappy eyebrows. Lee's mouth opened, his veined neck swelled in rage. "All right! Go On! You want a girl. A cunthole! Wait! And I'll tell you another thing! You read what Ava Maria Woodward say in *Movie Romance?* She say she Don't want none of them child young sissy boys! She don't be with them! She wants a Man! No little young sissy boys!"

"Awww." Jesse pouted, standing six foot, twisting in the room, waiting to escape it; but Lee had his exit blocked stark naked, waving his towel.

The older man spat out his words. "Wait now! Let me tell you something else! It's always them dirty old men be gettin' them little young girls! You never hear about them little young boys going off with young girls.... 'Cause they all goin' off with the Old Men. The Dirty Old Men, and Like It!" Lee spat.

Firmly, he clamped the towel around his lean hips. On one hand angrily, he began enumerating: "Frank Sinatra, Cary Grant, Sammy Davis! They get them little young girls, and They Dirty Old Men! Frank Sinatra is a dirty old man! Ava Maria Woodward. Elisabeth Hutton...You don't see them going with them sissy young boys! Look at Anna Maria Alberghetti. Look at Sally Ann Grant! Who they all with?

"Shit, Jesse! Go on out my door! You don't have no place to get in out of the cold! You don't have a pot to piss in! You little young boys, you get you a girl, and gonna take her in the alley somewhere!

"I have a bed up here, a place where she can wash up after. But YOU get her, you take her into the alley somewhere, up on somebody's back porch, in fact I bet you bes up under MY porch! And she got to wear her clothes all ditty after, with no place for her to lie down! Uh-HUH! YES! They just tryin' to get a NUT off? That's why them girls, they *LIKE* a Nasty old man! He knows how to treat them!

"Look at yourself! You a phony! I wear a dress, but you more phony than me! I fuck a girl, or a boy, and they come back! Both of them! I got me a woman right now in the Buchanan Street high-rise. A lady Nurse. I got Ralph. Bill. I caught two of your little boyfriends—look at you! You can't even catch! You can't even catch up with that cunt you caught up here before!

"Nasty old man? I'm a nasty old man! Well, you a Nasty YOUNG man!" Lee howled after the tall figure, whose giant strides had gained the threshold of the bedroom, and went into the living room. The amber light was brighter here. The record player was stuck, playing over and over the last album. Lee looked old in the light. A mature man, he was almost handsome—but for the high-pitched sense of desperation about him. His quick movements belied the soul of a man frantic to hunt down a sex partner each night, as if to stave off that ever-reaping scythe of age. Of time talking him out.

Lee rushed after Jesse. Without shoes, a full half-foot shorter, he still posed a threat; a muscular man, enraged at what he considered being tricked. Jesse stood near the lamp upon the worn carpet as Lee came around him again, blocking his path. "What happened to that little young girl you had with you last time you was up here? You didn't treat her right! You don't think she's good enough for you! You get her all full of dope and pills and shit, and get a nut off! Now where is she? Out makin' money in the street—and she won't give you a cent, will she? 'Cause you don't deserve it! She won't give you the time of day. She'll give that money to somebody who *satisfy* her!"

Jesse opened his mouth, his teeth gritting. "Aw, Man! Say, Man!" Kept trying to interject, but it was no use. The man was shrieking at him, a lesson that he needed to learn. "Oh, I see them! The Blue Grape. ALL them young boys. *Sissies!* The Arlington Airplane, I never SEEN so many sissies prancin' around on a stage! I used to go up there to the Fillmore West, I seen them! They don't think there's nobody but themselves!

Well, I'll tell you one thing! All them young little girls.... That's what they Want! Someone to make them *Feel!*"

Jesse gritted his teeth, pushed by the older man, who then circled around him again shrieking at him, with an icy blast. "And they all be singing about Love, Love, Love, Love, Love, and how I Love Her, and things.... Well, you know what you are! A phony! A phony! You get up in here to get out of the cold, and 'cause you want a girl, you won't even take off your pants! Ain't that some shit! You want to come, don't you? Well, what's the difference? Did you Love that little young bitch you had up here that time? Shit! That's all you talk about all night long is broads, broads, broads.... Well, there ain't none here—*I'm* here!"

Jesse was angry; wanted to retort, hands at his side. But his anger couldn't compare to the age-old anger of Mr. Lee. It had struck a nerve. The boy protested. Trying to defend his pride. Lee wasn't even listening. "Now how in hell, I just ask myself...How in the hell could I get mixed in with such a Measly little Pimp of a person. That's all you are, a little Measly boy!"

Jesse had said something, which Lee at last heard, and it only infuriated him more. "YOU SAID! YOU SAID! Now don't you interrupt! You don't say a THING! You HAVE said—Plenty! You *SAID!* HA!" His gold tooth showed. "Now, look I SAID down there in the street...I laid my cards out I said, 'We'll have a party! Well make a party...' You know what I meant! Down there you say YES.... Now, you gonna change your mind.... It's not your shot. Now you say, 'I like girls.' That's your excuse.... Well, it's all over, Jesse! You won't never come up here and USE me...."

BANG! The door slammed. The lamp shook. The record shut off. Inside the apartment, the voice came, echoing thru the silent halls. "Yes! I am a man! I know it! You more a lady than I am! Nasty young child! I am a man! A dirty old Man!"

BANG! Lee slammed the door again.

He went running down the foggy steps. Thoughts racing thru his mind. Third floor, strong smell of greens. Second floor, male and shrill female duos had an argument between them. Pots and pans clanked, throwing things. Ignoring any other noises in their building, intent on their own fight. But the woman's voice rapping to her no-good nigger husband. He in turn calling her all kinds of bitches and whores. And things her momma had never aspired to when delivering her at the hospital. Jesse's head still echoed with Mr. Lee's voice, shrieking at him.

At the ground level, Jesse slowed. His heart pounding. He heard no sounds of La-Di behind him—giving him that damn sermon, and worse, naked, but for that towel, chasing him, stark raving lunatic out into the night—embarrassing him so bad! He wanted to compose himself, to get lost on the street. At the door, he'd took the steps running, stumbling—his long daddy-longlegs crumpling under him, skinning his knee. He was afraid of that one thing—being followed by this maniac—of having his cool blown out on the streets, a naked Sissy chasing him, for all the big-time hustlers to see—being called out by a Sissy! He disguised his fear now. He walked out into the night jauntily. Hat tipped ace-deuce on his skull. Coat patted smooth on his slim frame, dip-walking the pimp strut, bopping, shaking his head from side to side, as was the big-league fashion; he walked out into the night.

Snake Charmer

Belasco

The Blue Globes

Thomas Glave

But first beginning with their secret. That of the blue globes.
Which are always blue, as
they always were. In the beginning. When he was thirteen
years old. When I was twelve
years old. When we were
sixteen
years old
:

But yes. Beginning with their secret. That of the blue globes, their secret, and his secret, which was also mine. The secret of "Smell," he said. Smiling down. "I want you to—" "Smell," I said, smiling up. My jaw, feeling the (but yes). My face moving toward what he wanted me to smell. Toward what was his, and his alone, until I made it mine. Until I breathed it in. About which I said I would never tell. "I'll never tell," I said. Said to him. To his face. His laughing, smiling face. His face that smiled as (in darkness, in light) the blue globes descended, came closer and closer and "Smell it," he said.

"Just like that. Now. That way," he said. And laughed. Both of us laughing, laughing now, as no one will ever know.

I breathed in. Am breathing in. But he has not yet danced. Danced over my "Face," he will say. "So that you can look up, even in the darkness, and see them. The globes. As I dance. Dance over your face. The globes, that will be blue, as you look up and call my name. My name," he will say, reaching down to pull that part of me closer to his (yes).

I am calling
his name. I am looking up and calling
his name. I am calling his name as he looks down at me and
then
"Oh, Jesus!" I say. Yes. *As he pulls that part of me closer to his (yes) and I am O I am and*
I
am and O.

He wants me to breathe. To inhale. He always wanted me to breathe, to inhale. To take in all of it and carry it "to your dreams," he would always say. "I want you to smell me in your dreams." But yes.

If they had ever known—any of them, the ones who were never there when we, the ones who never heard when we in that time or this one—if any of them had ever known, "They would have laughed," I said. "They would have said—" "Uh-huh," he said. "They would have thought—" "Of course," I said. "They would have—" "Exactly," you said. "And we wouldn't be—" "No," I said.

And so they who were we
will never tell. I will never. You will not. And no.

Years later, they will look back. Both of them. They will see
themselves holding
each other. See themselves smelling
each other (yes, and laughing). See themselves
doing those things that require a little assistance
with each other. Moving groceries, starting a car, or "Do that
to me," he said. You said.
"Like that." Dusting off furniture in the secret place they
kept, the place no one ever knew
about except themselves. Where they could go sometimes
and "Underneath?" I said.
"Between the—" "No," he said (you said), "right there, next
to my—yes, yes, that's it.
That's it," you said. Between the groceries, moving the hand
to pull the clutch.

Looking back. But so much ahead.

All right, then. And so the globes. That began when I was in (summer) camp. When we were in camp. When there was nobody around. Nobody because "They're all swimming," he whispered. "In the pool down by the—"

"Getting wet," I said, pulling at the—

"Yes," he whispered (you whispered). And laughed.

In camp. Where I was. Right there. Just there. Lying on my "Back," he said, quietly. "On your back. Stay there." "Why?" I asked. "Because," he said (you said), smiling. But I didn't have to ask. Because that would be the first O yes the first yes time that he would ask me to do that, to do just that, to put my face there in that way, near the blue globes.

He liked the color blue, he said. His mother bought it for him to wear when he was in water, he said. Which was often. He liked the water. He liked the blue thing his mother bought him. He liked the way it fit so nice and tight around his (yes, me too). He liked the way it slid so slowly off his (but of course. And I did too). He liked the way the blue shone in the sunlight and the way it glistened when he dove into the water. When he parted the water. When his form streaked through the water and he moved his legs and there was no smell, no sense of smell, only his open mouth and his legs, arms, moving. Stroking. Only watermovement and darkness there. His belly flat between the strokes. His open mouth moving through the water. His open mouth tasting it. Between strokes. His mouth moving above his legs, above the water's mouth, in darkness, yes, and light.

Smell it, you said
Why, I asked
Because you like it, you said
Because you like it, I said
Yes. Yes, I really like it, you said
You want me to smell it. You want me to breathe in, I said
Jesus, yes, you said. You groaned. Jesus yes. Yes yes yes yes
yes. As I did, and you did,
and no one ever knew. Because we can't ever tell. O no.

And so a dance. A dance of the afternoon. A two o'clock dance, a move out of dusty corners, a move of hips. Moves when all the others were away. Away swimming, getting wet. Wetting their mouths, soaking their thighs. A dance that began when we were thirteen and fourteen years old—began not quite with the blue globes, though they were there, but with "A skirt!" I almost shouted. Lying on my back, on that small camp bed that fit only one. "Where did you get that?" A skirt that you had stolen from—from her? The one whom you would later kiss while I watched? From her? "Do you like it?" you said. "Jesus Christ," I said. A skirt. The blue globes (though I didn't know it then) beneath. Shining. Beckoning.

Yes, I liked it. Just that way. The way the blue thing your mother bought you fit so slyly, ever so slightly, around your hips. They way it breezed, ever so slightly, when you did what you always did. "Wear it," I said, quietly, very quietly, as you watched me holding myself. Lying on my back. "Wear it," I whispered, as you climbed above me, stood above me, dancing over my "Face," you said. "Over your face. Look up," you said, "and tell me what you see."

"I see everything," I said.

He was dancing over my face. They were all away, away at two o'clock in the afternoon. Wetting themselves. Splashing each other's back parts, each other's chests. Away as he danced over me, as the skirt swished around his hips. As I saw everything. The blue globes beneath. Beneath the skirt. And everything pressing beneath them. I could see his ankles, his thick-to-thin ankles, on the bed on either side of me. His feet, at that time without shoes. Without the high heels that, while again dancing over my face, he would wear years later, in that secret place we kept, where groceries crackled in paper bags and the furniture sprouted dust. I could see his ankles as I would see them years later, when, on those nights that were still to come, long after camp and the bed that fit only one, long after hidden afternoons when they all were away wetting themselves with their shouts and splashes, long after the rings we would eventually place upon fingers in pledges to other people who would never know, long after the children we would each beget who also would never know, he would come to that place, that secret place that had begun long ago with a dance whispered out of dusty corners at two o'clock in the afternoon, and once more dance over my face with a skirt that swished about his hips, that swished to reveal—only now and then—the blue globes, and all that pressed behind them, beneath them. He would dance years later, as he danced only yesterday (but I will never tell), with those black patent-leather high heels wrapped tightly about his ankles. Those shining high heels close enough to lick. He would dance, and still, when the desire came, he would command me to "Smell it," he would say, and I would. Clutching myself. Smell it, O my God, smelling it as my face disappeared behind the blue globes and they, yes, they, became all and everything. Became my face.

No, we can never tell. He can never tell how much he enjoys when I "Smell it," he said, and "I'm smelling it," I whispered, and "I know," he groaned, holding my head there. Keeping my head there. He can never tell. Not ever tell the one who now delights in the rings about their fingers that both share, nor the many others who share merge reports and analyses, spreadsheets, of his days—the days when he thinks of me, I know, and of how, on some night soon to come, far away from the children he begat and the she who bears the ring that matches the one he wears, far away from the children I begat and the she who loves my smile as I delight in her face, I will smell him I will smell him I will "But just kiss it," he will say some night, "just this once, or twice, or three times." "What would any of them say if they knew?" I ask one night as he dances over me, trying to aim everything for right there, just there. "If they—"

"But they'll never know," he says—and though I cannot see him entirely, for the darkness of that place that is this one, I know that he is smiling, that he will soon laugh—yes, laugh the way he always does when he comes down over me, when the skirt billows over my face, when he knows that I am closing my eyes as he closes his and smelling it, taking it all in, about which we will never tell "anyone," I say. Say to the darkness. To the globes, that will become (but not for the first time) my mouth. Open my mouth.

The first time, you wanted me to touch them. You put them
in my face.
They were wet. And I
Yes. Was thirteen
years old. Was fourteen
years old. You were fifteen (sixteen?)
years old. You were
"swimming," you said,
"swimming. That's why they're wet."
"They're blue," I said. "Front and back. I like the color. Blue
like—"
"Don't say it," you said. "Just put your face there, and—"
"Smell it?" I asked.
"Yes," you said. "There. Right there!"

That was camp. When we were twelve or thirteen or fourteen years old. By the time I was seventeen and you were

"Eighteen!"

I thought with purest secret pleasure as you danced over me and I thought about doing so much more—yes, so much more than merely kissing it. You were eighteen and had graduated from lifting first one leg, then the other. From laughing so uproariously when you did what you did, and I breathed in. From sticking it out so that the blue globes, especially when it was time for you to do what you did, touched my face. From balancing over me just that way, gently, ever so gently, so that, when it was time, when you next wanted me to, I would inhale all of it and reach up just that way—yes, still lying on my back—to kiss the blue globes that would be "wet," you whispered, "yes. For you, always wet. Like the first time when

I came in from swimming and they were—"
"Soaked," I say, remembering.

No one else ever inhaled. Ever smelled. You promised me that they wouldn't. You promised me that you wouldn't do that with "Her," you said, "no, of course not. Are you crazy? How could I? She would think that I'm the ultimate—"
"Pervert," I said. "Yes."
"Yes," you said, blowing out the candle next to the place where we stretched, fully prepared. And then it happened, you did it, did it without lifting a thigh or arching your back (yes, even while lying on your back), it was one of your most reckless, and you commanded me to "Smell it," you said. And I did, O yes, but of course, as you pressed down upon me and kept me there. Covering my face. Covering. Allowing me to breathe in. Ensuring that I thought only of you and what your she or mine or any of the children we had begotten would say if they could "see us," I thought, closing my eyes. Sucking silent air.

But don't worry, I said years later. When I was forty-one years old. When you were forty-two years old. When we were
"in secret again," I said. "Yes," you whispered, taking that part of me in your hands and smelling it. "Yes."
Don't worry, I said, squeezing that part. You don't need to worry I said, for (but how powerful it felt in my hands!) there will never come a time when the globes are not blue and there. When you do not wear that thing that makes them blue, as you did when you
were
fourteen
years old. There will never come a time when I will not want to smell their secretmost things, those things shared only with me, about which I will never tell. You will never tell your her,

I whispered into one of your parts last night, and I will never tell mine. I will take my finger that bears the ring that pledges my self to my her and put that finger in your secretmost place that is only for me, and never (but no. How could I?) tell her that I did so. You will take your hand that bears the ring that pledges your self to your her and do that to me as severely as you can, yes, please, once more and again, just like that, with those circles, those spirals, all of those circlings around the secret part—you will do that, I will command you the way you command me when I smell you and open myself up to (uh-huh), but you will never tell her, her whom you never ask to smell anything as you ask me to and have asked me to since the two o'clock dance of that first afternoon. Don't worry, I said, because you are—of course—deep, deep down inside my lungs. You've been there deep down there for every year of all these years. The way I've been in your dreams and you've been inside my (yes) and we in all the secret places for all of these years. The way no one will ever know about it. No one knows about it. The way your ring shines when you move it around me that way and I can still smell you because the blue globes are only inches over my face. The way the globes move when you dance, the way they shudder when you want me to breathe in. The way the children you begat laugh when you come home. "Daddy," they say. "Daddy, Daddy!" The way she smiles at you when you're tired. Smiles, not knowing not ever knowing how you have been smelled for years, and how another face that smiles at her ("How are things, baby? Looking good, baby!") has disappeared within your secretmost parts for more than (fill in the years). The way you dance over my face, wearing that skirt (last week it was a Scottish kilt with pleats) and those shiny high heels prance close enough to lick. The way I inhale you—

No. No one will ever know. Will ever see. Will ever hear. Nor smell. Smell that smell that is for me. Me only. Only mine. In darkness, yes, and in light. The globes in blue.

Close to my face. As you do that. Yes, please do that. And
that and. About which we will
never tell. Never tell as I am smelling you. As I am fifty-one
years old. As you are fifty-two
years old. As you are

Above me. Dancing, yes. And the globes. Shining, always in blue, full and round.
Shining, before they descend. Descend to cover my face and I inhale and

Laughing. We who are laughing. We who are—

Kevin

Christopher David

If there's one thing I hate, it's a bitch telling me how to handle my fucking relationship! *Who the fuck does Jared think he is?* He acts like I'm one of their young bitches out there running around trying to keep a man! I know how to keep a man—*okay?* I've got one, does he? Hell no! Yet, he's gonna tell me how to handle my damn relationship! *Shit!* Friend to friend really, does that make sense? You know what, as a matter of fact, keep your opinion, because it doesn't matter! The point is he should learn to mind his business, and so should the *rest* of you bitches out there trying to judge me!

I don't have a problem with my man meeting new people, never have, and I never will, just as long as I know what's going on. I'm really not the jealous type, but the girls are fierce nowadays! Honey they will steal your man right from under your nose! You'll be sitting around, thinking, *"oh, they're just friends,"* and behind your back, they're justa humpin' and a fuckin'!

How do I know? Honey, 'cause I've played that scene before.

I remember back in L.A. I had this one ole' fine piece of trade! *Whew!* Girl she was TDH! Tall Dark & Handsome! And had dick for days chile! I mean a big ole' chocolate thang! We use to get down and nasty any and every chance we got—and it didn't matter where, just as long as we didn't get caught. Umm chile, just thinking about that man, and all that dick, is making me hot!

I met him one day while shopping at the Beverly Center. I walked into Crate n' Barrel to buy some candles with my friend Hector, when I noticed this vision of manliness strolling my way. He had on a charcoal gray velour sweat suit with Nike tennis shoes. First, I noticed the b-boy walk, then the face—but honey, as my eyes traced the curves of his body, I noticed the imprint of the dick that would forever change my life! He wasn't wearing underwear so his dick was just a swinging back and forth, and forth and back! I almost had a heart attack right then and there! I couldn't help but stare! But when our eyes met, he gave me the nastiest look like, *"what the fuck you looking at faggot!"*

I paid it, because honey, first of all I don't look like no faggot! I may cut up with you girls and talk this way, but out in the streets, I know how to represent—*okay?* So don't get it twisted! Second of all, I work out faithfully! I got body *downnnnnn!* If she would've even *thought* about stepping to me with some bullshit I would've beat that bitch with a bat!

Anyway, chile, like I was saying, she screwed her face up, and I just looked at her like, *"what, got a problem?"* He pretended not to notice my defensive stance, paid for his shit, and left the store. Hector and I purchased the candles and continued about our shopping spree. About an hour later we were walking through the parking lot, when I saw Ms. Trade be-bopping to his car. He stopped, turned, smiled, and then kept walking. I looked at Hector like, what was that about? He shook his head and brushed it off. So again, I paid it.

Honey, as I was preparing to pull my Toyota Corolla out of my parking spot, a fierce black convertible BMW 328i with twenty-inch rims pulled up and blocked my exit. Annoyed, I blew the horn to let whoever it was know I was trying to leave. But they didn't move, so I blew the horn again, yet still, no response. Mad as hell, I put the car in park, jumped out, and stormed to the car. Quite to my surprise it was Ms. Trade.

"What took you so long?" he asked in a comfortable masculine voice.

"What?" I frowned, annoyed by his directness. "What are you talking about? Could you just back up so I could get the hell out of here!"

"First of all niggah, take it down a notch alright!" he demanded.

Honey, my pussy got moist! He was a man! A real man! A man's man, and he wasn't taking no shit!

"Now..." he continued. "I saw you checkin' me out back there in the store..." He spit, his voice dead serious. "What was that about?"

I swallowed hard as I surveyed his position. He was sitting with his left hand on the steering wheel, but his right one was between his thighs, holding something. I couldn't tell if it was a gun or a knife or what, but I knew it was something.

"I don't know what you're talking about man..." I said backing up from the car, my heart beating a mile a minute. "But right now, all I want to do is get out of this space. I don't want any problems."

He laughed, revealing his pearly whites. "Chill man...ain't gonna' hurt you, I just wanted to know if you're feelin me, that's all."

The tone of his voice changed drastically causing me to laugh quietly to myself. Ms. Trade was cruising me.

"I guess you can say that." I smiled, feeling my confidence return.

"I thought so," he asserted. "So listen, let me get the digits so I can hit you up lata."

I looked back at Hector, and winked. "Sure, you got a pen?"

"Yeah right here, what is it?" he said revealing the hidden object. After taking the number, he smiled and said, "I'll call you tonight," then sped off.

True to his word, he called at exactly 1:57 A.M. I had just drifted off to sleep and was in the middle of one of my recurring dreams with Tupac, when the telephone rang.

"Hello?" I yawned into the phone.

"What's up niggah?" The voice boomed. "You sleep?"

Shocked that he had actually called I sat up in the bed. "Nah, not at all," I lied.

"Good, you up for company?"

"Now?" I asked surveying my apartment. It was a mess. Clothes, dishes, and CDs were everywhere.

"Yeah now! Why? You got somebody else over there?"

"Nah, not at all, it's just that," I paused searching for the clock, "it's two in the morning!"

"So what! It's Saturday night!"

"Well...I don't know—"

And then I thought about it—fuck principles! So what if I just met him! This man was fine, and he called at two o'clock in the morning to spend time with me. And here I was about to kick his ass to the curb—a fine one at that. What if he never called again? This could be a once in a lifetime opportunity, and I was about to let *pride* stand in the way?! Besides, what was the worst he could do? Kill me?

"As a matter of fact, yes," I said suddenly, "I do want company. Let me give you directions."

A half-hour later, there was a knock. I sprayed on some cologne and rushed to the door. Standing in my doorway, Ms. Trade looked better than I remembered, taller and definitely sexier, with his tank top and see-through nylon shorts. He smiled as he walked in.

"What's up man?" he said in his now familiar deep voice.

"Nothing," I smiled, "just waiting on your ass."

"Cool, cool. You got a nice place here," he said taking in my studio.

"Thanks."

"You hooked it up yourself?"

"Basically. You want something to drink?"

He paused. "Yeah, what you got?"

"What you want?"

"Some Mad Dog."

"Some who?" I shrieked.

He laughed. "Some Mad Dog? You know, the malt liquor?"

I shook my head. "Look. I have some vodka one of my boys left by here if you want some of that, but I know I don't have any Mad Dog."

He laughed. "That's cool. I'll take it."

We sat on the couch and talked for about an hour and a half. During which time, I learned a lot about him. His name was Hakeem Johnson, he was twenty-four and lived in Compton with his girlfriend. He had two kids by his ex-girl, a daughter She'kira, four, and a son, Ja'keel, two. He loved his kids, and did everything possible to ensure they'd never want for a thing.

He loved music, specifically hip-hop and he talked extensively about his collection of Too-Short, Ice Cube, and Easy-E CDs. One day, he hoped to manage his own rap group and, to ensure his future plans he was taking night classes at El Camino Community College in Business Management.

His favorite pastime was playing basketball with his boys from around the way, and spending quality time with his kids.

The more he talked the more I learned, and the more

interesting he became. He was smarter than he led others to believe, which he felt gave him an advantage. His reasoning, if people think you're stupid then they're prone to explain things in detail. The more they explained, the more he learned, and thus, the smarter he became. I thought it was bullshit, but hey, if it worked for him, it worked for him.

After about four drinks he leaned over and kissed me. For the next few moments, I allowed his tongue to explore my mouth. Confused, I stopped him.

"What about your girlfriend?"

"What about her!" he asked kissing me gently on my neck, causing every hair on my body to tingle.

"Aren't you in a committed relationship?"

He stopped abruptly and stared deep into my eyes. "Look, I love my girl ah-ight. And ain't nobody gonna take her place. But at the same time, you offer me something she can't."

"And what's that?" I asked, curious.

"This," he said grabbing my dick. "She can't give me what you can give me." With that he leaned over and let his tongue explore my mouth once more.

Gently, he began massaging the shaft of my dick and with each pull it grew larger and larger. I moaned in excitement, as I thought of how I met this man—this beautiful, beautiful masculine man. A part of me knew it was wrong to mess around with him, but then, the other part of me longed for the pleasure I knew only his strong muscular body could provide.

Before long we were both naked making out on my carpet. He gently kissed my body starting with my lips, then my neck, then my chest, pausing momentarily at my erect nipples. His lips, thick, full, and sensuous created sensations I never knew my body could feel. As they made their way lovingly down my stomach, I anticipated their arrival on my dick. With the grace of an angel, and the determination of a pro, he took my piece in his hand and gently guided it into his warm mouth. The feel of his tongue on my dick sent my hormones rocketing. Chile, Ms. Trade knew how to suck some dick! He caressed, and held it as if it were a long lost friend; one he missed dearly. Feeling myself nearing climax, I pushed him away.

"Whatcha you do that for?" he asked, disappointed.

I smiled. "I'm not ready to cum yet."

"So what you want?" he asked seductively. "Some ass?"

Honey, can I tell you something? There is nothing like a trade *down*—thugged out—masculine ass—motherfucker, asking you if you want some ass! Especially one as phine as Ms. Trade! My dick throbbed at the thought of pumping his tight ass. He felt it, grabbed his shorts, pulled out a condom and a small tube of lube, and proceeded to fit my piece into the rubber. Once done he turned over on his belly and added, "Handle your business daddy!"

Honey! I wore Ms. Trade's ass out! I had him climbing the walls, screaming all types of obscenities at me! Motherfucker this, Motherfucker that—you name it he yelled it! The sight of this man doggy-style clawing my carpet in excitement nearly caused me to nut. But, before I did, I pulled out. He wasn't getting off quite that easy.

"What the fuck you do that for?!" he yelled, annoyed I had tricked up his ride.

I smiled. "I'm not ready to cum."

"What? Why?"

"Because, fucking you like that has made me hot. I want you to hit this," I said tapping my ass.

He smiled, retrieved another condom, and squeezed, let me reemphasize that, *squeezed* his fat dick into a Magnum condom. Then, he lay on the floor, and began stroking it, as I readied my ass with lube.

I mounted him cautiously, then slowly—very slowly—slid down his massive dick. With only one third of it inside me, I felt both pain and pleasure I had never experienced before. He moved to slide the rest in, but I jerked, letting him know, not so fast, girl, mother can only take but so much at a time! A few minutes later, the fucking began.

Honey, I thought I knew how to fuck! I thought I knew how to smack it up, flip it, and rub it down! But that man, with that dick, wore-my-ass-out! He had my legs crossed, bent and pinned in positions I never thought they could do! My body trembled with pleasure with each stroke. We hit about eight different positions before I demanded he take it out! He obliged, removed the condom, and lay next to me. Within minutes we both jerked our dicks to climax, shooting warm cum all over each other's body.

We dated for a year and a half, and the sex just got better and better. During that time, I met his two children, his ex-girlfriend, and his live-in girlfriend. I was even the best man in his wedding. His wife thought I was crying out of happiness for them. If she only knew, I was crying because I was living a lie and so too was the man I loved.

When the priest bellowed, *"Is there anyone present, that knows of any reason why these two should not be joined together in holy matrimony, let them speak now, or forever hold their peace..."* I wanted to scream out to the top of my lungs *nooonooo!* But knew I couldn't. Hakeem watched me with knowing eyes. I had promised him the night before I wouldn't say anything when that part of the ceremony came. Through tears I told him how I felt about him. I told him how difficult it would be for me to stand next to him, and watch him dedicate his life—our life—to another. I told him I could no longer go on with this charade. I could not keep pretending, and hiding my feelings from him, and the world. I explained to him how every kiss, every touch, every moment spent with him had been recorded in my heart, and that the pain of loss, was causing it to break in two. I told him how it pained me to lie to his children, to his mother, to his fiancée! I wasn't ashamed to tell the world that I loved him, but he was! He was ashamed of our life and our love—but I wasn't.

Regrettably, I agreed to honor his day. But in my heart, I knew that that night was the last night we'd spend in the dark, sneaking around. It was time for a change.

Stank

Domingo Rhodes

Cambridge College, built in 1896 and the oldest of Branford University's ten original dormitories, is a four-story domicile that pretends to the world that it is a Gothic fortress, with white fluted spires that spurt exuberantly from the building's crenellated façade and a popsicle-blue sloped roof and towering black iron doors. Its interior, renovated after a small but spectacularly destructive fire in the '90s, is sleek and modern, its common rooms dark and high-ceilinged, dotted with small dark leather loveseats and bordered with tall frameless mirrors. Room 338—burnished blond wood floors, two full-sized beds, internet-wired, cable-ready—is a double on the southwest corner, looking out from its iron-clasped windows onto a green lawn that falls gently toward the slender shores of a small artificial lake, and from its double-locked door down the wide corridors of West Wing 3 and South Wing 3. The carpet that cushions the sound of 165 tramping Branford students is red and gold, the colors of the gleaming lion-embossed armor and Roman plume of the university mascot, the Warrior.

Residents of 338 during the current school year: Carmelo

Hildebrandt (a sophomore), Coby Bryce, and Trajan Ramos (both juniors).

Coby Bryce is tall, dark, with long heavy tattoo-layered arms and large hands, a knobby 'fro and a shaggy goatee, big lips, big eyes, perfect Egyptian bas-relief carven eyebrows. He and Carmelo hail from the same hometown (San Gabriel, California) and attended the same high school. They share a birthday: Both are Tauruses, but having been born one year and an ocean apart—Coby in Rieti, Italy; Carmelo in San Antonio, Texas—all but their sun signs differ considerably. They have been friends since Carmelo's freshman year. This is the first year they've roomed together.

Carmelo Hildebrandt is of a height neither tall nor short, and has acquired, through a gym regimen begun on the high school track squad, a musculature of appealing definition rather than pronounced muscle, though his shoulders are very broad and his hips very narrow. His colors are honey and brown sugar, depending on the body parts you observe. His accent is faintly southern, like his parents', his fingers long, his hair of the sort that his countrified relatives in east Texas still refer to as "good," but since February has been shorn so that it resembles the buzz-cut of a '50s roughneck. Carmelo makes straight *A*s, always has, and reads and masturbates a lot and has many female friends, no girlfriends. He is not at home at Branford, does not yet feel truly at ease with most of his fellow students. He relies upon Coby for the intermittent sensation of belonging.

Coby has many girlfriends. He occasionally models, and in fact because it is now spring quarter he's traipsed off again to Europe to prance along catwalks in Milan and Paris and otherwise amass the lucre necessary to finance his very expensive education. Coby's departure has put Carmelo at the mercy of the housing gods, who, in the mysterious way of all deities, have given him a troublesome new roommate.

Trajan Ramos, an Afro-Nuyorican, is one of Branford's top soccer recruits. Lean and burnt gold-brown like the crust of an apple pie, Trajan is a lanky frame filled out with knobs of muscle: His shoulders and biceps are like round yellow apples, his forearms slightly thickened; he has a small hard chest with pectoral muscles that round at the bottom, ribs of sinew on his stomach that you could climb like a ladder, and bulging calves above slender ankles. Trajan has an easy, friendly manner about him, a large grin. His nose is wide and oversized, and the smile sometimes gives him a clownish air. But his eyes can be distant and hard.

Trajan's easy on the eyes, somewhat less kind to the other senses.

Often Trajan strips in the room before going out to the shower down the hall. Knots of curly black hair cluster in the middle of his chest and reach up toward his neck; a trail twists down between the ridges of abdominal muscle. His crotch is bursting with dark hair, and its aroma is pungent. One might even say it reeks. In fact, though Trajan takes frequent showers, there is always a strong smell emanating from him, a kind of smell-aura you might imagine as the particle cloud that accompanies the character Pigpen in *Peanuts* comics. The odor is much more pronounced—more naked—when Trajan strips to go to bed. At best, it's a sweet funk like the inside of your mother's spice cabinet. At worst, it's a semi-stench reminiscent of the inside of a small windowless men's locker room on a humid day, a smell like fried skin and the thin patina of sweat that collects between a football player's bulging thigh and his oversized balls and saturates the edges of his jock. Powerful stuff.

It turns out Coby knows Trajan—fairly well, in fact.

Trajan makes Carmelo nervous.

"You go to bed naked?" Carmelo asks, unable to tear his gaze away from one of Trajan's nightly strip shows.

"Yeah, it's more comfortable."

Carmelo has never seen a dick so large (not even Coby's). It's a hose. It spills out from Trajan's pubic hair as if it were some kind of animal, as if it didn't belong on Trajan's body. The width of a cowboy belt, the girth of the lower end of a latte glass, brown, long so that it laps his hairy inner thighs, only lightly veined, uncut, with a slightly reddish bottle cap head peeking over a horizon of foreskin. The dick hangs down low, sometimes obscuring Trajan's balls.

When Trajan wakes at night to take a piss, Carmelo turns over on his bed and keeps one eye open to watch the shadow of Trajan's dick arch ahead of Trajan in the darkness.

"My dick hurts," Trajan sometimes says.

"Why?" Carmelo asks.

"It hasn't had anything to fuck. If it doesn't get squeezed every once in a while, it starts to throb. It hurts."

"Why don't you just—jack off?" Carmelo says. The words droop on his tongue, and he is sure he sounds like an idiot.

Trajan shrugs and his lips curl. "It's not the same."

It is a hot, humid night, unseasonably so. Carmelo enters 338 and finds Trajan lying in what he still thinks of as Coby's bed. Trajan, wearing only a pair of long, loose, red, and gold PROPERTY OF BRANFORD WARRIORS basketball shorts, is lying with his hands behind his head and his legs bent outward—so that his lower body resembles a vast hairy cup—as he watches the small color TV propped on the top of Carmelo's dresser. The gold ring in Trajan's left earlobe glistens, and his chain and silver Coptic cross is tangled in a mass of curly, black chest hair. Carmelo notes immediately as he walks in Trajan's shock of copious underarm hair—and how every bit of space between Trajan's splayed legs is filled.

The room smells like incense and a deer run on a forest preserve.

“’Melo,” Trajan murmurs. Carmelo just nods. “Where you been?”

Carmelo hesitates. They have been roommates for exactly a week now.

“The Dramat’s doing *The Toilet*, so I auditioned.”

“They’re doing *The Toilet*?”

“It’s a play.”

“Yeah, I got that. How’d it go?”

“What?”

“The audition.”

“Oh. Fine.”

Silence lingers fretfully in the room before Trajan says, with a mildness that underlines the aggression he’s concealing, “You don’t like having me around, Carmelo?”

“What?”

“You wish Coby was here, don’t you?”

“Uh...no...”

“Ah, so you do like having me around. That’s what I told Coby.”

“When did you talk to Coby?”

“When I talked to him ’bout requesting this room. Coby thought you might not be comfortable with me.” He gives Carmelo a smile—an evil smile. “But you like having me around.” Trajan reaches down, gives his crotch a squeeze, and watches Carmelo watch him.

Carmelo stares because he can’t help himself—then determinedly begins unloading his backpack. “Whatever.”

“How come you ain’t out gettin’ some pussy tonight? The hos like to fuck when it gets hot like this.”

“How would you know? I don’t see you out getting any.”

“Oh, I know. The whole summer is like this in New York. My boys and me used to run hos like they were breeding bitches in a kennel.”

“That’s disgusting.”

"Fuck, no, it ain't. That shit was fun. Everybody enjoyed those nights, man. We had girls comin' round to ask to be let in on it."

"Oh, right. Well, why haven't you opened a West Coast campus branch, then? Instead of sitting up here in my room watching..." Carmelo peers at the screen. "Bruce Lee karate movies?"

"I already busted my nut today. When the temperature goes up like this, I get impatient. Lucia and me skipped class and went out and fucked on the hillside near the trails."

Carmelo feels his groin pulse violently. But he sneers. "No, you didn't!"

"Yeah." He smiles again, sticks his hand down past the elastic of his shorts, and begins to ostentatiously fondle his balls.

Carmelo's shrug matches Trajan's ostentation. "Someone would have seen you."

Trajan shrugs back. "Maybe someone did."

"So why aren't you with Lucia now? If it was so good this afternoon, why not tonight?"

"Ah, she has some kinda bruising on her bladder or some shit. Doctor told her to take it easy for a couple days so she doesn't get a urinary tract infection. She banished me from her room tonight."

"This is because of the sex you had earlier?" Carmelo tries to sound both bored and knowledgeably disapproving.

"We were fucking too hard, I guess, yeah. I like to do that shit rough. What about you?"

"Do *I* like to do it rough?"

Trajan pauses to let Carmelo's logical mis-leap hang on the air, like flatulence. "No," he says brutally. "I mean, why aren't you out fucking?"

"For some of us it isn't that easy, you know. We don't have girlfriends and we don't pick up women just by smiling at them the way Coby does." He considers a way to change the subject. “Anyway, from what I hear, just because you and Lucia aren’t—getting busy—doesn’t mean that you wouldn’t be finding someone else to satisfy you.”

Big smile. “Oh? And where did you hear that?”

“Coby told me....”

“That’s a lie. Coby wouldn’t tell you that.”

“Coby and I are best friends, Trajan.”

“You lying anyway. Where did you hear that about me?”

“Well, don’t get upset.”

“I’m not upset. I’m just curious.”

“I don’t know where I heard it....”

“I think you do. Cuz there’s no way you could have heard it, except one way.... So why aren’t you out gettin’ some pussy?”

“Because!”

“Well, then why ain’t you givin’ up some hole?”

“What?”

“You heard me.”

“What are you talking about?”

“Are you a faggot, Carmelo?”

“What?!”

“That’s how you heard about me, isn’t it? Because I’ve been faithful to Lucia since I got to college, except I go down to the bathroom in the psych building sometimes or to the steam room in the gym and get my dick sucked by some of the little faggots, if I need it. And I have warned those little holes not to tell anybody or else I’d beat the shit out of them. The only thing I allow them to do is to tell other faggots. So that must be how you know, right? Who told you? Deke? That skinny blond guy with the crab tattoo, whatsisname Philip?”

“Uh...I don’t think I know anything about this stuff....” Carmelo had, in fact, overheard Deke talking, not two days after Trajan moved in.

"Coby told me you was a faggot."

"He did not!"

"When I'm not here, you suck on his piece after he fucks girls on this bed."

Carmelo can't stuff down the gasp before it gusts from his chest. "Coby would *not* tell you that...."

"So you *are* a faggot."

Carmelo swallows. "Look, what goes on between Coby and me is between us."

"Don't worry, sweetie. I got nothing against faggots. My twin brother is a fag."

"And you call him a faggot?"

"Why not? I like the word. It's nasty. Like *ho* and *bitch*. I like words like that—especially I like saying those words when my dick is in somebody's mouth or rammed up their cunt. Or stuffed in they ass. It makes me hot. Gets my bitches excited, too, in my experience. My brother liked it when I called him that. Back when we were fifteen, sixteen—you know, when you just have to come like six times a day or go crazy—I used to wrestle him and beat the shit out of him—but not for real, you know, just brother-on-brother ass-kickin'—and then I'd sit on his chest and feed him my cum. I'd call him faggot and beat his face with my fat dick."

Trajan stops, lets the image begin to cohere in Carmelo's busy, busy thoughts. "Then I'd rub my balls on his lips. Boy has some pretty lips."

"And he liked that?"

"He said he did."

"I can't believe it."

"Why?"

"Just—that anyone would like being degraded like that."

"Some like it a lot. I tend to hook up with a lot of people who like it—I guess cuz I like to degrade whoever I'm fucking. Gives me a thrill. You know what I mean?"

"You like to hurt your sexual partners?"

"Kind of. I mean, not bad. But, yeah, I like that shit. It's just a sex thing, for me and for them. Some people like gettin' their feet tickled with feathers. I like rough sex. I never do it with someone who's not willing. And I like it with someone I love. I love my brother. I miss playing with him like we used to."

"Are you like that with Lucia?"

"When she wants it. Sometimes."

"I don't believe it...."

"Oh, I think you can believe it. You're no different from my brother."

"Look, I don't know what the fuck you're talking about. Like I said, what goes on between Coby and me, that's not anything like what you're talking about. It's not even what you think, he just tells me about it and we jack off together, that's all!"

"I bet you'd like to be licking his ass right now."

"No, I—"

"Have your nose pressed right up to his asshole. Smelling it, licking it. Licking up all that sweat and butt-juice. I bet if you had the courage you'd go around all day smelling like men's asses." Trajan sits up. "You want to swing your tongue around in my ass, Carmelo? I'll let you. But then you have to do what I say. Always. And be very quiet about it, because I don't want Lucia to know."

"What?"

"Come on over here. Be my little faggot tonight, since Coby's not here with you. He won't mind if I use you. Matter of fact, he told me how he'd like us to share you. That your hole is so nice it shouldn't belong to one man."

"You're lying! Coby and me never—he said *what?!*"

"You haven't let him fuck you yet? I'm surprised he didn't just throw you down and ram it in, the way you twitch your little bubble ass around the room. It's *obvious* you want a man up in there, fucking it. Shootin' all his hot load of cum up in there, and then gettin' hard again, and fucking it again till it's sore and raw. If you'd been my roomie all these months, I'd a had that shit by now. You'd be a good, trained little boy."

"I am *not* trying to hear this."

"You've been fucked before, bitch."

"Fuck you!"

"Oooh, you haven't, have you? Damn. Mmh, mmh, mmh. So you'll let me take your cherry. I promise I'll make it good for you. Think about it. I got a nice one. Thick, ten and a half inches." He's holding his dick through his shorts. It's not completely hard yet, but Carmelo can see the plump length of it looping diagonally up from the base of Trajan's crotch. "Think about it. All that Puerto Rican dick going up in you. In, out, in, out, boom boom boom."

"Trajan, that's enough."

"I'll let you lick out my butt. It's nice and funky. And hairy. You like that. Coby told me."

"That is—disgusting—"

"If you don't lick it out now, I'll make you beg for it next time. You know you're gonna want it. If you make me wait, I'll have to punish you when the time comes. May have to humiliate you. Come to think of it, especially if you're still cherry, that could be good, too...."

"Okay. Trajan. Look. This is *never* going to happen...."

"Yeah, that is good. We'll wait. I'll fuck you like a little wife back in the old days. Throw a sheet over your ass so you can't even see, so you just a hole for me to abuse.... Hmm, yeah, thass good. Okay. Good night, Carmelo."

He whips his shorts down so that the elastic pushes his balls and dick out like a cock ring. Carmelo stares at the half-engorged dark brown beauty, salivates as the pent-up crotch odor suddenly fills the room. Trajan sticks his finger in the space between his balls and asshole, and swabs it around. He brings it to his nose and inhales. "Mmm, smells good down there tonight. I'd like to eat it myself, if I could. You don't know what you're missing. First hot night of the year—it never gets quite as good as that."

Carmelo can't sleep all night. Trajan sleeps soundly, except when he occasionally turns over. When he does, Carmelo can hear him softly laughing.

Later, on another night (Carmelo calls Coby in Europe, they leave messages on each other's phones for a few days, in one of which Coby denies having said anything to Trajan—but then Coby asks if anything Trajan says about Carmelo is true, which makes Carmelo furious, so he doesn't return the call), Carmelo hears Trajan stir from his bed. He hears his feet touch the cold floor. Slowly he turns so that he can see without Trajan noticing. But the lean, long shadow doesn't pass by. Trajan comes toward him. Startled, afraid his voyeurism has been discovered, Carmelo shuts his eyes tight and readies a fake snore. He feels Trajan near him, standing at the side of his bed. Trajan stoops over him. Carmelo can smell the funky odor of Trajan's body.

Then Trajan's hands are on him, touching his face. His fingers play blindly with Carmelo's lips and push at his mouth. Carmelo opens his mouth and suddenly it's full of salty knuckles. And then the fingers retract, and Trajan places his wet fingertips on the back of Carmelo's head. Carmelo opens his eyes and sees Trajan lifting his dick to Carmelo's face. The spongy head touches his lips and Trajan's hips push forward impatiently. Carmelo hesitates, but the grip on the back of his head grows stronger and pushes Carmelo toward Trajan's crotch. He opens his mouth and the dickhead and part of the shaft slips inside, bumping the roof of his throat. Thick: the taste is thick, and heavy, the solidness and strangeness of living flesh, and it's thrilling, maddening, that taste. In his mouth, melting on his tongue, it's intoxicating. Instantaneously, in his mind, he's a slut, he's a whore. He should be treated like a whore.

Trajan holds his dick in one hand and Carmelo's head in another. Trajan rocks his hips slowly back and forth, and suddenly Carmelo feels hot piss rocketing into his mouth. Carmelo tries to pull back when he recognizes the acid burn on his tongue and the acrid smell, but Trajan forces him to stay in place.

"Aaahhh," Trajan sighs as he finishes pissing in Carmelo's mouth. When he pulls out he keeps Carmelo's head in his grip and shakes the droplets of urine off over Carmelo's face. The dribbles sting Carmelo's eyes. Then Trajan turns and goes back to bed.

Horrified, horrifyingly more excited than he has ever been in his life, Carmelo watches as Trajan climbs back under his covers, turns over and goes to sleep. He listens for the snores. Carmelo touches his lips and finds them faintly bruised.

Trajan says nothing of this the next day, and he acts no differently than he did the day before. But Carmelo imagines that he sees that hard look in Trajan's eyes, watching.

That night Trajan strips in front of Carmelo again. "Good night," Carmelo says, barely able to contain his excitement.

"Night," Trajan says gruffly. "Damn!"

"What?" The anger in Trajan's tone makes the blood fill Carmelo's dick. *This time—if it lasts long enough—this time, I'll jack off,* Carmelo plots.

"I didn't take a piss." Trajan looks at Carmelo. "And I'm already undressed."

Silence. Carmelo can smell Trajan's rank crotch and see clearly the bristly black hairs.

"You don't want me to go down that hall and scare some poor girl with my dick, do you?" Trajan says.

Carmelo is numb. "No..."

Like an animal on the attack, Trajan is at Carmelo's bed, standing above him. He grabs Carmelo's head and in the full light from the lamp on the nightstand he wraps his free hand around his heavy, fat dick and slaps Carmelo's face with it, hard. "Open up." There is no emotion in Trajan's voice. Carmelo opens his mouth and Trajan shoves it in. Trajan has waited too long; he starts pissing even before Carmelo has the head fully on his tongue. He pisses for a long time, sighing happily as he finishes.

Trajan deliberately wipes the head on Carmelo's swollen lips, snaps off Carmelo's lamp, and without a word, goes to bed.

Later that same night Carmelo hears Trajan rise from his bed again. He gets ready for the piss (he's already had to run down the hall to the bathroom, twice). But instead of staying at the side of Carmelo's bed, Trajan climbs up on the bed with him. Before Carmelo knows what to do, he sees Trajan's trim, hairy ass above his face and Trajan's hairy legs on either side of his ears. Trajan sits down on Carmelo's face, forcing the black hairs in the crack of his butt—they part, like primly positioned curtains, around the amber-colored hole—down over Carmelo's nose. The smell is sweaty and just slightly, sweetly shitty: intoxicating. "Lick this motherfucker out," Trajan says and rubs his asshole over Carmelo's lips. Carmelo sticks his tongue out and starts licking. Trajan slowly swings his ass around and around, grinding down on Carmelo's tongue from above. He makes sure Carmelo gets his tongue way up there. This goes on for several minutes until Trajan begins to breathe hard. He moans heavily in the back of his throat. Suddenly he begins to whip his butt back and forth over Carmelo's face, making it difficult for Carmelo to keep his tongue lodged between the cheeks and in Trajan's slightly dirty hole. Faster and faster he saws his ass back and forth so that the bed begins to bump against the wall. Then, bracing himself with his hand on the wall, Trajan jacks on his fist-filling cock and shoots in quick succession three long whips of steaming white cum on the top of Carmelo's head and on his pillow.

Slowly Trajan returns to a state of calm. He backs up, rises from Carmelo's bed, and goes back to his own side of the room.

The next day, Trajan comes in from practice in his shorts and T-shirt, sweating. He bends so that Carmelo can see the wet perspiration running down from his back to his crack. He pulls out a stuffed army duffel bag. Then he strips his shorts and T-shirt off, and takes special care to peel off the worn white jockstrap hugging his brown, hairy buttcheeks. He fondles his dick a bit as it flops free from the tight confines of the jock, and Carmelo sees it thicken slightly. Trajan throws the jock and the other stuff into the bag. "You can wash these tonight," Trajan says simply. Carmelo looks at him with his mouth open. "And here, my shoes. Why don't you shine them while you're at it." Trajan's tone is flat.

Neither boy moves or speaks for a long moment. It is only when Carmelo, scarcely knowing what he's even doing, obeying some wordless dictate of his body—or, perhaps, his soul—bends to take the shoes in hand, that Trajan's dick climbs into the open air.

Carmelo has never seen it before totally hard in broad daylight. Trajan grabs the monstrous thing at the base and scoops his wrinkly sac in the grip, holding his genitals like a cock ring. He knocks the shoes from Carmelo's hands, and pushes Carmelo back down into the chair at his desk. Trajan waves his dick impatiently. Carmelo can't believe himself, but he leans over and starts sucking the big smelly dick. Trajan gets the idea of holding Carmelo's head by the ears and fucking his hips back and forth so that Carmelo almost chokes just taking a third of that dick into his mouth. Trajan thinks this is funny and starts laughing. When he tires of this amusement he grabs Carmelo by the back of his head and moves in close. Carmelo has no place to move, Trajan's all up on him, Carmelo has to bend himself backward in order to take it. Carmelo squirms, but Trajan seems to like this position and pumps roughly into Carmelo's mouth and throat. The effort of holding his mouth open wide makes tears flow from Carmelo's eyes.

Trajan shouts, sprays his load, brusquely pulls out, inspects his dick for a moment, then grabs a towel from his closet and his shower-shoes, and exits.

That evening, Trajan instructs Carmelo about how to properly fold and put away his underwear for him. "You have to kiss each pair before you put it in the drawer," Trajan says, deadly serious. When Carmelo, trembling, has finished this job, Trajan tells him to fall to his knees. Trajan has on big, loose basketball shorts and he pulls one leg of them up and in from the inner thigh: His dark balls flop out, dark as two large purple plums and spiky with hair. "And once you finish the underwear, you have to kiss what's been in 'em," he says.

Carmelo kisses Trajan's balls. He laves them with his tongue. Trajan likes that and rewards Carmelo by rapidly jerking his dick over Carmelo's upturned, worshipful face and spilling his jizz all over it.

A week passes. The frenzy of the days before seems to have abated. Trajan still pisses down Carmelo's throat every night, and once when Carmelo is busy studying, Trajan—apparently outraged by Carmelo's studiousness—demands a mouth to fuck. He puts Carmelo on his back, positions his crotch over Carmelo's face, and performs what he calls "swinging-ass push-ups." (Days later, Carmelo can still feel the tenderness of the lining of his mouth when it rubs against his teeth, and the raspy soreness at the back of his throat.) But otherwise Carmelo is left alone.

It is Thursday night. Trajan has left a soiled pair of scarlet trunks on the floor. They seem, though motionless, to strut across Carmelo's vision like the red plume of rooster's comb. Carmelo sees them on the blond floor, bends without thinking to put them away, and then stops. He looks around, listens. He goes down the hall to the bathroom, and doesn't find Trajan there. He comes back to the room and locks the door. He turns off the light, but leaves the curtains open so that the gibbous near-full moon, nearing its zenith in the late May sky, shines through. He picks up the underwear and gingerly holds it to his nose. He sniffs. The rank mixture of crotch sweat and hairy dark ass is powerful; it makes him wild. He starts rubbing it in his face. He unzips his pants, pulls out his rock hard dick and starts jacking off, faster than usual. Soon he has his pants down to his ankles and he's kneeling on Trajan's bed mashing his nose into the underwear, and his butt is up in the air as he pumps his dick into his hand. Then he kicks his pants off completely, lies down and holds the underwear to his face with both hands while he humps the bed.

"Oh, yeah, get all up in it, baby...."

Carmelo freezes.

It's Trajan, standing in the doorway. Through the scrim of the cotton underwear Carmelo can see Trajan grinning as light spills through the door, his teeth white and luscious lips wet. His goatee makes him look demonic, feral; his rugged, handsome face has become the visage of a satyr. He has on rumpled jeans and large sparkling beetle-black shoes and a short-sleeved blue silk button-down shirt that opens wide at the neck and hangs from his hard, muscular shoulders. Black curls clutch at the bottom of Trajan's sun-bronzed neck, and the silver of his chain glints in the moonlit darkness. He licks his lips, and starts pulling the zipper over the hump in his jeans. "Keep going. I want to watch you."

"No..."

"Keep going."

Carmelo flings the underwear aside and struggles to pull up his pants. He flushes with anger, with frustration. "No, I won't."

"You keep going or I'll open this door and turn on this light and call everybody in to see you. What would Tyra say? She already thinks you're a faggot. I wouldn't want to be you and live in this dorm with Abdul, Mr. Black Islam himself, if I got caught smelling a man's dirty underwear, butt nekkid with a hard dick." Trajan turns and nods down the hallway. " 'Sup, my brotha?"

"You wouldn't," Carmelo says hoarsely. "You're bluffing..."

Trajan slowly turns back to Carmelo. "I never bluff, bitch. I only threaten. I ain't Coby. You don't even want to know the kind of stuff I've done, the kind of mischief I've gotten into. Especially when the moon gets like *this!* Oh, I'm a nasty motherfucker, Carmelo. Don't think I wouldn't like exposing you. It would just make you all the more pathetic when you come begging for me to use you. And I'd like that." He licks his lips. "Right now, I'm startin' to think I'll expose you anyway, just for the fun of it, whether you do what I say or not."

"Okay, okay, okay. Fuck!"

"Watch your tone, ho." Trajan nods again toward the hallway, smiles. Carmelo shuts his eyes, and then he hears the door close.

Trajan's voice is just above him now. "Lie back down there like you were. Yeah. Smell them draws. Good, ain't it? Nasty, ain't it? That's me you're smelling, Carmelo. Inhale all that funk. Take it all in, like your wet mouth and throat gon take in my dick. Like your ass gon take in my dick. Breathe it all in. Move your ass around. Hold your breath! Yeah… Move that tight little bitch ass around. Make your ass squeal. Squeal for me like you'd die without me. Yeah, move it, move that pussy! Fuckin' punk-ass bitch. Move it round and round and round." Carmelo flinches as Trajan smacks his ass hard. "Keep holding the smell in, feel it moving around inside you. Like a snake. Like a serpent. That's me, coiling up inside you, everywhere, in every place, every pleasure-loving place, every pleasure-giving place, every vulnerable place. Uh huh, yeah, let it in to every needy place, every hurtin' space that needs Papi's soothing touch. Uhhh, yeah, you know how much you want it. Now breathe."

Carmelo exhales. The loud sound startles him. He feels like his blood is pounding through him, his every sense tingling, he feels savage, Neanderthal, lucidly insane, without name or memory. The rhythm of his yanking on his dick and moving his ass disintegrates. He just moves now, continuously.

Trajan frees his huge cock from his jeans and begins tugging the foreskin over its fat head.

"Say you want me."

It seems to take forever just to remember how to speak. "I want you, Trajan."

"Say you need me."

"I need you."

"Say you'll serve me."

"I serve you, Trajan."

"Say it'll give you pleasure to be used as I see fit."

"It gives me pleasure to be used as you see fit."

"You are now mine, Carmelo Delon Hildebrandt, until I release you. My cunt. Mine."

Carmelo sighs from his gut. "Yours, Trajan."

"You like that smell, don't you?"

"Unnh…yy-yes, yessss…"

"It's shit and piss and funk and cock cheese, ho. You like it?"

"Uh huhhh..."

"Then come."

Carmelo feels himself come: It's as if he vaults over the edge of a cliff, as if he were riding a motorcycle or a stallion that breaks the speed of sound, with cool wind in his face, beneath a moon the size of Jupiter white and bright in his eyes and flooding a desert landscape in bluish white, as if he leaps from the cycle and flies into the air, his arms outstretched like Superman. A feeling, intense, vivifying, consumes his feet, legs, groin, stomach, chest, throat, and head with hot fire as cold as piercing ice.

And then slowly, slowly, he spirals down.

Carmelo, exhausted, smiles. Then he feels a rough palm on the back of his head, yanking him up by the close-cropped hairs. Trajan's monstrous dick fills his vision. The head of it glares at him. Carmelo swears Trajan is standing more than a foot back, luxuriously stroking the truncheon at its base with his free hand. His hair-covered balls swing forward and swing back like a clock mechanism. Trajan winds his mean brown hips around slowly, sensuously as if to indulge every sensation of moving and stroking his dick—and then suddenly flicks his tight ass forward hard.

"A— ah! Aaaaaa!! Ahhhhhh..." Worms, slugs, sea horses of juicy, sticky, reeking cum—first in magnificent bolts, then mere baby gurgles—fly to land splat on Carmelo's face, cover his eyelids, stream down his cheeks and over his lips.

Trajan moves closer and wipes himself off on Carmelo's forehead. Carmelo dutifully laps up what covers his lips, and uses his hands to spoon off the rest.

"Mmmh." Trajan is smiling down at him—a mocking, superior smile, it seems. But there is something kind in it, too. He bends down and covers Carmelo's mouth with his. His tongue burrows between Carmelo's lips and sucks the inside of his mouth. The taste of his tongue—a faint taste of hashish, some beer, a day's breath, his saliva—is heaven to Carmelo. "I love my own cum," Trajan breathes.

"You know I just cast a spell on you, right?" Trajan says. He is zipping up. His dick flops inside his jeans and slightly balloons the baggy left trouser. Before Carmelo can answer, Trajan has grabbed him by the waist and in a deft movement Carmelo cannot account for, Trajan spins him around so that he lies on his stomach.

"What!"

"Shut up." Trajan jams his thumb right up Carmelo's ass. Carmelo screams, and Trajan immediately pulls his thumb out. He holds his thumb to his nose. "Almost like cherry." He spins Carmelo around again, looks him in the eye very seriously. "I'm gonna fuck the shit outta that." Then he smiles. "It's gon be good."

Suddenly Carmelo feels regret. Almost crying, he asks, "Will Coby know? I mean, about what—what we've done?"

"You mean how you seduced me and tried to make me into a faggot like you so I had to kick your ass?"

Carmelo looks up in horror at Trajan's calloused hands. He has heard about how Trajan and one of his teammates got in a fight with some Berkeley football players and seriously injured them. He didn't believe the story before, but...

Trajan laughs. "Just playin' wit'ya. As for our best friend—Coby and I have no secrets."

"Oh. Shit. Will Coby—?"

"The truth is, I'm just gettin' you ready for him."

Carmelo contemplates this, with excitement and fear.

"But don't worry. Coby's thing is only to be rough with white girls. I don't know why he limits himself like that, but to each his own. With everyone else he's very loving."

"Have you...slept with Coby?"

Trajan smiles enigmatically. "Go get washed up and come back in here. I'm tired, and I'm gonna sleep on you. You'll be my bed tonight."

Friday night Trajan has Carmelo get him dinner from the dining hall downstairs and bring it up to their room for him. In the dining hall, Carmelo tries to keep his head low. Tyra passes by with a tray in her hands and her glasses on and her head in a silk wrap. "Studying in our room this evening, are we?" she says with strident brightness. "Why're you taking *two* dinners?" Carmelo mumbles the answer. Trya gives him a squint-face. "Uh huh. Well, you are coming to the baseball game tomorrow, aren't you? They're going to be in the College World Series!" Carmelo says he probably won't be there. "You have two crumbs on the corner of your upper lip," Tyra says, making another squint-face as she walks away.

Carmelo brings Trajan his dinner. Later, he takes the tray back down. Around ten, after trying to study, Carmelo falls asleep in exhaustion.

Trajan goes over to his bed and climbs on top of him. Carmelo is on his stomach. Trajan's weight pushes him into the mattress. Carmelo listens as Trajan wets his fingers in his mouth and then jumps as Trajan's fingers poke at his asshole. "Wait...," Carmelo says. Trajan takes his fingers out and rearranges himself on Carmelo's back. He pushes Carmelo back down when Carmelo tries to get up, lifts Carmelo up when Carmelo tries to shrink away, arranging Carmelo's body to suit his pleasure. Then, butt raised just so, as if suspended by the power of Trajan's will, head down, neck tingling from the slaps Trajan has given it, Carmelo feels the massive head of Trajan's big, thick dick pushing hard at his hole. "No!" Carmelo cries to the pillow, but then Trajan's hand is over Carmelo's mouth. While Carmelo hisses and half-screams and twists and turns to get free, Trajan relentlessly pumps forward, one hard thrusting move followed by another. Without thinking, without meaning to, Carmelo pushes back by instinct, trying to throw Trajan off, trying to keep him out, but the movement is just enough to make his sphincter give way. "*Nice*," Trajan grunts. "Stop!" Carmelo whispers desperately, and then, "Wait, just please wait, let me get used to it...." But Trajan pushes each inch inside Carmelo until his chute is completely filled and stretched.

Trajan resettles his weight, placing his hands alternately on Carmelo's hips and on his shoulders like a rider testing the angle of his feet in stirrups, and then he begins a slow, agonizing fuck. Slight lift of the hips—Carmelo sighs—hard, full push back in: deeper. Trajan's ass lifts again, his dick slips further out—Carmelo tenses—Trajan lunges fiercely, swerves round, grinds: deeper yet.

Carmelo's tears run down over Trajan's hand clamped on his mouth, but Trajan's increasingly satisfied *aaahhs* and sighs excite him. He finds that he likes it better when Trajan fucks him fast, the big shaft thrusting in and out quickly like Carmelo's asshole is a sheath made for Trajan's dick. Somewhere in the midst of it, when his body is too ravaged to resist and his mind too tired to catalogue the sensations of pain, the jabbing heat, the way his body just opens and contracts, inflates, and empties, completely without regard to his own will or his own rhythms, Carmelo hears himself spit out, "Oh fuck...fuck...you're filling me, you're filling me up...."

"Wha...Wha'd you say?" Trajan pants, but Carmelo cannot answer, his moans fill the room, slip beneath the door, expand south and west down the hallways.

But Trajan heard. And replaying the sound of Carmelo's pleading in his mind, he loses control of his hips and starts to give it to the boy hard. You thought I was fucking you before, his hips, his dick, say: Now watch, bitch. Now see.

Trajan's thickness in Carmelo's ass is like a club, pummeling him, widening him, forcing the inside of Carmelo's body to grow larger, softer, more yielding. Trajan yells out, "FUCK!" and in three chicken-like thrashes floods Carmelo's pulsing colon. When he pulls out, he pats Carmelo's butt.

Carmelo, dazed, looks down at himself. He sees a wide brown spot on the sheets. "You bled a little," Trajan announces—with approval, it seems.

Trajan sticks a finger up Carmelo's ass so that Carmelo shivers. He pulls it out and puts it to his nose. "Nice boodie," he says.

The next night, Carmelo tries to complain about how Trajan's dick hurt him before they turn out the light and go to sleep. "If you'd just be a little gentler...," Carmelo says. Trajan watches him with cold eyes, and says nothing. He goes to sleep.

Later that night, Carmelo finds himself writhing uncontrollably on Trajan's lap as Trajan spanks him with his belt. Then Trajan pushes Carmelo down on the floor on all fours and rams his dick up Carmelo's butt. He doesn't use any lube but his own saliva, and it takes a while to get up in there—but not as long as it took the first time. Before he's finished, Trajan pulls out, stands up, and throws Carmelo on the side of the bed on his stomach. "Tired a your whining," he grouses. Trajan lathers the brawny shaft of his slightly drooping cock with some body lotion. His fingers cannot reach around the whole thing. Carmelo watches with his face pressed against the sheets: watches it push Trajan's fingers wider, watches it reach its full thickness, its complete rigidity. It is all Carmelo sees: a mass of flesh that slightly bounces as Trajan turns, and that spits once, twice, when it sees Carmelo staring at it.

Then Trajan sticks it up Carmelo's ass again. Not slowly. Carmelo feels that his skin and muscle, the organ that the rectum is, is being scissored, is ripping away to the bare fat beneath. "That feel better?" Trajan snorts as he dicks Carmelo with fierce all-the-way-in, all-the-way-out strokes. Carmelo thrills to the pain that lances through him and throws his butt backward to meet each of Trajan's punishing thrusts. They both come, muffling their cries.

Carmelo awakens late the next day. He looks at the clock, then looks down at the strip of blood-red cloth on his pillow. He has spent the last nine hours with his face buried in Trajan's dirty trunks.

Trajan isn't in the room.

When Carmelo can finally rouse himself from bed, his body feels tender, its balance precarious. The cheeks of his ass chafe miserably against each other, and all the muscles of his legs ache. His hole, of course, is sore, and seems to echo inside his body every time he moves. All the way to the bathroom down the hall, while he's on the toilet, and back to 338, all Carmelo can smell, the only aroma that the nerve cells in his nose and the smell center in his brain can distinguish, is Trajan. Carmelo's own body, his excrement, the room, Carmelo's own underwear (which he lifts briefly to his face, wondering: Do they smell like a rape victim's?)—everything smells like Trajan. Everything, drenched in the perfume of Trajan's juices.

Carmelo flings open the window on the west side of the room. The sun is high, the breeze light. From a distance he hears what sounds at first like a rumble, and then resolves clearly into a collective roar: the crowds in the stands at the ball field, cheering on the team. As he listens to the shouting, the loud shapeless massive noise, Carmelo feels oddly moved. Warmth suffuses his body (he thinks immediately of Trajan's piss, the way it seems to seep osmotically through the membranes of his cells as it cascades down his throat). The feeling oozing through Carmelo's entrails matches exactly the sound that he hears: frenzied adoration, fanatic love. And he finds himself cheering, exultant, for the Warrior's victory.

Sniff

Belasco

Sniff by BELASCO
SNIFF...
Sniff sniff
Sniff
SNIFF
SNIFF...
BELASCO ©

The Gift

Reginald Harris

"Well, I guess I better go," I said, shifting in my seat. "Gotta stop by to see my mom, then figure out what I'm gonna do tonight."

"You goin' out?"

"I don't know.... Doesn't seem like much point, really. Nothing but the same tired places to go to around here, with the same tired people in 'em. Still, I haven't been out in a while, so..." I shrugged and sighed, staring out the window at the clear late afternoon sky. "Maybe I'll drive down to DC for a change. I don't know."

"And here I am thinking I'm missin' somethin'." Andre scratched at the bandage holding the IV into his arm.

"Baby, you ain't missin' shit."

"Mr. Webster? Time for your meds." A tall male nurse entered the room, carrying a pair of tiny white paper cups on a faded orange tray.

"At least they gave me someone nice to look at while I'm up in here this time." Andre smiled at me.

"I hope he's not giving you-all too much trouble," I said to the nurse. Andre was right: he *was* kinda cute. In his twenties, I guessed, and the color of a latte grande, the nurse was tall enough that he'd had to bend slightly when he came in the door. But perhaps he was a little too "swishy" for me, too "obvious" or "clock-able." I'd been on a "straight-looking, and -acting, brothas on the DL only tip" here of late when it came to the men in my life. This guy could have been a drag queen somewhere when he wasn't working at the hospital, I thought, inhaling his strong cologne as he passed me.

The nurse looked like the type of guy I *used* to go out with. If I had seen him in one of the clubs (...and *had* I seen him? I couldn't remember...) I would've thought he was attractive, but stayed away, imagining he had the word *MISTAKE* tattooed all over his body, hidden under his clothes. Of course, as the hour got later, my objections would have evaporated faster than the ice in my glass and I might've said something to him, bought him a drink, asked him to dance, turned on the charm just to get into his pants. We might even have gone out a few times—depending on how good the sex was—then let the whole thing fizzle out. After some time not seeing him, perhaps we'd run into each other in a club and talk. Over the months that talk would spiral downward, first into a smile and a nod, then a wave, until eventually we wouldn't say anything to each other at all, just a quick dismissive, "*Him*? Oh yeah: been there done that," if our friends happened to ask one about the other.

I shook myself awake. Jesus! Here I've met the guy, dated him, slept with him, and dumped him, all in the space of about two seconds. And I don't even know his name. This is horrible....

"Oh no, he's no trouble at all," the nurse had been saying. "When he starts acting up, we know to just pay it no mind and move on."

"That's how we have always handled him." I laughed. "My

name's Eric, by the way, since *this* one's got no manners and doesn't know how to introduce people." I glared at Andre.

"Albert." He smiled sheepishly, then glanced away. Who knows, it might be fun.... I shook my head and got up to look out the window. "I'm not being disrespectful, it's just that I want to keep him to myself," Andre said. Albert helped him to shift up in the bed, so that he was sitting almost upright to swallow the pills. "I know how you Watsons are, remember? You see somebody good-looking and the next thing you know you-all are off banged up together someplace.

"And don't make me read you about that 'Mr. Webster' shit either." He turned on Albert. "I done told you I ain't writing no dictionary up in here. Call me *'Dre*, damn it, just like everybody else. I may look like an old man, but I'm not. Makes me feel like I'm two-hundred years old, goddamned 'Mr. Webster,' " he muttered.

Albert and I glanced at each other and rolled our eyes. "You just can't treat nobody right, can you?" I asked Andre. "Always gotta be giving grief."

"What grief? Mr. Webster's my father, God help him, not me and never has been. And before too much longer I never will be, either."

"Don't talk like that, baby...."

"Oh, please," Andre waved a thin hand. "Spare us both. We all know what's happening here. I'm dying, right? You know it, I know it, and he knows it. It should be no big deal. I've had a good life, had lots of fun, but now it's time to pack my shit and move on. Why pretend that things are any different? And, since I *am* going, I should be treated the way I want to be treated, right? After all, you don't want my black ass haunting you, do you?"

"You're right about that. You were pain in the ass enough when you were up and well. As a ghost, you'd be a real motherfucker."

"Right! So...," he pointed to Albert, "'*Dre*, right?"

Albert nodded. " 'Dre. Do you need something else? More water or something?"

"No, I'm fine baby, thank you."

"See, now he's all sweetness and light." I shook my head.

"Nice meeting you." Albert grinned at me before he left. "Hope to see you again."

"Nice meeting *you*."

"Isn't she cute?" Andre asked before Albert had even left the room.

"Yeah, yeah." I tried to sound noncommittal, but felt a familiar stirring between my legs. "He's so *young*, though! All these kids are so young nowadays. I feel like I should bring a box of Pampers with me every time I go out."

I looked over at Andre. He'd leaned back onto the pillow and closed his eyes. Perhaps his medication was beginning to take hold. His face was gaunt and sere, splattered with dark splotches from a malignant paintbrush. 'Dre's short brown hair was thin and graying, his skull almost visible beneath his skin. He could've been my grandfather's age rather than one of my contemporaries.

He opened his eyes slowly, like a lizard awakening from a sunbath, until they widened to their full extension, practically filling his face, as if nothing were left of him but his eyes. I knew his eyes were failing him, too, like so many other systems in his body. They opened wide to catch their last remaining sights before they went dark.

"How you doin', baby?"

"I hate this shit. It makes me feel so awful. And I must look a fright."

"Nah...you're still beautiful." I walked over to the bed and held his hand.

"Liar...but I don't mind."

"You look like you need some rest and I really gotta go."

I hesitated. Part of the reason why I'd come that day was to face this, to say this one thing to him and now I wasn't sure if I should or not. I looked into Andre's enormous eyes. In many ways, he really was still beautiful.

"You know...I always had the hots for you." Andre looked at me sideways. "I'm serious. How you looked, and the way you used to dance all night in the clubs...hell everybody wanted you. Why not me? I remember the second or third time I saw you, years and years ago. You were wearing a tight-ass pair of black jeans and a dark shirt, purple or some such color. We ran into each other in the street...not that far from here, actually, over on Rideout. You were going somewhere and I was headed home. You looked hot as shit and I thought, *Damn...* But I couldn't say anything since I knew even then that you were living with Sherman and all. Maybe...maybe I shouldn't have said that...I'm sorry...." I looked down at the floor.

'Dre slapped my hand. "*Now* you up and tell me this? If I'd a known something five or six years ago, I woulda been all over you!"

"Oh, don't tell me that. Now I'll be kicking myself for not coming on to you!" I laughed. "God, what am I saying—you were my cousin's boyfriend, for Christ's sake. He *and* my family woulda kicked my ass if we'd messed around."

"Neither Sherman nor your family didn't have to know, baby, you know that. Shit, I'm surprised when anybody in *your* family can keep their damn pants on for five continuous minutes at a time, as hot-assed as you all are. Your father running around on Vickie 'till she kicked him out, your sisters and all their damned boyfriends, your brother always off God knows where creeping around...and you too! And you and I both know you ain't no saint.... Is there anybody in this town some member of your family *hasn't* slept with?"

"Well...new people *are* moving in all the time, you know.

It's getting harder for us to keep up." We both laughed. "And we do kinda stop at close family members too, none of that incest shit."

"Yeah, but second cousins are fair game, right?"

I rolled my eyes. "I'm sorry I ever told you that, now. Jesus, it was only one time. We were kids for God's sake."

He held up a hand. "It's okay, it's okay. No one knows about that but you and William and me. Shit, as good-looking as he grew up to be, I woulda jumped him too... But the two of us? Your family wouldn'ta cared. They'd a thought it was just 'faggots being faggots,' that's all. No big deal."

"Maybe that's one of the reasons I *didn't* want to do anything. I mean, we may want to, or think about it, but not all of us are out fucking everything that moves every night. Besides, I needed one or two friends I hadn't slept with, you know?"

I regretted what I'd said a second after it slipped out, but if Andre thought it was meant as some kind of judgment on him, he didn't act like it.

"At least I'll be seeing him again soon," Andre whispered. "That's a comfort. And to not have to deal with his damned family...present company excepted, of course."

"You know we all hated what Mary did to you when Sherman died, freezing you out like that, not letting you sit with them. Made it seem almost like there were two separate funerals."

"At least your mother didn't act like the rest of them. Give her my love, will you? And I appreciated you and Mike's sitting out there with me in the lobby like that. How *is* Mike, anyway? I'm surprised the two of you broke up. Now there's a *fine* looking man."

"Yeah, well...these things happen. He's a good guy, but I'm an idiot. I don't know how to handle being in a relationship with someone normal, I guess. I need trauma in my life. No drama, no big scenes and I'm bored." And scared, I thought to myself. No one had ever gotten as close to me as Mike had, and I'd felt compelled to push him away.

Andre sighed. "You need to meet somebody. Or go back to Mike."

"He'd never have me back after the way I just kicked him to the curb."

"Humph. You'd be surprised." Andre wagged a finger at me.

"You'd know, wouldn't you? You and Sherman broke up for a whole year then got back together again."

"He thought he wanted someone...younger? Different? Humph—someone *else*. I let him play around with children for a while..."

"...While my family jumped on him to get married and settle down once they thought you were out of the picture..."

"...And I'm sure he had a good time. Until he realized he couldn't talk to them about anything. Or that all they wanted was the money they thought he had. He came crawling back. They always do. I let him beg for a while, then took him. You men are all the same." Andre coughed. "Always looking for something else when you've already got something perfect. Never satisfied with what you have."

"And you were some kind of angel, huh? I know you weren't always faithful to Sherman either."

He put up a hand to stop me. "I'm not talking faithful if what you mean is sex. I'm talking about commitment. I'm talking about throwing your shit away just because some piece winked at you in the bar. Sex is something the two of you can work out if you try, even if one of you just truly can*not* keep your dick in your pants. Love is something different. You got to hang on to love tight when it hits you. 'Cause when it hits, it hits hard, and it's not easy to get over. You're not going to fall in love, I mean find someone who *really* loves you, very often. You gots to hang on to that, make it last, build on things together. Fuck the dumb shit."

I looked down at my watch. I really did have to go (...and what *was* Mike doing that night anyway...?).

Andre leaned his head back onto the pillow again and yawned. "Shit, all this love and sex talk...as long as it's been since I've had somebody, I don't think I'd remember what to do."

"It's just like riding a bicycle, baby. You never forget how to do it."

Andre slipped me a look. "Maybe you should lock that door and remind me...."

I laughed. "Child, you as crazy as ever. Let me get outta here. Now—your chocolate chip cookies are over here on the nightstand if you want more. But save room for dinner, aw'right?"

"Dinner? Ugh."

"Yeah I know, I know. But try to eat it anyway. I...I wish there was something I could do for you."

"I told you what you could do—*me*! You think I'm kidding? I'm serious. I need some dick one last time.... Okay, fine, then. Be that way. Get the fuck out, then. Just get out." We laughed. "Take care, baby."

"Take care." I leaned down and kissed Andre on the forehead. A sudden jolt went through me as my lips touched his skin. Wild thoughts began running through my head. I stood up straight. "I'll see you later, boo. I gotta go shopping...."

"Pick up something for me. Anything, I don't care."

"Don't worry, baby, it'll all be for you."

"Hmmm...I like that," Andre murmured softly, lying back into the pillow. "And if you *do* decide to fuck that boy, let me know. I want a stroke by stroke description. Since I'm not getting any anymore, at least let me imagine it...." I nodded and went off in search of Albert. That description thing wasn't a bad idea either....

Albert snuck me back into the hospital at eleven P.M. The corridors were empty but for the low hum of machines. I went quickly to Andre's room, trying not to make too much noise with my bags. "I can give you maybe an hour," Albert whispered. "But no more." I took a deep breath. I wasn't sure I could do this, but it was too late to back out now. I pushed my way into the room.

I pulled my boom box CD player quietly from one bag and set it up next to Andre's bed, choosing a compilation of Brazilian music from the selection of discs I'd brought with me and pressed Play. The items from the other bag—rubber gloves, the still warm oil, cologne, a small container of cut-up fruit—I arranged on the table as well. I lit the vanilla-scented candles, placing them around the room. I shrugged off my jacket and gently shook Andre awake.

"What's going on?"

"Shh..." I turned on the light over his bed. "I'm here with your present."

I sprinkled a few drops of Aramis on Andre's pillow. It had been Sherman's favorite cologne, and I wanted to surround him once again in the scent of his former love. Andre smiled and wiggled his head into the pillow. I opened the container of fruit.

Maybe I'm strange, but I find papaya incredibly sexy. Something about its firm but pliant texture; its exotic, delicious, not-too-sweet taste. I helped Andre sit up in the bed and sat next to him, slowly feeding him a few slices. I knew he wouldn't eat much, but wanted to fill his mouth with something other than hospital food. I'd cut most of the fruit up into tiny pieces, but left one a fairly good size, about three inches in length and width. When Andre seemed close to having had his fill, I picked up the final piece. Slowly tracing around his mouth with the slice, I wet his lips with juice. I eased the papaya between his lips, gently sliding it into and out of his mouth, hoping he would get the hint.

Andre looked at me with consternation. "You mean it's been so long you've forgotten how to do this?" I asked. After a moment's confusion, Andre's brow relaxed and he pursed his lips. He began to suck on the papaya slice in mock lasciviousness, licking around it, running his tongue up and down the slice, quickly licking my fingers. He then took the whole thing in his mouth, slurping loudly and moaning. "Somehow I thought you'd be bigger, darling," he said, batting his eyes.

Chuckling, I got up and slowly unbuttoned my shirt, swaying to the samba unfurling from the CD player, playfully covering and revealing my bare chest like an exotic dancer. A slow smile played across Andre's face.

"My own Private Dancer! You Watson men...." He shook his head. Andre ran his hand across my bare torso, pausing to give my slight pre-middle age bulge a gentle squeeze. "You need to go to the gym, honey," he whispered.

I rolled my eyes, slapping at his hand. "*Bitch!* Only you would diss a motherfucking gift! Shut the hell up, I'm going back next week." I shook my head and slowly undid my jeans, casually letting them slip down to the floor.

Andre's eyes widened. He shook an admonishing finger. "Didn't your mama ever tell you to always wear underwear?" He reached out for me. "Humph! I really woulda tried to have you if I'd known all-a this was here."

I tried not to burst out laughing, or into tears, bending down to pull my pants back up around my hips. "Okay, now you." I reached for Andre's sheet.

"NO!" Andre grabbed it tightly. "No. Please. No way..."

"No, baby, it's okay, it's okay." I kissed him lightly on the forehead and both cheeks. "You have nothing to be ashamed of. Don't worry. Come on, let me see."

I eased the sheet from his hand and slowly pulled it back. I sighed in spite of imagining I had prepared myself for this. The flimsy hospital gown could not cover the fact that Andre's once beautiful body seemed to have been drained of fluids. He reminded me of photographs of African famine victims. His body appeared almost lost in the hospital bed, a dry black seed in the middle of the sheet's white husk. My voice was choked when I said, "You still got it goin' on, baby. Best-looking man in town."

Andre began to cry. I wiped away his tears. "Hush... hush.... Let me do this, please. If you start to bawl, I'm never going to make it. You don't want both of us up in here gushing like schoolgirls, now do you?" I turned the music up.

I put on a pair of thin, royal purple gloves. I'd never seen surgical gloves in any color other than faded beige, but somehow Albert had come through. "He needs a little color, don't you think?" he'd said earlier that day when I'd told him about my plan. I picked up the small bottle of warm oils and started with his feet.

I felt very strange. All the years I'd thought of this, dreamed of seeing Andre naked, longed to put my hands on his smooth bare body. And here we were. And were not. Andre both was and wasn't there. Or rather he was still here, trapped inside a fading body. His wit, his beauty, the person I had wanted still glowed there, like a light coming from deep inside a shell.

Moving the thin gown aside, I wanted to remember how he'd looked, to bring him back into his body. I wanted to remember how beautiful Andre's skin had been, just like polished mahogany. I want to remember him with my hands, bring him back to life with a loving caress. Starting with his hammer-toed dancer's feet, I wanted to touch every part of his body, to remind him of the pleasures of a man's hands on him. Crazily, I thought—if I do this right, then his bones will strengthen. If I do this right, maybe he'll stop wasting away; he'll regain muscle, retain his food and liquids. I can repair his beat-up body; smooth away his cuts and bruises, the scars illness had lashed across his body. His lungs will clear, his color will return, all will be as it was before. *I can bring him back,* I thought. *Please, God, let me bring him back. Change him back into the person I knew, the man my cousin loved, the vision we thought was just too sexy for words and all deeply cared for.*

I worked without a sound, except for the music and Andre's slow breathing, my silence a form of homage, a thing to be reckoned with. His skin inhaled the oils, drinking deeply. I moved inside the music in a subtle counter-rhythm to the *bossa novas* and *boleros* on the CD, gently working my way up his body, cupping his rough heels in the palms of my hands, slowly massaging his once strong calves and thighs. I tickled his "outie" belly button; caressed his stomach, sunken chest, and extraordinarily large, dark nipples; then moved across his shoulders and down his withered arms, carefully avoiding his IV. I rubbed Andre's throat and neck, and lightly played my fingers across his cheeks and eyebrows. Running a quick hand through his thin hair and kissing his forehead, I whispered, "Still beautiful, baby, still hot." Again Andre began to cry. I quickly kissed his opening mouth before he could speak.

I oiled my hands again and moved to Andre's crotch. He opened his legs slightly, and I slipped between them, searching. Carefully I slid a finger between his asscheeks, worrying the entrance to his hole. Andre moaned. I wrapped my other hand around his dick, gently stroking his maleness. Andre sighed, reached his hand out for me. I moved closer to the bed, lowering my pants, and placed my warm cock in his hand. His first touch brought me to life.

Gently fingering his asshole, I again thought of how much I'd longed to do this years before, the thrill of imagining myself with someone so attractive, the electric jolt tasting the forbidden always sends through your body. I thought back to another dancer I'd had a brief affair with—how his strong legs would wrap around me in our bed like a vise. His ass had gripped me tightly, pulsing as we fucked, as if he were trying to suck the jism from me with his butt. He, too, had had a smooth sleek body, and I closed my eyes, remembering. Andre had closed his eyes as well. Sniffing at the cologne on his pillow, he began murmuring Sherman's name. Andre remained flaccid, but my dick grew to its full length and hardness in Andre's hand, under the influence of my imagination and the memory of sweet afternoons spent with other men. We slowly stroked each other like ancient lovers, lost in our separate visions of the past.

"Huh uh uh..." Andre's hand slowed then stopped and he leaned back onto the bed. His breathing quickened and his head began to move from side to side. I continued fingering him, pushing in a bit deeper and pulling at his cock. Andre turned to look at me, running his eyes down my torso to my exposed crotch. "Beautiful, so beautiful," he whispered softly. Without a sound he ejaculated into my hand.

I wiped up Andre's cum with a towel and rubbed oils into his dick and ass again. I slowly covered him with the hospital gown, and pulled up the sheet and coverlet. Taking off the gloves, I moved to the head of the bed. Andre started to say something but I laid a finger across his lips.

"Shh.... Get some rest." I gently ran my fingers over Andre's face, lightly brushing his hair until his enormous eyes closed and I could hear the soft purr of his sleep. I quietly packed everything up, wiping the water from my eyes as I left the room.

Two days later the phone rang at exactly 3:13 A.M. I jumped, startled from the black-bottomed pool of sleep I'd been swimming in. I stared at the insane thing screaming in the darkness, reached for it, and then stopped. I didn't need to hear what the person on the other end had to say. One look at the time told me all I needed to know.

I lay back down, plugging my ears until the madness stopped, then pulled the sheet and blanket closer to me. I leaned back into the pillow, and began to gently rock slowly from side to side to a quiet rhythm only I could hear. My eyes filled with tears; my nose was haunted by the scent of vanilla candles, patchouli oil.

The Passion

Tip Langley

"My brother, may I ask you a question?"

I was just about to lift my head, when he continued, "Have you accepted the Lord Jesus Christ as your personal savior?"

I contemplated not acknowledging him and maintaining focus on my book, with the hope that my "brother" would decide to move along to the next prospective heathen. But something in the quality of the voice made me reconsider: His tone had a deep, sexy resonance and the cadence was of a particularly well-spoken man—one of my weaknesses. I caught sight of his hand clasping his Bible in my peripheral vision—richly dark, veined, with thick blunt fingers. He was wearing a nice suit along with a pair of well-polished, radiantly black Kenneth Cole shoes.

I looked up. I found myself gazing upon a deep-chocolate-colored man in his late twenties or so, with brown eyes that reminded me of sparkling marbles accentuated by his long lashes. This presumably Christian fellow also had full lips that lengthened into a smile, revealing a set of beautiful teeth, yet another weakness of mine. He had a noticeably tight frame, broad and taut and filled out in all the right places—reminiscent and even faintly redolent, in the imagination, of a darkened sepia photograph of the former Cassius Clay. I too smiled. Suitably disarmed, he brought me back to my senses with his importunate question. "Have you accepted the Lord Jesus Christ as your personal savior?"

Uncharacteristically, I stammered. His brilliant smile unwavering and his eyes conveying something between curiosity and friendliness, he held my gaze and awaited my response. Commanding myself to attention, mustering up briefly-forgotten powers of speech and elementary motor skills, I finally said, "Would it please you if I said yes?"

His face morphed into an expression of amusement, then contemplation. "I guess it would please me some. But now I would have to question the truth of it."

"You may be on to something," I said. "I have not accepted Jesus Christ as my personal savior. Based on what I assume to be your intention, that would make me in need of salvation." I stood and extended my hand. "I'm Dr. Richard Gentry, pleased to meet you."

He shook my hand. "Chris Stuart. Pleased to meet you... doctor?"

Smiling, I said, "I'm a professor of African American literature at the university. And not quite as pretentious as my introduction might have suggested. Would you care to continue our chat over a cup of coffee?"

"Yes, I would," was his soft reply—spoken with a gentle lowering of those feathery lashes as well as his voice. His reply I felt as well as heard, as a gust of his breath met my face, and a tremor moved through my body that I could barely suppress and rather enjoyed.

We decamped to the nearby Tully's.

Over my mocha and his chai, I learned that Chris had attended the university ten years prior. He had worked a variety of jobs, but still hadn't found the ideal vocation. To become a firefighter seemed to be his current career aspiration. He was raised in a religious household, headed by a loving, supportive mother. Father was not in the picture. The Church of God in Christ was a special place for the family and he, being the oldest of six, had embraced and accepted his appointed role as the dutiful inheritor and guardian of the family's faith. In the midst of my probing of a devotion I frankly found a bit baffling—*You believe that really? But what about...? What if...?*—I was deliciously surprised to learn that Chris felt his primary weakness was his ample appetite for sex. He reported this failure to maintain Christian purity to me with little to no irony. Apparently, since his college years, he had done a fair amount of "indulging," but he'd decided that this sexual indulgence was less than exemplary behavior. In order to fortify his religious ideals, he had recently joined a new COGIC congregation, also partly because it reminded him of his childhood church. He'd found this church on a visit with a prospective girlfriend. They were not having sex, I discovered with a few softly-spoken, professorially paternal questions, because she was just coming out of a breakup and needed time to heal before getting serious with anyone. He had not had sex with anyone for some time. *My, my, what a coincidence,* I thought. I had also been doing without sex since joining the faculty. Was this divine intervention? I had no concrete indication that Chris's "indulgences" involved sex of the homosexual variety, but my senses told me it was entirely possible he might consider such a union.

His new Church of God in Christ urged all its members to commit to a volunteer mission that would promote the teachings and spirit of the Lord Jesus Christ. As our fate would have it, Chris had chosen to share the word and teachings of the Lord with as many of his fellow black brothers as possible, from the streets of Berkeley to the cellblocks of San Quentin. How fortuitous that I happened to be in his path that day. And that day—that week—had been such a difficult one. I'm still surprised I even looked up at him. Maybe it really was salvation. Maybe I really was destined to be saved, resurrected even.

We talked for an hour or so. He clearly enjoyed a good conversation—which is to say that he enjoyed talking and I enjoyed listening to the sound of his voice and watching his mouth move. I grew gradually quieter and quieter, confining myself to smiles and simple questions and noises of assent, losing all reliance upon my usual intellectually rigorous tendencies as if shedding the scales of an old skin. I now simply desired him: definitely body, and likely soul. When the time seemed right—we had drifted companionably into a discussion of basketball, about which I know little but was faking rather well, I thought—I seized on the moment to say, "Chris, I feel like I need a change of scenery." (No, it's not a very compelling line. But you'd be surprised what a confident tone can pull off—especially when the listener's real agenda has nothing to do with sense or logic.) "Would you please accompany me to my home?" I paused, let my fingers dance across the tabletop. "And perhaps provide me with the spiritual enlightenment you purport to have for your black brothers?"

He hesitated. I expected the hesitation, and of course since I couldn't manage to breathe while awaiting the answer, I busied myself contemplating the shallow ravines flowing back from his wrists between the muscular tendons of his forearms. Finally, tentatively (those lashes fluttering again), he responded. "Yes, Dr. Gentry, I would be happy to provide you with some spiritual enlightenment and accompany you to your home."

I breathed at last, and couldn't stifle a chuckle I hoped

didn't sound too Satanic. "Very well, then, shall we be off?"

At home, as Chris discoursed on a variety of topics, I prepared tea and placed the tray on the coffee table. I put on a CD of rhythmic and melodic belly dancing music I'd acquired in Istanbul. (Did this evangelical Christian consider Muslims pagans, I wondered? Probably. Or maybe not—People of the Book, and all that. But my interest in Islam tends toward the ecstasies of Sufi mystics and the lustful pursuit of beautiful boys you find in unexpurgated versions of *The Arabian Nights*, and I doubt those would pass muster in the Church of God in Christ.). I lit a few strategically placed scented candles and surreptitiously dialed the thermostat up to a sultry eighty degrees. Fetching the large gold leaf Bible I had inherited from my grandmother (and had only ever perused to hunt down passages the writers I taught made reference to), I gingerly settled its great sacred bulk on the table next to the tray of tea and some chocolate fudge cookies I'd rustled up. He had mentioned earlier that he was a "chocoholic." It felt fortuitous to have them to indulge his eager palate. I watched, pleased, as he devoured them.

Feeling comfortable with the ambiance created, I said to Chris that this seemed like a good time to begin my spiritual enlightenment, or at the very least make an attempt to dredge my soul up from the pit of depraved idolatry to which it was, sadly, all too accustomed. He looked startled, then laughed. I went on to say that I am more labile to the reception of spiritual information when I'm unencumbered. "I trust you won't mind if I remove my clothing. This flat does run warm."

This time I didn't wait for a reply. I was glad that I had made it to the gym over lunch. My caramel-colored body had a fresh tautness from the day's workout. I am over six feet, broad-shouldered, and—dare I say it?—handsome, in an elegant and dapper Langston Hughes sort of way (but bigger). As I undressed, neatly folding each garment as I removed it,

I glanced over at Chris sitting on the sofa, and noted that he appeared to be taking my thinly veiled striptease in stride (eyelashes raised, then lowered, raised again, like the passing of a fan over of a geisha's face; mouth set, impassive—but lips suspiciously lubricious). His body affected the posture of an attentive choirboy, as he leafed reverently through my ornate Bible, expressing how beautiful it was. So coy, I thought.

When I'd finished undressing, I sat down on the high-backed armless chair opposite him and told him that I was ready to receive his wisdom—but for one small matter. He looked up from the Bible, his eyebrows and the corners of his mouth rising like the calligraphic curls that adorned each verse of the scriptures, and slowly drank me in with those beautiful eyes of his. "What is the small matter?" he asked.

I said to him, "It is very warm in here and we're both gentlemen." Ahem. "I think it a good idea that you take your clothes off as well. I would be much more—relaxed—if you did. Of course, if you'd be more comfortable, feel free to keep your undershorts on."

He sat very still. For what seemed like a lengthy deliberation, but was probably only a minute, perhaps two, he did nothing. I feared he might be considering the distance to the front door (I shifted imperceptibly to my right, intent on blocking his way if need be).

But then he smiled, shrugged, and began disrobing. Unabashedly, I focused on him as he undressed. He didn't make eye contact, but his stripping was executed with titillating finesse. Each piece of clothing came off slowly: jacket, tie, white lightly starched shirt, belt, pants, and so on, each piece neatly placed on the sofa. During this gradual revelation, he bent and flexed at varied times, his mahogany muscled body seeming subtly to dance. His movements were interestingly in sync with the Arabian rhythms around us. (*Ah!* I thought. *Who is converting whom?*)

Upon completion, he stood before me in nothing but a pair of brilliantly white briefs, more sexy than I had even imagined, and my body, most notably my dick, responded.

"Shall we begin?" I pointed to the Bible on the table (my arm innocently brushing against my rising dick as I pointed). "Please share with me your favorite passage."

He squatted down and opened the Bible, his thigh and leg muscles contracting and delightfully bulging. I sat before him, legs splayed, dick hard, sweat forming, and heart racing. I could not remember the last time I had felt this stirred and excited. Still squatting, not having looked up, he began reading. His voice was deep, resonant, and smooth. Each word carried a weight and emphasis as perfectly balanced as a gymnast astride a pommel horse.

AND, BEHOLD, A CERTAIN LAWYER STOOD UP, AND TEMPTED HIM, SAYING MASTER, WHAT SHOULD I DO TO INHERIT ETERNAL LIFE? HE SAID UNTO HIM, WHAT IS WRITTEN IN THE LAW? HOW READEST THOU? AND HE ANSWERING SAID, THOU SHALT LOVE THE LORD THY GOD WITH ALL THY HEART, AND WITH ALL THY SOUL, AND WITH ALL THY STRENGTH, AND WITH ALL THY MIND; AND THY NEIGHBOR AS THYSELF...

He was clearly passionate about this scripture. As I listened to his reading, I luxuriated in his voice and for the first time the verses seemed more accessible, more suggestive, and less didactic than I ever remembered them being.

The exhortations to take up a fervent devotion to the Lord thy God however did not abate my sexual desire. As he read, I grew increasingly desirous. My heartbeat steadily increased.

Perhaps sensing my discomfort, he rose, and, picking up the Bible as he continued reading, walked over to me and knelt at my feet. Still reading, he placed the Bible on the floor between my opened legs. There were now short pauses between sentences and intermittent glances up at my face—or maybe he was looking at my turgid pulsating dick (it would be difficult to miss).

...AND HE SAID UNTO HIM, THOU HAST ANSWERED RIGHT; THIS DO, AND THOU SHALT LIVE...

The pauses lengthened, his breathing was a bit deeper and I noticed a few beads of sweat on his brow. I could feel the heat emanating from his body. The wave of it swept across the hairs on my skin, and sent blood thundering through my veins as another tremor rocked me. All at once, almost violently, he stood. His crotch was at eye level. Some considerable lengthening had begun there as well. The snug cotton briefs were straining to contain his engorging staff. I reveled in this hoped for moment, and though I imagined I might feel more triumphant, I wasn't conscious enough of myself, my ego, to feel that I had accomplished my goal. I was overwhelmed, enraptured with the intensity of it all. He continued to read without the Bible. Apparently he didn't need it.

...BUT HE, WILLING TO JUSTIFY HIMSELF, SAID UNTO JESUS, AND WHO IS MY NEIGHBOR? AND JESUS ANSWERING SAID...

Raising my eye level, I noted his glistening torso, his chest rising with every breath and his eyes closed as he recited. Freely following my primal impulse, I reached, grabbed on to the waistband of the briefs and determinedly pulled them down and off. His divining rod, twitching with anticipation, jutted out toward my mouth, grazing my lips. Slightly opening my mouth, I circularly flicked my tongue around the head. Hearing first a soft gasp, then moans between his words, I took more of him into my mouth and sucked and licked along his dick with mounting hunger. I felt his hands, their thick fingers, clasp my head. His pelvis gently thrust forward, stuffing more of his dick into my voracious mouth. All the while, I heard hums descending from above, moans and sighs and gasps amid fervent snatches of breathy scripture. His thrust became more urgent, more deep, stabbing against my epiglottis, burrowing for the deep cave of my throat. I sensed impending climax. The volume in his reading and his riding increased, but I wasn't yet ready for a culmination. Firmly gripping his hips, I first pushed back, and then determinedly stilled his thrust. Reluctantly, I relinquished his dick.

He looked down at me, his lashes lazily caressing the glowing bulbs of his eyes, exhaled, moaned—and recited.

A CERTAIN MAN WENT DOWN FROM JERUSALEM TO JERICHO AND FELL AMONG THIEVES, WHICH STRIPPED HIM OF HIS RAIMENT, AND WOUNDED HIM, AND DEPARTED, LEAVING HIM HALF DEAD...

I stood, and took Chris into my arms. He hugged and kissed me back with ferocity, then buried his head in my neck, kissing, sucking, guzzling. Somehow still he continued his recitation, kissing, pushing "And lo, there was..." and "And then the prophet said unto them..." into my mouth, deep into my throat, filling my body with the verses, filling more than my body. Our dicks met and oozed between us. Our moist bodies commingled. The passion rising in me was—transcendental. More than hypnotic.

In spurts Chris told me of the parable of the Good Samaritan, how one should love God with all of his heart, soul, strength, and mind. Love one's neighbor as one loves oneself.

And I did. I loved him, and loved me, and loved him loving me. I surrendered to his passion, had no choice but to give in to it, not just the sex but all of it, the tsunami of primal need that seemed to make him shake with every word and movement. I grabbed his head, nearly snarling, nearly wailing, and put my mouth to his and kissed him with the fierceness of a tiger. I sensed some merging had occurred, was occurring:

Our spirits and our flesh were lost to the rhythms of lust and revelation, pulsating as one.

I listened.

...BUT A CERTIN SAMARITAN, AS HE JOURNEYED, CAME WHERE HE WAS AND WHEN HE SAW HIM, HE HAD COMPASSION ON HIM...

My legs began to wobble. Chris turned us around, sat down on the chair, and hoisted me onto him. Now straddling him, I felt his staff, nestling between the cheeks of my ass, gliding up and down, providing me with yet another ecstatic sensation. His mouth sucked at my neck and at each nipple with relish. My dick between our sweaty bodies brushed and bounced against his muscled abdomen. He clutched on to me. This man was full of love and passion. I held on to him, digging into his skin and muscle as our sexual rhythm matched that of the Arabian melody playing around us.

I could have stayed that way in perpetuity. In a fleeting moment of lucidity, before trying to kiss him again, I gazed at his tender face and noticed tears streaming from his eyes. All the while, he was still moaning, groaning, and mumbling scripture. I found his tears touching and I almost wept along with my own moans of pleasure. We were both cresting, and nothing now could quell our respective explosions. He grabbed tighter. I reciprocated, and intensified my ass glide along his dick. I reached back, lightly grasped his pulsating dick, slightly rose and positioned my rarely entered asshole onto the head of his moist dick. The new package of studded Beyond Sevens and lube in my drawer came to mind. But the desire to become connected with Chris completely, to surrender to this passion which felt so right and somehow "safe," outweighed my usual caution. I quivered, he moaned, and I slowly eased down as he fervently thrust upward and entered my snug and surprisingly receptive ass with a feral intensity. His mouth found my right nipple and he sucked with abandon. Traveling upward, his mouth nestled in my neck. He licked and kissed and growled. The sensations were otherworldly. Our rhythm was perfectly synchronized, with the Arabian percussion seemingly reaching a crescendo just as we were. I felt transported, and merged with another in a way I had never before imagined.

Moments later, I experienced an orgasm like no other. I had heard about the tantric-based kundalini, internal full-body orgasms, but such an orgasm up to that point had eluded me. As I held on to Chris, I first began feeling a flame of sorts ignite in my groin area, but deeper inside, deeper than dick, deeper than flesh, far down in the swirling energy centers that lie like a furnace within. The fire began growing and growing, leaping higher, radiating throughout my body, touching every nook and cranny of my being. I heard Chris cry out, "Oh Jesus, oh God! Ugh! Ugh!" and we both erupted. I felt partly in my body and partly out of it. Everything tingled and vibrated. My spirit seemed to expand beyond my body, it seemed to rise up and inflate, enveloping Chris in our connection.

We both laughed and cried and held on to each other tightly. It felt—it was—rapturous.

We didn't leave that chair for an hour. It took that long to come down. I did not want to let go of him, nor he I, yet we realized we couldn't stay in that chair forever. At the last moment, before I reluctantly disengaged from my Christian lover, I kissed every part of his face and thanked him. "This was...it was the most *profound*...the most *sexual*...," I stammered.

He said, "God is good and we all did it together." I smiled and agreed with him.

Chris and I have since become very close friends. We discuss an array of topics, including Christianity and a host of other spiritual practices. I remain a spiritual free agent, delving into and adopting a variety of creeds and belief systems. He continues to enlighten our brothers, not in the extensive manner in which I was enlightened, he maintains, but his Christian resolve and mission have remained intact. We have reflected on our first night together and decided to treat that night as a sacred gift, something that does not and maybe should not occur habitually. Recreating it might be daunting, but not impossible. I believe we both have it in the back of our minds and in the depth of our spirits to one day resurrect that particular passion. Who knows if we will succeed, yet I must admit, his openness and passion have created inroads in my heart and spirit that I never thought possible. Sometimes I wonder, have I fallen in love with my prey? Uncharacteristically, I don't try to name it or analyze what we share. I simply continue to enjoy our friendship and this feeling. And occasionally, I find a friend on friend blow job is in order.

Horse Philosophy

Robert F. Reid-Pharr

He is a reasonable young man, the one over-bundled in khaki and blue, carefully shielding himself from the dampness that clings so nonchalantly to the red-green glitter of late December New York. He is reasonable and true, this pleasant, unspectacularly brown young man, edging himself neatly into the hard, dingy plastic of one, just one, corner seat on the Manhattan-bound F train, all the while holding his knapsack politely on uncrossed knees. He is self-contained and cool, trim and unspectacularly brown, with hands, as trim and brown as the man himself, that expertly balance a worn copy of a difficult, hermetic, badly translated work of race theory on the makeshift tower he has produced from knapsack, uncrossed legs, and hard dingy plastic, the entire structure rocking like a well-built skyscraper to the rhythms of the slow-moving train.

With reason and care, his vaguely full lips tightly shut, he reads, refusing even the suggestion of that vulgar mouthing of ideas and emotion so often practiced on the F line. He finds, however, reasonable, bundled, pleasant, trim, and true as he is, that he is puzzled. His heavy eyebrows pinch together in consternation, furtive fingers ring the inside of his collar, pausing briefly to pull at the wiry, unruly hairs that peek out from the top of his cotton undershirt. He has read this text many times, studied it extensively; indeed he teaches it often himself, always with great success. And yet, this thing, this clumsy, bitter, and somewhat impolite companion remains a stranger. It seems somehow to take from him but never really to give back, much like the fat gray kitten who resides with disconcerting feline self-composure in the luxury of his Brooklyn flat.

Reaching into his knapsack, his irritations and urgencies shielded from the other Manhattan-bound passengers by the composure that he maintains as the train leaves the tunnel, revealing the humdrum squalor of Brooklyn's southwestern border (the ugly bridges, the clapboard houses, the hideous canals, the oversized billboards, the funky, ridiculous splendor of it all) he retrieves from deep within a small notebook. It is a handsome, delicate, red leather rectangle, the size of a cheap romance novel. He likes the feel of it, both physical and mental. Indeed he overvalues the words that he has carefully copied into it as the book, with its blank pages, red leather cover, its weight the same as that of cheap romances, was presented to him by thoughtful friends on the eve of a long trip abroad. They have penned, *bon voyage, and remember to write!* on the inside of the front cover. He unfortunately forgot their entreaties on his long European tour but he keeps it with him constantly now, reprinting in his clear, even hand, passages from texts that confuse him, words that he wants to believe but that he senses are necessarily incorrect. As the train wobbles along and as his knees press even more tightly one into the other he writes:

> *There is a zone of non-being, an extraordinarily sterile and arid region, an utterly naked declivity where an authentic upheaval can be*

> *born. In most cases, the black man lacks the advantage of being able to accomplish this descent into a real hell.*[1]

He finishes his task, not an easy one on the hard plastic seats of a wobbling, damp, poorly heated train, and rereads the passage as the F line plunges again into the steel and concrete gloom of the tunnel. Then after much consideration and with absolute seriousness he adds his own dull commentary beneath the difficult passage: *I wonder if the man had ever been to Brooklyn.*

Things had gone well at the club. Brown was, in fact, somewhat of a hit. Rather, he had been able to turn his awkward posing into shockingly valuable sexual coin. The only problem was that as usual everybody wanted to be fucked.

"New York, city of eight-million bottoms," Brown mumbles out loud as he finishes his shower and uses the already damp towel to wipe water and little rubbery balls of leftover cum from pecan-tinted skin. Still, one shouldn't complain, he thought. Though he had not been fucked himself he *had* topped two guys and turned down at least two others. Moreover, he had been very satisfied with the quality of the men who had pressed themselves on him. The first, a forty-something, chestnut-haired chatty fellow from Chelsea turned out to be an incredibly proficient kisser with blue eyes exactly the color of the summer sky over North Carolina. Blue had spotted Brown almost the minute he'd walked into the club and followed hawkishly as he made his way around the simple maze of rooms and cubicles. Eventually, after maneuvering Brown into one of the darker corners of the maze and then again into an unused cubicle, he proved conclusively that he knew exactly what to do with the tongue, how to suck with hunger and passion on the pink softness of vaguely full lips.

Blue kissed, in fact, like a top, hard and aggressive, with wetness and passion that portended athletic fucking, as did the thick hairy belly, muscular chest, broad pink-tinged back, a good-sized arched cock, all enveloped by pecan arms and mahogany legs.

"Wow!" he had said, in that friendly chatty Chelsea fellow sort of way, "What do you like to do?"

Brown, still infinitely reasonable with his sweaty back, pouty lips, great dark almond eyes, tense mahogany nipples and buttocks that looked as firm as unripe melons but felt in the hand like great mounds of milky cheese wrapped in silk, said with both reason and conviction, "I like to get fucked."

"Damn! *You're* a bottom?" the chatty, forty-something had responded with blue-eyed incredulity. And with that the young man looked with his dark almond Brooklyn eyes into the watery round blues of Chelsea and the two, a bit embarrassed but still polite, settled down to a friendly bout of sixty-nine and frottage. They ended when one or the other suggested that they find a third and the two left the room together. Only by then the simple maze of rooms and cubicles had somehow grown infinitely more complicated and Brown became separated from Blue and attached himself to Red.

> *Not surprisingly, then, and even though his prose and some of his reasoning depend upon it, Fanon rejects the European model entirely, and demands instead that all human beings collaborate together in the invention of new ways to create what he calls "the new man, whom Europe has been incapable of bringing to triumphant birth."*[2]

The facilities were of course less than perfect, the health inspector having been by sometime earlier to shut down both steam room *and* sauna. And of course New York being New York a Jacuzzi was completely out of the question. Predictably then the young man became bored by all the stalking and cautious self-monitoring that took place between rooms and cubicles and decided, reasonably enough, to take a seat on one of the uncomfortable metal benches that were constantly sprayed and wiped by the particularly conscientious cleaning staff.

"*Reinigungskraft,*" he thought, priding himself on remembering this random word from the lists of German nouns he had long since studied. *Reinigungskraft, Volkshochshule, Lebensmittel, Schwul, Sauberkeit, Gesundheit, Blut.* And then after he had tired of counting common German nouns and nearly exhausted himself conjugating irregular Spanish verbs, he slipped—again predictably—into the regrettable gloominess brought about when one starts imagining a world in which it would not seem totally uncouth to lose oneself in a difficult, hermetic, badly translated work of race theory while seated on an uncomfortable metal bench in a sex club in the middle of Manhattan. But fortunately before boredom gave way fully to gloom Red appeared.

It is perhaps worth noting here that it is not nearly as easy as one might imagine, this process of maintaining a reasonable, level-headed demeanor. What with the wobbling of drafty trains, the vacant chatter of pleasant forty-something Chelsea fellows, the unceremonious closures of steam rooms *and* saunas, not to mention German nouns, Spanish verbs, and pressing, if incongruous, desires to pick up where one has left off in difficult, hermetic, badly translated works of race theory, it is understandable that even the most reasonable of reasonable young brown men might forget themselves, might forget to avert their almond glances away from red-headed, barrel-chested, boyishly attractive bodybuilders, the ones dressed only in standard issue white towels, just barely large enough to cover their deliciously ballooning, bodybuilder buttocks.

We might properly overlook Brown's lack of discretion then as Brown caught the eye of Red, who also lacking discretion made the uncouth gesture of dropping his hand below a heavy clutch of stomach muscles to squeeze himself in a thoroughly vulgar fashion through that ridiculously impractical towel. Moreover, we will certainly have to sympathize with Brown's amazement, his provincial Brooklyn wonder, as Red smiled at him broadly and winked just before slipping his key into the lock of his door. And as a matter of simple Christian charity we will have to ignore Brown's forgetting, at least for a moment, badly translated race theory, pulling himself with alacrity from his uncomfortable metal bench and following Red into a small, dimly lit room where to Brown's amazement Red quickly removed first his own then Brown's undersized towels, sat himself on the single bed that filled the small space and began to give Brown a vigorous blow job, the kind that hurt: teeth, tongue, suction, the occasional strand of spittle dropping from Red's mouth to the white sheets of the single bed; so that Brown, still attempting to maintain composure, and thoughtful enough to place a reassuring hand on the half-dollar-sized spot of pink skin in the midst of Red's tangerine-colored hair, found himself grimacing, flinching, and wondering if Red intended to bite the thing off.

And perhaps if we muster enough generosity and tolerance we might be able to empathize—if only briefly—with Brown's sense of surprise as Red hauled his two-hundred-plus pounds of muscle onto the bed and positioned himself in front of Brown's young, trim pecan-tinted body to reveal an impossibly chiseled expanse of gym-manicured masculinity; tangerine hair, giving way to thick neck, oversized, rounded shoulders beginning the great inverted triangle of flesh that culminated in a schoolgirl's waist only to explode again in two great, perfectly symmetrical mounds of gluteus flesh. One begins, in fact, to gain a sense of Brown's struggles, his many demons, reasonable and otherwise, as one watches him drop his face to those mounds, separate them with trim fingers and begin his greedy ministrations with a tongue that perfectly matched the pink of the hole that puckered and wept with each naughty flick. What forces one to draw in the breath, however, that bit of narrative detail that may force my dear readers to place delicate hands at the napes of sculptured necks, is Brown's taking that stinging pecan penis of his and pressing it, slamming it some might say, hard against the pinkness of Red's small deliciously weeping and puckering hole. Indeed Brown became so, dare I say it, unreasonable, that Red, previously silent except for the odd moan and the occasional, "yeah baby," was forced to tilt back his tangerine head, pull thin lips over perfect teeth and interject a bit of caution into this already impossibly unreasonable moment.

"Hey there, let's keep it safe," Red offered with much decorum, sending Brown hunting for latex and lubrication.

And then the fumbling, trembling, pressing, aching, spitting, pushing, sweating; the shifting, probing, arching, wrangling, squirming, shaking, biting and Brown was inside. Then Red, his muscles overwhelming the small bed, his tangerine head tilted back like a she dog baying at the moon, revealed to Brown the one place where he was *not* tight. For Brown knew, moments after rolling the condom onto his penis, seconds after offering a reassuring kiss and instantly upon entering the warmth and wetness of Red's body, that he was most certainly not the first person to have enjoyed this ride.

So with force and speed and not a small amount of rhythm Brown threw himself into Red, fast and faster still, the sweat from his forehead landing like wet snow on Red's great muscled shoulders, pecan penis pulled out to near withdrawal then quickly returned with an upward stroke that kept time with Red's downward arch. And when he tired Brown leaned hard onto Red's back, pressed him down to the small bed, grabbed a lock of tangerine hair with one hand and pressed the thumb of the other into Red's mouth until continually pumping into those yielding mounds of gluteus flesh he began to sense, to intuit, to feel.

"Oh my God, Oh my God, I'm close."

With that the crazy tickle began somewhere deep inside Brown's own hole. He felt it advance between tensed buttocks, course through the wickedly sensitive space between penis and anus to attack his taut testicles. And then he pulled out so quickly that Red gasped, yelped really. And again that fumbling trembling, pressing, aching, spitting, pushing, sweating as Brown struggled with the condom, getting it off just in time to come, without reason, direction, or the least bit of decorum all over Red's expansive back and his own pecan stomach.

> *The "white man" is a distinct image in Asian-African minds. This image has nothing to do with biology, for, from a biological point of view, what a "white man" is, is not interesting. Scientifically speaking the leaders of Asia and Africa know that there is no such thing as race. It is, therefore, only from a historical or sociological point of view that the image of "white man" means anything. In Asian-African eyes, a "white man" is a man with blue eyes, a white skin, and blond hair, and that "white man" wishes fervently that his eyes remain forever blue, his skin forever white, and hair forever, blond, and he wishes this for his children and his children's children.*[3]

After passing several very pleasant postcoital moments with Red, who informed Brown that his impressive musculature was due in part to his having lost his job some months earlier allowing him to drastically increase his gym schedule, Brown left to clean his own semen and Red's saliva from his body.

"New York, city of eight-million bottoms."

Brown was of course preparing to leave the club now that he had spent time with Blue and Red, turned down two others, showered, and meticulously removed soap, saliva, and semen from his body. He only wanted now, as would have been the case with any reasonable Brooklynite, to get back onto his train before the afternoon rush. Indeed he intended to dry himself, gather his things, head for the station, and return to his struggles with that difficult, hermetic, badly translated work of race theory. But then of course there was the matter of White.

White had been watching Brown shower and Brown had carefully ignored him though he had, in fact, noted the nonchalant manner in which White stood against the wall, his hands resting on the top fold of his towel, one foot crossed loosely over the other. He had also noted that White possessed neither the physical presence of Red nor the Chelsea fellow friendliness of Blue. At least he assumed not as White stared at him with an expression that might have denoted either desire *or* malice. No one could have been more surprised than Brown then when after rubbing the already damp towel down a long graceful expanse of pecan thigh, flipping it over buttocks the shape of unripe melons, using it to massage taut almond nipples and carefully drying each well-manicured toe on his buffed and polished feet, he followed White out of the showers, through the maze, past both Blue *and* Red and into another nondescript cubicle, without a single word being exchanged. Things were indeed going very well at the club that day.

It could not have been the kissing. For indeed White kissed

no more proficiently than Blue. Nor was it White's body. For as Brown felt the slackness of the muscles in White's arms, back, and thighs he found himself missing the careful sculpturing of Red. One might have concluded that it *was* the drugs, the poppers that White had offered and Brown had accepted. And certainly when the rush came and Brown felt his heart quicken and the top, only the top, of his head lighten, he did not resist as White laid him on the bed and pressed his even-sized cock between his pinkish lips, while simultaneously bowing his own head between pecan-tinted thighs searching out that sensitive hole, the color of which Brown himself could not have described. Indeed Brown yielded quite easily, sucked greedily at deeply thrusting penis, slobbered over hairy testicles the size of walnuts, while his partner smothered himself in the milky cheese texture of splayed buttocks, the two settling into a rhythm of six and nine that far exceeded what Brown and Blue had accomplished earlier.

And when White pulled himself away and roughly pulled the length of Brown's pecan body along with him, lifting one, just one, leg over his shoulder while turning the reasonable young man onto his side, Brown did understand what White had to offer. He did relish the secure, even, relentless push of White's even-sized cock against his own tightly sealed hole. And when White pushed too far and the reasonable young man feared of yielding too much he did pull away. So White pushed again and again Brown did pull. And they went on that way, pushing and pulling, pulling and pushing until Brown stared hurting, felt pain in his stomach similar to the kind he felt right before the onset of the burning insult of a cramp. It was then that he repeated a sentence he had heard someplace else.

"Hey there, let's keep it safe."

With that White pulled away, gathered himself, and fished out a condom from a small kit that he kept on the table that stood beside the bed. And without fumbling or trembling, sweating or wrangling he rolled the thin layer of latex onto his even-sized penis, placed one, just one, of Brown's gracefully shaped pecan thighs over his shoulder and in a moment of push and pull that Brown would later think of as symphonic White and Brown were one.

Do you know, gentle reader, what it is to be fucked and fucked well by a man who holds one's body like the pages of some ancient and precious manuscript, the very man who stinks with the smell of the sweaty funk he has drawn from between one's own thighs, the man who relishes the animal look on the face, the delicate quiver inside the body as passion surpasses reason? For Brown, White was such a man. This is indeed why he arched his trim body so elegantly onto White's thrusting form, why he stretched out his thin hands to more firmly grip White's straining buttocks. And when White changed rhythm, somehow managing to maneuver Brown onto his stomach without removing the joy of that even penis, Brown did not resist or falter. Instead his pose was more elegant still, his body that much more securely attached to White's.

There was grace beyond comprehension then, passion beyond understanding as White again slipped Brown the bottle of poppers, somehow incongruous with its shade of pecan so similar to Brown's. So when White pulled away again and removed the condom, when he kissed hard against Brown's pinkish lips, leaving behind the funky smell of Brown's own colorless hole, Brown did not this time pull as White pushed. Instead he achieved that grace, that stretch, that impossible arch and gave himself, gave everything, lips, tongue, mouth, hands, ass, cock, poppers' rush, to White.

"Goddamn! Goddamn!"

White withdrew and stained Brown's pecan-tinged back.

Done. Free.

He is a reasonable young man, the one over-bundled in khaki and blue, carefully shielding himself from the dampness that clings so nonchalantly to the red-green glitter of late December New York. He is reasonable and true, this pleasant, unspectacularly brown young man, edging himself neatly into the hard, dingy plastic of one, just one, corner seat on the Brooklyn-bound F train, all the while holding his knapsack politely on uncrossed knees. He is self-contained and cool, trim and unspectacularly brown, with hands, as trim and brown as the man himself, that expertly balance a small red leather notebook on the makeshift tower he has produced from knapsack, uncrossed legs, and hard dingy plastic, the entire structure rocking like a well-built skyscraper to the rhythms of the slow-moving train.

As he writes in his even, clear hand the train suddenly leaves the gloom of the tunnel to reveal the humdrum squalor of Brooklyn's southwestern border (the ugly bridges, the clapboard houses, the hideous canals, the oversized billboards, the funky, ridiculous splendor of it all). But Brown sees none of this. Instead he is immersed in his task, absolutely resolute in his desire to settle some difficult concept of race theory that seems to bother him now more than usual. He reads the note that he has just written, his lips moving slightly as he ponders whether he has really gotten at the true sense of an important matter he hopes to settle:

> *It may indeed be true as all of the most significant students of revolution have informed us, (Fanon, James and Wright come most quickly to mind) that the revolutionary act is by necessity a destructive and violent act. Rather, the work of the revolutionary is always to tear down the basic structures of society as these are the very structures by*

> *which his domination (dominion?) is managed and maintained. That said, I must wonder why it is that no one has imagined a necessarily self-pleasuring and indeed celebratory aspect to this destruction. It seems somehow counterintuitive to suggest that one should not only sacrifice oneself but that one should have a bad time while doing so. Instead, I wonder if the element that is left out of revolutionary analysis is precisely pleasure, the way in which if the revolutionary is to give himself over to the cause, the movement, the unforeseeable and unknowable future, then he should (I really want to say must) enjoy himself.*

With that, the young man replaced the notebook, opened his legs wide, placed his knapsack squarely on the seat beside him, and looked out the window before the last of the ugly billboards passed from view as the car wobbled into the tunnel again.

Notes

1 Frantz Fanon, *Black Skin, White Masks* (New York: Grove Press, 1967).

2 Edward W. Said, *Freud and the Non-European* (New York: Verso, 2003).

3 Richard Wright, *White Man Listen* (New York: Harper, 1957).

Miracle 5

Shane Allison

"Hey, a lady just came out of two and said it's too loud," Darryl said from behind the counter.

"It's in THX sound, it's supposed to be loud," Collin said as he made his way over toward the concession stand.

"Run upstairs and tell John that it's too loud."

"Why can't you go?" Collin asked insubordinately.

Darryl rested his elbows on the gray surface of the counter. " 'Cause I have to stay down here and work concession."

Collin stood in the lobby, his fingers fidgeting with a ticket stub.

"I'll stay down here and watch the lobby while you go tell him," Collin said.

"I'm not working door today, Collin, you are."

"Yeah, but..." Darryl interrupted him in mid-sentence.

"Man, will you go and tell him, dang! Why you always gotta be such a dick?" Darryl hollered.

Collin tossed the stub on the counter, and stood at the door that led up to the projectionist booth. "I got your dick right here," he said, yanking the crotch of his black pants.

"Yeah, you wish," Darryl retaliated weakly.

Darryl hated working with Collin on Tuesday afternoons. He was the coworker at the theatre he found to be the most irritating and most annoying.

Noticing that he was low on candy, Darryl went in the storage closet to retrieve more stock. Kendra came out of the box office for a short break holding a brown bag. She reached around the soda machine, filling her Looney Tunes mug with Diet Coke.

"I heard y'all out here," Kendra said.

"What's that?" Darryl yelled, peeking from around the chicken-wire door of the storage closet holding three heavy-bulked boxes of strawberry-flavored Twizzlers.

"I said I heard y'all out here hollering and screaming like y'all crazy," she repeated.

"Yeah, that was Collin's butt acting stupid." Darryl sat the three boxes of candy on the square sheet of glass above the candy case.

"Can you fill this up with popcorn?" Kendra asked.

"You want butter on it, baby?"

"No, just plain," she said.

Darryl opened the fiberglass doors to the popper and shoveled popcorn into Kendra's bag.

"That's why I don't like working with him, 'cuz he act so stupid."

"I tried to get Reece to change days with me, but he got class on Tuesdays, so he couldn't do it," said Darryl, as he handed her the brown-bagged snack.

"Come on D, he ain't that bad," said Kendra.

Darryl grabbed the box cutters on the table behind him and cut across the duct tape of the boxes.

"Yes he is, girl. I don't know why Rob sticks me with him. He knows how annoying he can be," Darryl said as he stacked the Twizzlers in stacks of five in their respective slot in the candy case. Kendra giggled as she listened to Darryl ramble on about Collin.

"You know what I think?" said Kendra.

"What?" Darryl said.

"I think deep down, you gotta soft spot for Collin. I think with all that arguing and fussing y'all do, you actually like him."

Darryl placed the last pack of Twizzlers in the candy case and broke down the empty boxes, throwing them in the white garbage can beneath the butter machine.

"Hell no, girl! Not the way he gets on my nerves." Darryl said.

"D, the thing with you is, you like attention. You're all about the drama. You are the biggest damn drama queen I know. Why don't y'all just fuck and get it over with?" Kendra remarked as she smacked and crunched on kernels. Kendra grabbed her mug of soda and headed back to the box office.

"Girl, you so crazy," Darryl said, laughing. "But he don't look half bad," he said to himself. "He's definitely fuckable."

Collin returned from upstairs.

"Did you tell him?" Darryl asked.

"Yeah, and he bit my head off. I told you there was nothing that could be done about the sound," Collin declared.

He walked over and reached down for a small courtesy cup from beneath the register where Darryl was standing. In his efforts, he knocked the entire column of cups on the floor.

"Now pick every one of them up," Darryl instructed. Collin picked up the cups that rolled like spilled beans across the gritty linoleum. He sloppily replaced them in the cubbyhole below the register.

"Man, don't put them back under there. Throw them away, they dirty."

As Collin gathered up the contaminated cups, Darryl's crotch caught his eye. He noticed the bulge in his pants and gawked at Darryl's package like a hungry vulture. He licked his upper lip with the tip of his tongue. His mouth was only inches away from Darryl's dick.

Collin threw the cups away, all accept for one, which he used to fill up with root beer.

"Get from behind here," warned Darryl.

"Why?" Collin asked in a somewhat childlike tone.

" 'Cuz you're a jinx."

"I'm not a jinx," Collin grinned.

"Yes you are, too. Anything or anybody that come near you, bad shit happens to them," Darryl said as he filled a cup with pink lemonade slushy.

"Man, whatever!"

"I might get struck by lightning or something—round you," Darryl said.

Collin walked from behind the counter and sat in one of the rowed chairs that decorated the lobby. "*The Specialist* is about to let out," he said.

"Well, I guess you better get ready to go clean it then," Darryl said snidely.

Collin pulled the folded, tattered movie schedule out of his pocket and studied it. He grabbed the broom and dustpan leaning in a corner next to the women's restroom and took some trash bags from the janitor's closet. A few minutes later he opened the double black doors to theater one. Gloria Estefan's cover song "Turn the Beat Around" echoed out into the lobby. Collin waited until the theater was empty to begin cleaning.

Darryl realizing he was running low on medium cups, retrieved a new stack from the cabinet, and shoved a second batch between the soda machine and the ice bin. He started to think about what Kendra had said to him earlier about liking Collin. "He is kinda cute. I like his eyes; he got nice eyes," Darryl whispered to himself as he scribbled a number on the count sheet. "I guess I can be a little hard on him sometimes. He's not my type, though. I can't really see myself getting with somebody like him. He's so geeky looking."

Collin came behind the concession stand with the broom and trash-filled dustpan.

"I told you not to come around me," Darryl said.

"Man, shut up," Collin said playfully. "I just need to empty this." Darryl opened the lower half of the popcorn popper to check the oil container. It was just about empty.

"Shit!" he murmured under his breath. "I gotta change this." And then louder, "Hey, can you give me a hand with the oil?" he asked.

"Oh, so now you need my help? I thought I was a jinx?" Collin asked.

"Don't be a smartass, come help me," Darryl demanded. Collin followed him into the storage room. "Hand me the stepladder from over there."

"There you go bossing me around again," said Collin as he grabbed the stepladder leaning against stacked boxes of Sprite. Darryl climbed up and cupped his hands around the oil can, pulling it toward the edge of the top shelf. Collin was standing directly below him. His head came point-blank to Darryl's robust, bubbled butt. Collin found himself caught gazing at Darryl's ever-perfect scrumptious booty. He tugged at his crotch, his warm dick pressing against his thigh. Collin wanted nothing more than to sink his pearly whites into Darryl's robust booty. Collin lightly glided his hands up Darryl's pant-covered thighs, lazily making his way toward his ass.

"Okay, I'm gonna hand this down to you, are you ready?" asked Darryl. Collin was caught in a rapture of lust. "You ready?" Darryl repeated. Collin snapped back into reality, jerking his hand down away from Darryl's booty before he could notice.

"Yeah, I'm ready, I got it," Collin confirmed.

Darryl slowly handed the bucket of canola oil down to him. "You sure you got it? Don't drop the shit, Collin," Darryl warned.

"Come on D, man, I got it." Collin sat the oil outside next to the semi-empty oil can. Darryl grabbed the screwdriver lying next to the cappuccino maker, while Collin slid out the old can of oil. "So what were you thinking about?" asked Darryl.

"Thinking about when?"

"It looked like something was weighing on your mind."

Collin's eyes shifted like he didn't know what Darryl was talking about. "No, I was just waiting for your slow ass to hand me the oil, he said.

"Oh, okay, 'cause it looked like you was looking at my ass."

Collin looked coy and dumb-founded. "What? No! Hand me the screwdriver," he demanded.

"I mean, 'cuz if you were looking..."

Collin stuck the flat head screwdriver into the holes in the lid of the oil can. "I wasn't looking at your ass, man," he grinned.

"I was going to say if you were, that's cool, I don't mind," said Darryl.

"What do you mean you don't mind?" asked Collin.

"I mean I'm cool with it."

Collin replaced the oil and pushed it back under the popper. Darryl handed him a paper towel to wipe the excess oil off his hands. "Well, I wasn't looking," he said. Darryl drank the last few sips of pink lemonade slushy. Collin refilled his cup and rested his elbow on top of the black napkin dispenser.

"Can I ask you a personal question?" asked Darryl. "Have you ever been with a dude?"

Collin took another sip from his cup. "What?"

"Have you ever done it with a guy?"

"I've had a few experiences, but I prefer tits and pussy over dick and balls," Collin said assuredly.

"So what did you get into with guys?" Darryl inquired.

"Kissing, that's about it."

"Nothing else?" asked Darryl.

"No, nothing else, man." But Collin had had more than just a few experiences.

"Do you consider yourself bi?" Darryl asked.

"Yeah, I guess. I've kissed guys, but I'm more into chicks."

"So you've never fucked a guy?" asked Darryl.

"Man shut up, someone's gonna hear you," Collin murmured. "No, I've never fucked a dude."

Darryl laughed silently as he took a damp washcloth to wipe stuck-on syrup off the sides of the soda machine.

"So let me ask you something," Collin said. "What was your first experience like?"

"It was a while back. His name was Francisco, but everybody called him Cisco."

"Oh, like Cisco Kid?" Collin asked.

"Yeah, something like that," replied Darryl. "Anyway, I had the biggest fucking crush on him. We had wood shop together but never talked. I remember having to wear an extra pair of shorts under my sweats in gym class 'cuz I would get a huge fucking hard-on seeing him in his basketball shorts. We were always the last ones left changing in the field house. I didn't think he was into guys, 'cuz he was always macking the girls in school.

"So once, when we were changing, he was sitting on the bench with his shirt off. He'd always put it on last. Oh my God, Collin, he was so fine. He was about your height with big, pretty lips. He used to lick 'em like L.L. He had arms like damn sledgehammers and smooth, coffee-brown skin that glistened with sweat. I was putting on my socks when he started talking to me...

" 'Hey, aren't we in wood shop together?' he asked. 'Your name's Darryl, right, people call you D?' I couldn't believe this guy was even acknowledging my ass.

" 'Yeah, that's me.'

" 'So what do you think of ole Coach Ash?' he asked.

" 'I don't really like him,' I said. 'He thinks that making a fucking candlestick is something you need to know how to do in the real world.'

" 'Oh man, I know. I hate it when he stands next to you to show you how to use a drill or some shit. He stinks,' Cisco said.

"So we started talking about other shit like girls, basketball, sex. You know, typical shit straight guys like to talk about. He was telling me all this stuff he would like to do to girls like stick his dick in between they tits and jerk off on them, right. His ass was freaky, which is why I liked him. I would fantasize about sucking him off and licking the sweat off his balls."

"Eh-ew, he nasty," Collin laughed. "So did y'all mess around?"

"Well, when we were talking about fucking, he told me he heard all these rumors about me being gay. 'So I hear you're a punk?' he asked. I felt like he had jabbed a hot knife in my gut. 'Hey, if you are, that's cool,' he said. 'That's your choice, man.' He asked me if I had ever sucked dick before."

"Shit, this guy didn't waste any time," said Collin.

"I continued getting dressed. He said, 'Yo, D, I'm not trying to dis you or nothing, I'm just asking. So you suck dick?' I wasn't sure if he was being an asshole or was genuinely serious about wanting to know. I looked around to see if his boys were hiding out ready to jump me or something if I said yes. I looked up at Cisco as I was tying my shoe.

" 'So what if I do?' I replied.

" 'So...you want to suck my dick?' Cisco asked, fondling his crotch. He leaned back against the lockers, spread his thighs, unzipped his pants, and took his dick out of his underwear and started jacking off. I had the biggest fucking hard-on, and he knew it 'cause he was staring down at my dick and shit."

Collin glanced down at Darryl's crotch as he observed his hand gestures describing the moment.

"So I walked over to him and stood in between his thighs. He ran his hand up my stomach. I couldn't fucking believe this was happening. I reached down and started rubbing his dick."

Darryl lowered his voice to make sure that no one could hear. "He moved his hand away and let me do my thing. His eyes were closed and his mouth was semi-open like he was waiting for me to shove something in it. I went to check to see if everyone had left 'cause I didn't want anybody to walk in on us. I pulled down his boxers. I didn't think he was a boxers boy. Strictly fucking tighty-whiteys, you know? He had the thickest bush of pubes.

"When I ran my fingers across his groin, that got him hard and I hadn't even touched his dick yet. I stooped down and pulled his jeans off his legs."

"Was he hung?" asked Collin.

"Oh my God, he was huge. His cock was fat like a damn pork sausage. I dropped to my knees, pulled back his foreskin, and licked the moist, supple head with the tip of my tongue. Hell, I didn't think I was going to get it all in my mouth, but I was like, fuck that. This shit was like a fantasy come true and I was going to do it up right.

"He reached down and pulled up his ball sac. 'Lick 'em,' he demanded."

Darryl leaned in close to Collin and whispered, "I could taste the juices on his balls."

Collin let loose a burst of uncontrollable laughter, enough to turn the heads of a few departing theater patrons.

" 'Damn this dick is good,' I said.

" 'Yeah, you like sucking dick don't you?' he asked.

"I slurped, slobbered, and bobbed down on Cisco's hard dick like it was a Halloween apple. 'Suck it, suck my fucking dick!' he yelled.

"I ran my hand across his stomach and up to his nipples, tweaking them like two radio knobs. That got him even hotter. He stood up off the bench and drove his dick down my throat. Every now and then, he would pull out and beat it against my tongue.

" 'You want it, you want this dick in your mouth, boy? Open your mouth, punk!' Cisco demanded.

"He fucked the shit out of my face. His dick was soaked with spit. I started to gag when, holding the back of my head, he forced me all the way down on his dick. 'Eat my dick!' he kept saying. 'Eat my fucking dick. Suck that black dick!'

"My lips massaged the thick, purple veins that ran up Cisco's shaft. I could taste a little bit of pre-come. Slobber ran from the corners of my mouth, trickling down Cisco's dick into his pubic forest and balls."

"You didn't get pissed when he called you a fag?" Collin asked.

"We were so into the shit that I didn't give a fuck," Darryl murmured.

"No one saw y'all?" Collin asked.

"We thought we heard someone coming downstairs. It scared the hell out of us and we jumped up, got dressed, and ran for the exit doors. When we got outside, he pushed me against the wall. 'You better not tell anybody or I'll kick your ass,' he said. I never said nothing to nobody. You the first person I'm telling this shit to."

"So did you ever hook back up with Cisco to finish 'the job' so to speak?"

"Oh, there were plenty of chances, but he was scared of getting caught. We never spoke to each other after that day."

Collin walked over to the soda machine for more Coke.

"Damn!" he blurted out.

"Yeah, so that was my first time." Darryl noticed Collin's crotch. "Man, you hard?"

Collin tugged down on his dick with his right hand. "A lil' bit," he replied.

Darryl stood next to him, reached down, and grabbed Collin's dick in his right hand. "Feels like more than a little bit. I know where we can go."

Collin followed Darryl to the janitor's closet where they crammed in between shelves of degreaser bottles, wet mop heads, and other cleaning supplies. Collin and Darryl unbuttoned their pants, pulling them down around their asses, and simultaneously began stroking their dicks.

"That shit got me hot, man," Collin admitted.

"Yeah?" Darryl sighed as he squeezed Collin's erect dick. A pearl of pre-come formed at the tip of his piss slit.

"Hold up!" Collin whispered. "I think I hear someone."

"Let me go check," Darryl said.

There was no sign of anyone in the lobby.

"We better hurry, a movie is about to let out in twenty minutes," Collin said.

Now fully erect, Collin and Darryl gripped and mutually beat each other's tender dicks.

"Suck me, dude," Collin demanded.

Darryl squatted down, his bare, chocolate-brown ass grazing against the rim of the yellow mop bucket. He took Collin's dick, pulling back the foreskin, and tongue-tickled the head.

"Suck it," Collin sighed. "Suck it just like you did Cisco's."

Darryl buried his head in Collin's lap, hypnotized by the musty aroma that came up from his crop of pubic hair. Darryl grabbed on to Collin's hips, pulling him closer into his face with every sensational suck. Sounds of a dick being slurped distracted them from the scent of floor wax and disinfectant. Collin held on to the lip of the sink as Darryl took full control of his throbbing dick, which poked against the wet insides of Darryl's mouth, hitting his tonsils. Darryl jacked off with his left hand, as he roped his right one around Collin's engorged boner.

Darryl pulled Collin's foreskin down and up, taking his dick and bouncing the head on his pink-lemonade-stained tongue. He ran the tip across his full, butterscotch lips. Darryl's spit coursed down Collin's shaft into a thicket of crotch hair. With his mouth full, Darryl slyly slid his third finger into Collin's warm buttcrack. He was surprised how easily his finger slid into Collin's hungry shithole.

"Damn your ass is wet," Darryl whispered.

His lips massaged Collin's spit-clogged dick.

"I'm about to come, man," Collin said seductively.

Darryl held on, sucking without reluctance.

"Shit, you give good head," Collin said.

Darryl lifted him, pressing him back against the faucet in the sink behind him. He sucked even harder, his cheeks caving in with every blow.

Collin fucked Darryl's hole, taking hold of the back of his greased head and thrusting his dick deep and steady. His eyes were shut and perspiration dripped from his stubbly chin. Without further warning, Collin let loose his load in Darryl's spit-filled mouth.

Darryl jerked away immediately as he tasted the salty globules of semen, spitting into the mop bucket of dirty water behind him.

"Fuck man, my bad," whispered Collin.

Darryl stood up in between Collin's legs and persisted in pounding his own dick. Collin took hold of Darryl's eight inches and commenced jacking him off.

"Milk my dick," said Darryl. "Make me come."

Collin jerked Darryl's dick hungrily.

"I'm about to come..." Darryl shot semen on Collin's white shirt and paisley vest. Blotches of come landed on the grimy floor beneath them.

"Damn!" Darryl screamed.

"You shot a big load!" said Collin.

They grabbed a roll of paper towels and unfurled a couple of sheets, cleaning off the last bit of come that drooled from their piss slits.

"Shit! You got come on my vest," Collin said.

"It'll come out. Just take it home and wash it," said Darryl.

"It's almost time for a movie to let out," said Collin.

"Yeah, we better get back out there."

They got dressed, buttoned pants and vests, buckled belts and tied shoes. Collin walked out first in case Rob was around. Darryl followed, purposely lagging behind Collin to cop one last feel of his ass until another Tuesday afternoon.

One for the Road

Canaan Parker

I

Knock on wood, but Marco the Magnificent may have saved my life when he fucked my brains out fifteen years ago. It was the last time I was ever screwed, perhaps the last time I ever will be, but, honey, it was one to last a lifetime.

Fifteen years! I miss it in the ass. I often dream about it vividly. I remember *thunderclaps against my buttcheeks.* Marco pinning my prostate gland to the bulletin board. I could use condoms, but my experience hasn't given me enough faith in them. In the early eighties, we didn't know quite how to use them. (They are tricky little things; it does take a bit of finesse to get one on.) And so my memories sustain me through these dry years of abstention.

Thanks to Marco, I was able to change my sex habits (as far as passive anal sex goes) in the early days of the plague. I still got horny, but once Marco was done with me I was no longer in heat, which is a very key difference. When you're horny and a guy refuses to put on a condom, you kick his nutty ass out of bed; in heat, you fuck anyway. You feel incomplete; you are *searching* for sex. You are on a mission. Better to stay out of heat these days. Fortunately, I found what I was searching for *once and for all* with Marco, whom I think of as His Majesty. It was May of 1982 when the Great King fucked the Holy Molies out of me, and all these years later my bunghole is still content.

Well, perhaps not content, but I'm not going nuts like my friend Nicky either. Nick is buzzing like a queen bee for a good boning, but he too is wary of men who don't like or don't know how to use rubbers. Five years ago a man promised to use a Trojan to fuck him, but as soon as Nick was facedown in the pillow the guy tried to sneak his unsheathed prick into Nick's ass. "They make me lose my boner," the trick complained when Nick turned around and caught him just in time.

Nick hasn't had a dick in the bum since. He was doing his "fuck-me" walk last week—his hyperkinetic swish, fast-forward knock-kneed zigzag with panicked shoulder glance *bend my pelvis pop my cherry* splayed jellyfish salmon wriggle *yes yes* high-step jump out the window *oh God Christ Jesus please*—and Nick is not especially fey.

"What are you doing to me, Nick?" I asked, fighting the urge to mount him right there in the street. Nick is in heat, you see. His primal mating instincts are driving him mad. There're two theories about this. One, a virus gets into your brain and its reproductive instincts become your own. And two, when the mortality rate in an ecosystem is high, reproductive urges intensify to make up for the losses. Nick's butt apparently doesn't know he can't get pregnant.

I worry that Nick can't hold out forever. One day "Top Man" Johnny is going to follow him into an alley, and when Top Man won't use a condom, or tries to but the damn thing turns inside out and sticks to his dick like chewing gum, and the plastic lip tears off and gets tangled up in his pubic hair, Nick is going to fantasize that Top Man is "probably negative" just long enough to get lovingly seroconverted. I could easily do the same, but Marco let the hot air out of my balloon, so to speak, a long time ago.

II

I had beautiful legs when I was twenty-two. I lived in Boston then, and every day after a run along the Charles River I'd finish with a sprint up Beacon Hill. Neighbors hollered from their windows, "Lift! Lift!" as I kicked up the hill most normal people had trouble walking. I also lifted weights, but sparingly. I didn't want too much muscle. I was in my oral phase then. All I wanted was to give head and I wanted my body to look like a dish of pudding. Up and down the Esplanade I walked in barely legal corduroy cutoffs, shredded in homage to Tina Turner. I hadn't been screwed yet, but the idea must have been germinating in my brain cells. Bobby, whom I knew from music class, came walking toward me from about a block away with an abandoned-in-the-desert look on his face and didn't look up from my crotch until he was a step away. His face beamed when he realized he knew the person in those shorts. He took me back to my apartment, opened the living room window, turned me around in my recliner, and tried his best to get inside of me, but I was too tight, and Bobby couldn't hold it.

Kevin May lived across the street. He was weird and obnoxious and vulgar, and hot after my cherry. No one else talked to me the way he did. Sitting on my doorstep, eye-level with my hip pockets: "These buns will suit me fine." In the bathroom at Buddies disco: "Wait 'til you see the log I got for you."

I had never been pursued so aggressively before. I told Kevin to drop dead, but he kept after me. "I'll fuck some of that snot out of you." "Shish-ka-buns, shish-ka-buns." He had to be joking, I thought. Why would I let someone crack open my ass and pump cum inside of me? After all, I wasn't a girl. Kevin paid no attention to my male ego, which was a red herring. He ignored my prissy rejections like so much irrelevant red tape. "Damn, I want your big butt," he sputtered, speaking directly to my body. "Shish-ka-buns."

It took me a year to figure out that I liked Kevin. After months of insulting him, I sent him an anonymous letter asking if he wanted a hot piece of ass. Somehow Kevin knew I had sent the letter. When I came downstairs he was waiting for me, a doubtful but smoldering look on his face. My roommate was still upstairs so we went over to his apartment.

He hadn't lied about his log. It was heavy as a big-job wrench, black, solid, and industrial. It would have hurt if he hit you in the head with it. While I fretted and fussed like a baby Kevin wedged it into me.

"Stop crying, it's all the way in," he said.

All I felt was numbness. "Easy. Oh please, easy," I whispered. I scrambled away, trying to pry myself off his cock. Kevin pulled me back, but I bucked and lifted him up off the bed. Fed up with my nonsense, Kevin gave up and pulled out. I felt a gusting vacuum where his cock had just been.

I complained about how rough he was. "You have to go slowly. I'm a virgin!"

But Kevin didn't appreciate my blessed state. "You're just a piece of ass to me," he said, giggling with an eccentric glee.

I was exasperated. "I let you be the first, Kevin!"

He put his arm around my shoulder, his eyes vital with a private joke. Resting my chin on his chest, I looked down a long, rippled brown landscape past nipples, knees, an iron mine in a loose bag of skin, and tall feet in the distance. I felt like crying—I wanted Kevin so badly, but he was too much for my cherry. My ass felt damaged and raw. Kevin saw my eyes dampen, and smiled impishly.

"Nothing special. You're just another piece of ass," he laughed.

I spent the summer after my last term in graduate school in Boston so I could be with Kevin. I was scared to let him fuck me again, but there were other things we could do to enjoy ourselves. Though I fucked Kevin several times, emotionally I felt I was his wife. That was the relationship I wanted with him, and it was true in all ways except mechanically. It didn't matter to Kevin who fucked whom. "It's like having sex with myself," he told me once, so the difference was ephemeral. Kevin and I were practically twins. I was slightly taller and my skin a shade lighter, but we were the same age and built alike—brown, leggy, and lean. He was a painter and I a musician. He was more talented, I was more educated, but we were both eccentric, young, and broke. I saw him once on the corner by the Greyhound station, where he turned tricks when he needed money. "Come here," he said, grabbing at my belt as I walked past. He held me warmly against his crotch, one leg on a standpipe, his arms comfortable around my waist. A man walked past, stopped at the corner, and wiggled a finger at him.

"Wait here," he told me, and walked with the man around the corner toward the Boston Public Garden.

After he made money, we spent the day together, strolling the length of lovely Boston, toe-dancing in the grass on the Esplanade. Down by the edge of the water we hugged and French-kissed, hidden from the straighties by the thick hanging leaves of a tree rooted in the riverbank. "Let's go home," Kevin suggested. He was enormously hard and I could tell he wanted to finish the job he had begun on my butt. But I was in a fickle mood—a cockteasing mood—so I said no.

That afternoon I wanted to drive Kevin to a dreamy level of unrelieved horniness. If possible, I wanted to make him come in his jeans in public. In Kevin's pool-hall hangout, in front of several of his friends, I brushed my bum on his zipper, rolled up my cutoffs, spread my legs, unbuckled his belt. I rolled up his shirt and licked wax out of his navel. The bartender, letting soda run on his hand, looked on the verge of tears watching us. Under Kevin's shirt I played patty-cake with his penis.

"Come home with me," said Kevin.

"No," I answered, to my eternal regret. Kevin was ready to turn what was left of my cherry inside out and peel the pits. I was tempted, but fearful. I didn't want to fail again. Was I just too tight, a lousy lay? Not woman enough? What was I supposed to feel anyway? Perhaps I should try again and tough it out? But cockteasing was also an intriguing experience and I wanted to explore it a while longer.

Two days later I left Boston with an unanswered question a foot deep in my behind.

III

Marco, the Great King, adorned his neck with a small gold chain—flat, soft links that brought out the undertint of his skin, *gold shining through mud.* He was built to fuck, ass in particular. The shape of his hips, rump, and thighs implied a great chemical potential of power lying in rest, like plastique or nitro. His fat, Cajun penis was the bait in his mantrap. His brown boy's eyes, both blinding and soothing, prepared his sex partner emotionally for a natural, moral aggression. His golden skin. Lightly tinted pubic hair.

Once inside his circle of reflected light my mind slowed and I groveled. I wanted to be fucked by gold. I hoped to become gold next to him. Marco's gift was to conquer gently, and yet presumptuously. Which is to say, he had a regal bearing.

I was with him twice, a sonata in two movements. The first, *Allegro cantabile.* The last, *Allegro con fuoco.*

Our first time came in the bathhouse on the Upper West Side of Manhattan. I was living there, night after night, having failed at coexisting with my parents. I saw Marco in the steam room, and even through a cloud of vapor he was beautiful—compact, powerful, the young middleweight champ. I groped him, but he slapped my hand away angrily. Afterward, by the heated swimming pool, Marco took my hand and led me upstairs to his private room.

"Did you think I was straight when I said no downstairs?" he asked.

"No," I said. "I thought you just didn't like me."

Marco's body felt like a warm bath. His pubic hair was fresh and sweet. He was nineteen; he didn't live anywhere. And he came from so far away, Louisiana of all places (he talked while I sucked his cock). I wouldn't have guessed. He had no drawl. He reminded me of no one and no place.

He seemed conspicuously untroubled for a homeless gay youth on the streets of the City of Predators. No one, I sensed, had ever fucked him over. He was luckier, so far, than Baldwin's Giovanni. The hardened tricks with spare rooms or a carpet for him to sleep on, who might have wounded him, preferred to adulate him. He was their favored guest. For Marco had a reputation, I later learned, in Greenwich Village. He gave priceless anal sex, the best in the world. You couldn't buy a more wonderful screw with a million dollars. Men smiled at him as he walked the street. Some poked their faces in his path and made tentative gestures, bids for his interest. Everyone wanted to lie beneath him. Which is to say, Marco enjoyed the royal prerogative.

"Nice ass," he said as I crawled toward him on my knees. He had grown bored with the blow job and nudged me onto the bed. "How old are you?"

"Twenty-three."

"Twenty-three?" he asked, as if that were ancient. "You

got a nice ass for twenty-three." He brushed his hand up and down between my cakes. Then he swiped lightly at my down, giving me a start.

"Do you want to get fucked," he asked politely.

Of course I did. I wanted to get stitched into the mattress. But I answered with that tired, silly cliché:

"Only if you promise to take it easy and pull out when I say." Which was nonsense *and* a lie.

Action: Marco fucks me in a dozen positions—on my belly, on my knees, standing up, upside down. He shoves my legs over my head and tells me my asshole looks just like a pussy. "I'mah get some of this pussy," he says. I whisper in his ear, "Oh Marco fuck me," as I wrap my arms around his chest and my knees around his neck. "Please fuck me." Someone knocks on the door and interrupts the warmest, richest pleasure I have ever known. Marco stops and opens the door. It is his friend, a tall, older man with a bushy Afro. I sit up on the bed with my arms crossed on my knees and grin with embarrassment; I can tell he heard me. Marco glances at me and then smiles at his friend, who looks at me with jealousy and hate. Evidently he had expected to be with Marco. Later Marco tells me his friend had paid for the room.

After his date left I wanted to start right up again, but Marco leaned toward me with a worried look on his face. "When did you become so, uh, feminine?" he asked. He seemed concerned that he might one day enter a feminine phase himself. After all, I was an athletic young black man much like him, perhaps physically stronger and only a few years older.

"*You* made me feminine," I said. "Usually I'm the one that fucks."

Marco winced, mistaking my meaning. "I don't give ass," he warned.

"I wouldn't want to fuck you," I said. "You're too masculine." He smiled like a ten-year-old. To make him smile again, I told him his cock was really enormous. Jumbo-sized.

"This is nothin'," he said, with absurd modesty. "Down in Louisiana they got those *big* dicks." The image of Marco in bed with a giant knee-dangling Creole (doing what?) was terribly provocative. From his curiosity about my feminine urges, and his statewide survey of Louisiana trade, I could tell he had budding questions in his own bottom. Marco was no schoolboy on top. He was dominating, long-lasting, egotistical, and experienced. But in his strong, round ass, he had not yet been, but clearly one day *would* be, fucked, which made him, technically, a virgin. (This wonderful paradox, the virginal stud, exists only in gay sex.)

On the subject of dick, true, Marco's wasn't the biggest I had ever seen. It was the ideal size, as big as one can get without being impossible. It was surely enough to dry your mouth on sight, to shut your brain off for the night. No one would ever say, "I wish it were just a bit bigger." Thankfully, it came to a pointy tip so it could slide through a frightened little pucker and smoothly split it open. If it were a person, I'd say Marco's dick had a slight weight problem.

It had softened during our conversation. "Make it hard," he insisted, expecting me to use my mouth, but it was coated with shit and so I used my hand. Marco fucked me beautifully on my back for a long while and then came inside of me. It was 1981.

A year later, in the spring, Marco found me sitting on the stoop of a dumpy hotel off Christopher Street, where I had moved. "Don't I know you?" he asked. I nodded and he sat next to me, still remembering me only vaguely. As his memory returned in detail he winced with guilt, then smiled. We talked a bit. Marco had on his gold necklace. I complimented him on it and ran my finger down his neck. *Gold in shadows.* "Where do you live?" he asked. I pointed overhead, indicating my room upstairs. Marco's hair needed combing. I took out my Afro pick and undid a tangle in back of his head. The sky was clear; it wasn't too hot. I could smell dead fish in the Hudson River just across the highway. The drone of four-lane traffic only yards away was calming. There were queers everywhere, pushing their luck in early spring, wearing hot pants, going topless. I took off my sneakers and socks, pulled off my T-shirt, undid the top button on my shorts.

Marco leaned over and whispered in my ear. "You want to do something?"

"All right," I said. We went upstairs.

IV

Marco fingered my rump as I bent over his thigh and blew him, unraveling my fleshy curlicue. It was my favorite thing, too, when I was the top; to twirl a few shit-caked hairs between my fingertips, to press that pouty little button like a doorbell when you're caught in the rain. Using his whole hand, Marco brushed and smudged like an artist working in pastels. I knew firsthand how good that felt. Who cares about the blow job? I can do better with my hand. But to scrape and pinch and tickle and poke. Up to the knuckle and shake. Sometimes fingers are the best things in the world.

That's what I mean! It was wonderful to give ass. I stuck my rump out until my back hurt and my big cheeks opened wide to Marco's touch. I knew he would love that. Marco scratched me with his fingernails. He didn't slap me, though I would have let him. "He's not mean enough," I thought, prematurely.

"Do you want to get fucked?" he asked, just as before. How sweet. It was the unfucked virgin in him, his darling nature, a schoolboy raising his hand for the bathroom pass. Asking permission to fuck me to pieces, as if there were any chance I might say no. This time I didn't ask him to go easy. I thought I could handle this. I didn't know yet that, our first time, Marco *had* been taking it easy with me. I thought he had fucked me as hard as he knew how, ignoring my plea for lenience, but no. As I had asked, Marco had held back a good half of his strength.

But not knowing this, I answered simply and directly, "Yes." No conditions. Marco made room in my bed for me to lie down. Then he gestured with his hand where he wanted me to stretch out. He wanted me to lie on my stomach, though I wanted it on my back. I tried to roll over but he coaxed me back down on my belly. That ancient gay dilemma: On your back feels more like you giving than him taking. You feel more skin, and you can kiss and wrap your ankles behind his neck (behind your own if you're very good). On your belly you can't see much, so other senses perk up to compensate—in this case, the feelings in the rectum.

Facedown, blind in my pillow, I felt revolutionary nuances of pressure. An alert, graceful insinuation past folds and curls, sticking hairs. Marco hitched and locked me with his thigh. A snakebite deep inside me, then pop! and a trickle of fluid as Marco crashed a tiny, inflated, fleshy obstacle. What finesse, I marveled. Marco was experienced to the point of being a sage. He was an enlightened despot, brutal right up to but not past my breaking point. But he was not considerate; he simply knew what he was doing.

My philosophy of anal sex

In music, jazz drummers play drumrolls on fresh eggs. The violinist shuts his eyes and cocks his head to hear the resonant frequency—one cycle per second off and the whiskey glass won't shatter. In painting, it is the invisible point where blue is no longer blue but green. In my hotel that May afternoon, it was Marco's fine, measured blend of lenience and stabbing, splitting violence. He was looking for an invisible point on the spectrum of physical sensation. I could relax just enough to make penetration possible, but no more—Marco wanted it to hurt. It should hurt until my squinting eyebrows touched the tip of my nose, but not a bit more—Marco wanted me to enjoy the pain.

Finding his fine balance, he made pain register in my mind as pleasure, fantastically transformed into its opposite through a trick mirror in my nerves. Which is to say, the aim of art *and* anal sex is the realization of paradox.

I did scream. I screamed to make room for more agony. I heard myself grunting desperately. I wanted to say, *Oh fuck me Marco,* but I no longer controlled my voice. Marco did. He played me like a saxophone, pressing my keys, blasting air out of my lungs. This noise was what he was really after. He fucked not for orgasms but for the dance on his eardrums, the quaking vibration in his solar plexus from involuntary squeaks and honks, groans and frightened squeals. Perhaps as a baby he had heard his parents fucking. Did his toes spasm in his crib that night?

I was his musical composition, a rhythmic tone poem. Oh (THRUST) OH (thrust) (thrust) (pinch) Ouch! Sheets of sound. Marco played conga drums in my ass. He made me sing like Leadbelly, like Sonny Rollins's horn in low register.

My rib cage rattled. The shock waves escaped through the top of my head. My eyelids flapped like a window shade in a windstorm. Then came gale-force winds. Then a typhoon.

I thought he was in all the way. He wasn't. He had a secret weapon, an extra inch, an inch I would never have consented to. An inch that wasn't funny anymore. A lonely inch that even great cocksuckers couldn't suck, a shortchanged youngest child. A neglected inch of cock filled with rage. Marco was blind and deaf. He was humping, pounding, grappling, jiggling.

Blast off! With one thrust, he speared me with that last inch of cock and added depth from his furious hips. The pain surprised me, and I hollered in great alarm. But it was over, and before I could resist he had come. It was an instant of true violence, unendurable if it had continued....

It was just a flash. A vicious half-second I've relived a thousand times in all the years since...

In my memories, I don't feel the pain. I remember it but don't feel it, and so I can alter the sensation; I can change it into gold. I squiggle in my chair. I flex my cheeks and sap the energy out of a blind, old moment. I nurse the memory to keep it alive....

Marco was enough of a virtuoso to have tricked me on purpose. Holding that last stretch of cock on reserve, knowing I would have hurled him off the bed if he had tried to get it all in sooner. And I'm sure he had done it to other men. Waited until they were drooling and thankful, their legs limp, their thoughts trapped in a box. Then launched a missile up their ass and came and was done, before they could object.

It was rape, calculated from the start behind a mask of grace, more childish than criminal, but still brutal. That single, splitting, foot-long thrust was Marco's aim from the minute he sat down next on me on the stoop, smiling with the sweetness of ancient sugarcane. Still, I would have happily consented again if I had ever had another chance to be with Marco. I would have asked him to take it easy, though.

A Spanish man who had been after me in my hotel for some time must have been listening at my door. He gave me an amazed look later in the hallway. Maybe the sound carried in the stairwell and he followed it. "Can I do that to you, too?" his eyes asked. There was envy in his eyes as well. I felt like a celebrity—I had put on a concert of sorts. I took his amazed, almost incredulous look as a testament to Marco. *Sorry, but I belong to the Great King.*

Dear Marco, Amon-Ra, sunburst shadows and golden mud of the Nile, Your Majesty, for a thousand nights, until death will I serve you.

V

That was the last time I was ever fucked. By the next year AIDS was on television and I saw my first friend who was to die, Mark, twenty-two years old, struggling down Christopher Street with a cane. My passive desires vanished, though I'm sure they are still buried somewhere in my unconscious. I'm in an odd state, now. I fantasize about Marco and about Kevin. I've been with Marco perhaps a thousand times in the past ten years. Yet I have no actual desire to get fucked. I'm not fighting temptation constantly like Nicky, zigzagging his way up the street and trying to stay alive. Though much less than a perfect solution, it is enough for me to remember Marco.

I suppose if I had never been with him, I would be much more confused about the epidemic. But I look back over nearly half my life, I look into what I hope will be a distant future, and say *I had it really good at least once.* My sexual regret is not so profound that I would risk my life for a hot cock in the bum.

Whereas I might for a fresh, beautiful ass.

My deeper sexual regret is that I've never done to anyone what Marco did to me. I haven't screwed a man I found truly beautiful so fantastically, so long and hard and strong, that it exceeded my fantasies, and his. Anxiety, awkwardness, a lack of finesse, and now a lack of practice, all due to the plague, have interfered every time. It is a hard thing, to feel sexually cheated by life. It presses me blindly. It stirs in my bonnet. If I get another chance—to lay a virgin, or to throw the fuck some teenager will remember in *his* middle age—will I stop if the condom breaks?

Pray for me. My dick is still out there, on the riverfront, on Weehawken Street, out in the gay wilderness, searching. My ass, though, has been put to dreamy sleep.

The Sleepwalkers

Samuel R. Delany

Dear Sam,

Sorry it's taken so long to answer yours of October 3. Probably it's a strange time for us all. I was particularly taken with your comments about AIDS. Suddenly it raised in me an urge to talk about some things in my own life.

You haven't asked to know them. They may not interest you at all.

But they want to be told. (I want to tell them.) Something about me yearns to put my communication with someone or other on a new footing—that seems, somehow, in this time, this situation, important. So here's some of what I've been doing over the last few months—it's up to you if you want to show this to Irving or not.

In a sense this letter started from the shared concern between me and Irving, Timothy Hasler. What impelled it, more than anything, was my realization of all those things Hasler and I share that Irving doesn't. That, at least, is the insight that fell to me as I began thinking about it. But weeks on, as I actually sit down to write—and this is specifically what your AIDS comment took me to—my thinking arrives at the realization of further separation, distinction, difference.

Some months ago I went down to "GSA Night" at the Mine Shaft—stayed out till six-thirty in the morning. (Rare for old nine-to-five me.) On the first Wednesday of each month, my friend Pheldon told me, GSA (The Golden Shower Association) sponsors a Wet Night—catering to guys with a taste for recycled beer. "Since from time to time you've said you were interested in that kind of thing," said Pheldon, leaning on the counter of the Fiesta, "go on down there and check it out. I did. It wasn't that bad. Here's the address."

So I did.

The bar's in what must have been, at one time, the second floor of a warehouse. A couple of stairways angle down to the first floor, where there's also a bar. (Once the lower space must have been a garage.) The floor's concrete, with half a dozen built-in drains. Water hoses, in green or black coils, hang here and there on the dark wooden or brick walls, near old-fashioned spigots with iron handles. In the largest room, under dim blue and orange bar lights, sit three bathtubs. Some of the other rooms contain a variety of slings, tables, and—yes—wash basins.

On Wet Night they open at nine, and for fifteen dollars you get all the beer you can drink till midnight. In the upstairs bar, there's a room to check your clothes. (About three quarters of the guys in line do. But not wholly sure of what was coming up, I didn't.) For fifty cents extra you can rent an old jockstrap, if you want. You go downstairs, get your beer free from the two hard-working bartenders there, drink it, and...

After three different guys just walked up to me, while I was standing in a corner, whipped it out, and started peeing on the leg of my jeans like big fucking dogs!—I began to realize why so many of them had opted to get rid of their clothes.

Well, you see some pretty strange stuff—in those rooms

where it's light enough to see. I started out pretty much on the "pitching" end of things. I guess that's only natural with a bunch of guys you've never seen before. (I thought I might have some trouble in that department, but after the fourth or fifth beer, I lost my inhibitions—since it was going on all around me.) Generally it's fairly quiet there, considering forty or fifty men are moving around and drinking beer. Every once in a while, in one of the darker back rooms, you hear an echoing slap—from someone getting his butt smacked. Sometimes you'll hear a couple of guys laugh. But generally everyone kind of whispers—or at least talks pretty softly, especially once you get away from the beer counter. And, of course, there's the general trickle and chatter of spilling urine—sometimes louder, sometimes fainter.

Purposely I'd worn my rattiest pair of jeans and an old green workshirt. To be accurate, I hadn't known about the clothes check when I'd arrived, so I kept my clothes on for most of it. But, if anything, that seemed to make me more attractive to the committed pitchers in the crowd. Once, in a *sotto voce* conversation with a little pudgy blond guy, I was told about the clothes check place upstairs. "Well," I said, "next time, I guess." But I was already sopping from my chest to my pants cuffs. Inside my sneakers, it felt like I was walking on wet sponges. Finally I had to take my shirt off. (Some of these guys aim high!) I stuffed it behind a folded-up ping-pong table that was leaning against one brick wall in one of the hallways.

Eventually I decided I'd better take my turn in the barrel—that is, in one of the tubs—since that was, really, what I'd come for. That night I did at least one thing I'd never done before: I got in a bathtub while some nine guys (with several more standing around) drifted over, unbuttoned their flies (the ones who weren't already naked or in jockstraps; zippers, I guess, are not too popular with these guys), and let go all over me. You know what it feels like, to be pissed on by nine guys at once while you lie spread-eagle on your back in a bathtub, Sam—I mean, more than anything else?

It feels warm!

At one o'clock they closed the downstairs for cleaning—shooed everybody up the brick-walled stairs into the upper bar. The work lights were all on and the hoses were coming off the wall when I left.

About ten minutes after they'd locked the door to the downstairs area, though, I remembered my shirt was still behind the ping-pong table. The upstairs bartender—as shirtless as I was, but in a studded black body harness—told me I had to wait till the whole bar closed; then he'd let me down there to see if I could remove it.

So I sat down at the counter, to drink my first beer of the evening that I'd paid for out of pocket. Miracle of miracles, only the edge of the money in my wallet was wet. A wiry little older guy was there, who, like me, also had no shirt on—but I think that's the way he'd come. He just wore jeans, a big, silver, longhorned belt buckle, and cowboy boots. Bow-legged and a little unsteady, he was strutting about the bar and wanted to joke around with everybody. Some tattoos were blearily visible in the white hair, over his arms, and he had a twangy southwestern drawl. He looked like a well-preserved fifty or fifty-five and, myself, I thought he was kind of cute. But when he went up to two fellows at the bar (both of them still just in jockstraps), put a hand on each of their shoulders, and proposed loudly that they all go off in the back and have a threesome—well, first the two guys were clearly into each other, and second they were clearly put out by his intrusion. Finally one said, "No," loudly and firmly and I realized most of the customers there were finding the little codger a pain in the ass.

But I went over to start a conversation with him; he told me—hanging on to my shoulder—that tonight was his sixtieth

(!) birthday. He was celebrating, and he was (I quote) "out to show as many of these young cocksuckers what I can do as would be interested." He seemed disappointed so few of us were taking him up on his offer.

Boxes and crates were piled up at the back of the bar, and after I bought him a birthday beer, he went over and climbed up to drink it there, knees wide, horny hands on them, banging his boot heels on the boxes below. I stood in front of him (with my own beer bottle raised before my bared pectorals—moderately okay from my morning push-ups, I guess—like a protective sword between us), looking up at the snarled white hair over his tanned chest and, above that, his wrinkled brown-red neck.

"I mean," he explained to me, "I'm a fuckin' trucker. No joke—a real one, with a real *truck*—parked outside right down the street. No kiddin', boy! It's no eighteen wheeler or nothin'; it's just an old Dodge cube. I work pretty much between New England and Delaware. But I always stop off here, when I'm coming through the city—especially on Wet Nights, if I can make it. I've had some pretty good times here—usually I make out like a fuckin' bandit. But I don't know what it is tonight. All the cocksuckers is supposed to be crazy for goddamn truckers, and here I am—horny, hung, and ready for bear—and can't get a taker nowhere! It's enough to make a birthday boy break down and cry!"

"I'll suck you off," I said.

"Yeah?" he said, brightening up. "You will? Hey, how about that! Well, let's see what you can do, boy." And he set the beer I'd bought him down, pulled open his fly, and tugged out a respectable, uncut six-incher. While I was working on him (his jeans were still wet from his stint downstairs—as were mine) and he was holding my head, the bartender came up to us and said, "Come on, Tex." (This old fart was actually called—at least in the bar—"Tex"!) "Take this guy in the grope-room in back or into the men's room or something. You been here enough times to know you're not supposed to do it out front here, with everybody walking around. Even if you *are* an exhibitionist!"

"I know, I know," Tex said. "But this cocksucker's good. It won't take me long. Just gimme a minute—just a minute now!"

"Okay, but if I come back here and there's a fuckin' puddle on the floor in front of these crates, I'll eighty-six your hillbilly ass out of here for good! I'm not kidding, now—birthday or no birthday, you hear me? The stuff you like to do is downstairs—and it's over with for the night, anyway!"

Then the bartender walked away.

And Tex, still holding my head, said: "Fuck him! *Suck* my dick, black boy!"

So I did; and in two minutes he grunted, "Oh, shit!" and dropped a small, lumpy, old man's load. I stood there milking him with my mouth. He sat above me, breathing hard. As I started to pull off him, he caught my head with one hand. "Aw, come on now. I saw you downstairs. I know what you come in here for, tonight. You just lemme get my breath back, and I'll give it to you. You can take it all, now—can't you? Just don't spill any—then I really *will* be in some trouble. You heard the bartender—we just can't leave no mess up here on the floor like you can downstairs. But you'll take it for me, won't you, cocksucker?"

From his movements, now, I could tell he'd up-ended his bottle of beer. Then, with his softening dick still in my mouth, he began to pee. It wasn't very salty. But it flowed and flowed, long, warm, and hard. I drank. And I didn't spill anything. Finishing, he sighed. "Boy, that felt good!" His hand relaxed on my head, as at last I came off him. "That was some birthday present you give the old man." He held down his hand. "Wanna shake?"

So I shook his hand. His palm was sandpaper rough, and his fingers gripped me hard. Without letting go, he leaned down and said:

"Gimme a kiss."

So I stood up on tiptoe; he bent way down—and thrust his tongue way the hell into my mouth. I thrust mine back, and from the slippery hardness I hit, behind his teeth and under his palate, I realized those were dentures that had filled his friendly grin. Finally he sat back wet-lipped and smiling. "Now, that's what I call a real happy birthday! If you don't catch a little of what you pitch, you can't really appreciate it, now, can you? You better get on to the men's room, 'fore you fuckin' bust!"

"Yeah," I said. "I was thinking on the same lines."

"If you're still up for it," he said, "you should try the Real Men's Room."

I wasn't sure what he meant as he patted my head and I turned to amble across the bar floor. Three or four people who'd been watching us—one stopped masturbating to put his cock inside his leather pants—turned away. The restrooms were marked MEN'S and WOMEN'S. But over the woodburned panel that hung on the women's room door, someone had taped a piece of paper on which was scrawled in magic marker: REAL MEN'S ROOM.

I opened the door—on a space with three commodes in it. Two were occupied. On one sat a small, muscular blond. His jockstrap was around the ankles of his basketball sneakers. In front of him stood a black guy, about forty, maybe forty-five years old. He was about six-foot-three and, though not particularly muscular, big. I mean he weighed a good two-hundred-fifty, two-hundred-eighty pounds. He had glasses on and a baseball cap with the visor turned to the back of his head—which I assumed was from some time spent sucking cock downstairs. From a stubby uncut dick protruding from dark fingers like a still darker sausage, a full stream of yellow glittered, a gold staple between it and the white fellow's open mouth.

It kind of surprised me.

I decided to sit down myself, though, and took up the one free commode. Moments after I did, I realized there weren't any urinals in here. We—the ones of us who were sitting—were it. And just to confirm that, three more guys came in, as I was settling: One took up his place in front of the other guy sitting next to me, a bony fellow with a black leather hat on, black boots, and not much else.

Two more took their place in front of me—one a pretty good-looking guy with a brown beard who'd obviously done some working out with weights; he had on a leather vest and jeans. The one in line behind him was in marine fatigues and shirtless. (But looked more like Phyllis Diller than a marine.) The bearded man unbuttoned his fly, pulled out both cock and balls—from a moment's stagger, I realized he was drunk—and just began to piss in my face, letting me get it in my mouth.

This guy had a real horse bladder and the pressure of his water was immense—greater than I'd thought somebody pissing could muster. Swaying in front of me, as I gulped and gulped him, he looked over his shoulder and motioned to the kind of ugly looking guy in the fatigues, "Come on up here, man—and piss in this guy's face with me, huh? He loves it! Look at him." The guy stepped up and in a minute, I had both cock heads in my mouth, with their vastly differing flows.

I don't know why. Maybe it was because this was the first time I'd done anything like this—I mean, in a bar, in a controlled situation, where all (or most) of the people who'd come were into the same thing—but I found myself with an obsession not to spill any.

The guy on the commode next to me, every once in a while, would hold the cock delivering into him in his hand, sit back, and play it over his face and chest, letting it waterfall down between his legs, over his dick and balls, and into the toilet. Then he'd go back to drinking. But me—and, I realized the little white brick shit-house on the other end—were not about to lose a drop.

I had about a six-minute rest before the next three guys came in. I took them, one right after the other. Just before I finished the last—a squat Puerto Rican, who grinned down at me all through it, nodding drunkenly, approvingly—I felt an overwhelming urge to shit. Since I was on a commode, I let it go. It was shit yeah, but it was awfully loud, a whole lot of it and very wet. And not a full two minutes after I'd reached back to flush, I had to go again. This one was even wetter.

Two more guys—and I took them.

A couple of minutes later old Horse Bladder pushed through the door again: the big, bearded fellow with the leather vest and the muscles. In the thirty-five minutes since he'd been in here before, he hadn't gotten any soberer. His cock—as I saw this time—was (as I already knew) fairly sizable; cut—but pretty raggedly. And he had some of the most pronounced veins webbing his shaft I'd seen. At one place on the side, one seemed to have ruptured beneath the skin, to form a smooth little dime-sized planetarium. But it didn't seem to bother him. He grabbed my head with one hand, more to steady himself than anything else, and thrust his cock, already spilling tasteless waters out its quarter-inch slit, hot on my face, hot in my mouth. "Oh, shit...!" he grunted. "I didn't think I was gonna make it, man!" and leaned with one fist on the wall behind me—while I felt my asshole open up again: below, it let a stream everyone could hear roaring into the toilet.

It came out of me like water from a fire hose.

What had happened, I realized, was that all my sphincters had opened and were letting liquid through and out as fast as it came in! Nor had it been traumatic—or even vaguely painful.

Damn, I thought; I'm going to have the cleanest gut in Manhattan! When he was finished, Horse patted my face with his wet hand. "Thanks, fella'. See you again in a little bit."

But, frankly, as he left, I wasn't sure I was up to another half hour in there.

I wiped myself—really I was completely clean—pulled up my pants (still pretty wet from downstairs), and—had to go again! So I pulled them down again, sat once more, and hosed out another quart.

Then I wiped and pulled up my pants a second time. The bony guy in the boots and black cap had gotten up and gone by now, but the little, muscular white fellow in the jockstrap was still going strong, it looked like. One guy stood with his dick in the fellow's mouth; one guy waited in line behind him—even though the other commode was free.

I pushed out of the restroom, back into the bar.

The first thing I noticed was that the place had pretty much cleared out—there were maybe a third as many guys at the bar as there'd been when I'd gone in. Horse Bladder was still at the counter, in his leather vest, talking to somebody. I came over beside some character in full leather I didn't even remember seeing before and sat on a stool. The bartender immediately came up to me with a beer. "Tex bought you this—he said to give it to you when you came out."

"Oh," I said. "Did he go, yet?"

"Nope." The bartender nodded toward the counter's end.

I looked but didn't see anybody—at first. Then I noticed, up on that pile of crates and boxes, somebody lay stretched out on his back. The toes of a pair of cowboy boots pointed toward the beamed ceiling a few feet overhead.

"He said he wanted to buy you a drink," the bartender repeated, "before he fell out."

"Oh," I repeated. "*Uh*...thanks."

I looked at the clock. It was a couple of minutes after three. I'd gone into the Real Men's Room just a bit before one—though, if you'd asked me, I would have sworn I'd been in there closer to one hour than two.

I put a forearm either side the bottle, and wondered if I should drink it. Should the urge hit, I was all set to scoot back into the john and loose more water. Finally, though, I picked up the bottle, and took a swallow...and realized, as I set it back down, that I felt...good!

Incredibly good!

And peaceful.

And content.

I didn't feel any need to talk to anyone. The feeling that gets you up, looking for this and that, that starts you off doing one thing or the other, just to have something to do, was in abeyance—an abeyance I usually associate with tiredness; only, though it was after three in the morning, I didn't *feel* tired.

I thought about that strangely and rarely attainable condition Heidegger called "meditative thinking" and wondered if this was it.

I was sitting there, the time going just as unconsciously for me now as it had in the Real Men's Room, when suddenly a heavy arm landed around my shoulder, and a bearded face pushed up into mine. "Oh, man there you are. I was hoping it was you! I'm ready man—I'm about to fucking bust. You gonna take it for me...?"

I was startled. But I didn't even pull away. "Hey, I'm sorry," I smiled. "But I think I've bad my fill—"

"Oh, no, man! You gotta take it for me," Horse insisted, shaking his head drunkenly. "There isn't anybody left in the bathroom. And I gotta piss so bad I'm about to bust. You know, I can't piss in the fucking toilet—not in a place like this: That's the rule, you know? Tonight. I mean, that's my rule. I gotta do it on somebody, in somebody please, baby.

Lemme piss in your face. You know you love it, you know you want it! And I'm not gonna make it if I have to hold it too much longer—"

Though I'd never said that to anyone, I knew what he was talking about: It was the same voice speaking in him that—in me—had said I had to drink it all. "Okay," I said. "Yeah, sure. I'm just afraid I'm going to shit out piss all over myself again if I drink any more—"

"That's okay, guy. That's okay, I'll help you..." and he was forcing me down from the stool, pulling at his fly.

I got his big, veiny meat before he started. I was holding on to his leg with one arm and a rung of the bar stool with my other hand. While I knelt there, somebody else came up. And a western drawl: "Oh, shit—is this cocksucker still workin' out? Cause, Jesus—I gotta take me one wicked piss. I just woke up back there—an' I gotta piss like a fuckin' race horse, boy—"

Swaying above me, Horse said thickly: "Well, come on. Stick it in his month and piss, you scrawny-ass motherfucker! You can see he's taking it!" Hands moved over my head, and a moment later a second, uncut cock prodded and pushed in beside Horse's—and let go!

"Jesus Christ, Tex—? What the fuck...ah, come *on*, guys!" It was the bartender again. "Who you got down there? Will you let him up, man? I told you, you can't do that up here in the bar. That's for downstairs. Or in the men's room!"

"Get the fuck out of my face," Horse grunted. "If I make a mess, then you can say somethin' to me. But I know my piss drinkers, man. And that's not this one's style." He bent over me a little. "Is it, cocksucker—it better not be! Or we're gonna be in deep shit!"

Tex just chuckled.

"I swear," the bartender said, "I'm gonna kick the both of you out of here—shit, it's time to go, anyway. All right, drink up! Mugs and bottles and glasses on the bar, guys!"

I drank.

Tex said: "*He's* sure drinkin' up, ain't he?"

"Drink up and turn 'em in, guys!" I heard the bartender call again. "All in, now. All in!"

Tex finished first. His dick slid out from beside Horse's thicker, longer tool. The cleaning lights came on about twenty-five seconds before Horse finished. Five seconds before he pulled his dick out my face, I felt that pressure building in my ass.

As soon as I was off, I rasped: "Oh, shit, guys...I think we've got an emergency—!"

Maybe it was the look on my face.

Maybe it was my tone of voice—

"*Uh-oh*," Horse said. "Come on, Tex. We gotta get this cocksucker into the bathroom." They both were over me, lifting me by the arms, dragging me, practically carrying me across the room. Clearly they had a good idea what was going on—like they'd both been here before.

They pushed into the john with me. Horse was pulling at my pants. "Let it go, guy. Just let it go..." A moment later, my ass hit the toilet ring, already splashing loudly below.

Sitting there, my butt spurting water like a stuck balloon, I began to laugh. "Well, I guess we made it...!"

The whole thing seemed crazily comic.

Tex squatted beside me, rubbing my belly "How you feelin' there now, boy?" He seemed to think it was pretty funny too.

Horse was swaying again—like maybe he was too drunk to find it funny. His hand on my back, he rubbed down, up, rubbed a few more times, and the next time went right on down, over my buttocks, through the commode ring and under my ass; he moved his hand around in the hosing waters—once even stuck a finger three joints up into my spilling hole. Which made me laugh more.

I leaned against his jeans. (And I still had that same good

feeling. I wondered if, in their drunkenness, Horse and Tex did too.) Horse's pants lap was wet, as though he'd had some trouble holding it in awhile now. Or maybe it was left over from downstairs.

Still bending over me, Horse looked at his big, wet fingers: "Cocksucker, you're clean as a fuckin' whistle!" I was still smiling; suddenly he thrust his forefinger into his mouth between his mustache and beard, then the second; then, surprising me equally, he dropped his hand to my face and ran his third into my mouth; he followed that with his little finger. "If you don't catch a little of what you pitch," he said when he'd finished sucking off his fingers, "you can't really appreciate it."

"Yeah," Tex said. "That's what I told 'im, before."

Horse stood, wiping his hand on his weight-lifter chest. He pushed his vest back enough for me to see a really thick-gauge tit ring piercing a nipple five or six times the size of the nipple you'd see on most guys—five or six times the size of mine, anyway. Still rubbing, absently he moved the vest back from the right one. No ring. But his male teat in its quarter-sized aureole was still as big as some women's.

When I stopped spurting, and the sound died beneath me, Tex asked me, "You okay now?"

"Yeah, I think so."

"Good." Horse took a breath. "'Cause I gotta get home. I have to be at work at eight-thirty this morning." He staggered a moment, then stood up. "I'm a computer programmer, working on electronic music—only now I double as a sound engineer at Columbia Records. And just don't ask me," though, drunk as he was, I wasn't sure what I wasn't supposed to ask, unless it was, What are you doing here...? "Hey, man—thanks for everything," he said, with that alcoholic seriousness of someone who's managed to rise to some emergency. "Especially that last one—that was the important one, you know? Thinking about all the piss you had in your belly, guy—and how you still took mine: Man, I'll be beatin' off to that one for a long time!"

"Yeah," I said. But I was grinning again. "Good. I'm glad..."

I think Tex was fixing to stay in there with me, but Horse gave him a kind of push on the back of the head: "Come on, old man—get on out of here. Let the guy get himself together, huh?"

"Oh, yeah...," Tex said, and stood. "Yeah, boy. Okay. You get yourself together. You okay now...?"

I nodded.

The two of them left.

And you know, I felt even better?

When I came out this time, Horse was gone. The bar's work lights were still bright around the place. Tex was lingering at the door.

I went over to the bartender, who, behind the counter, in his studded leather jock and his body harness, was dunking glasses in one sink, twisting them on the pair of brushes in the next, then moving them to the rinsing sink. As soon as I went up, he said: "You see, man—these guys are always trying to abuse the place here. You gotta follow the rules. Or we won't be able to do it no more. At least they didn't mess up the floor—but there's a place for everything. And you still have to follow the rules."

"Sure," I said. "I understand that."

"I know it wasn't your fault. Some of these guys just don't give you a chance to say no. Still, you gotta be kind of firm with 'em—some of these piss masters. For their own good—and yours. I mean, you like this shit; I like it too. I'm not trying to be holier than thou. But—still—you gotta obey the rues."

"Look," I said. "Before, you said that when you were closing up, you'd let me go downstairs to see if I could find my shirt...?"

He looked up, frowned, then seemed to remember. "Oh, yeah. That's right." He wiped his hands on a towel. "Come on, then."

I followed him to the door that had been locked for the last few hours. After he unlocked it (with a key on the ring at the side of his leather jock), I followed him downstairs.

He turned on some work lights. I found the ping-pong table in a hallway in the back, but when I pulled it away from the wall, my shirt wasn't there. "You know," he said, while we walked back up the brick-walled steps, "when they clean that place out, after the guys get finished with it, they really hose it down good. The walls, the ceiling every-thing—then they slop a couple of barrels full of disinfectant around—and hose it out again. Anything that's in there, it goes out as garbage. I mean, you can understand that, can't you?"

"Yeah," I said. "Sure. I understand."

Then, when we were coming out between the raw brick walls into the upper bar again: "You see, we don't have it set up to clean out upstairs the way we can clean it out down there. We don't get the hoses and stuff. That's why we have the rules we do."

"Yeah," I said.

Tex was gone now—besides the two bartenders I was the last person to leave.

But when I got outside, on the porch, with the meat-hooks off under the awning to the left, in just his jeans and boots, Tex was waiting on the sidewalk—still shirtless. (Like me.)

"Hey, boy," he said. "I got my truck. You going to Brooklyn, or maybe down toward Canal Street—I'll give you a lift! I can't stay over or nothin'. But we can go in my truck! You like that, boy? You like to ride in a real trucker's truck? It's all mine, too—all paid for over three years ago, now. Ain't a big one. But it's mine."

I grinned. "Thanks, Tex. I'd appreciate that. But I'm heading uptown."

"Oh..." He looked really sorry. "Well, then. I gotta get going too. I'm gonna be late as it is, boy. I should have been out of here and back on the road by midnight. And it's fuckin' four in the goddamn morning!"

"Hey, Tex," I said. "I was just wondering. Did anybody ever tell you that you weren't supposed to call black guys 'boy'?"

"Oh, shit...!" Tex said, looking down and stepping aside. "Just about once every six weeks as far back as I can fuckin' remember—and, well, goddamn it, I must be gettin' fuckin' senile already—" he reached up and scratched his short brush of white hair "—'cause I never can fuckin' remember it! Look—" he raised a hand in front of his face, rough palm toward me "—I swear up and down, if it makes you feel any better, I sure don't mean no offense by it. So help me, I ain't callin' you boy 'cause you a nigger; I'm callin' you boy 'cause to me you look like a fuckin' *kid!*" Believe me, I ain't out to offend no nigger! It's my fuckin' *birthday*, man! I just wanna have a good time! Hey, why would I be out to hurt some nigger's feelin's after a blowjob like that? And if I did, so help me, I'm sorry. I'm sorry—!"

"—Okay, *okay*!" I said. "Okay."

"Why am I gonna go out and try to make people feel bad on my fuckin' birthday? That's fuckin' *crazy*, ain't it? I'm just tryin' to have me a good time, gettin' my dick sucked, tryin' to let you have a good time swingin' on my meat—that's all! There wasn't nothin' bad meant by it! I swear, up, down, sideways, and on my momma's grave! I didn't mean nothin', not a thing, I tell you—"

"*Okay!*"

A child's bewilderment in his aging face, he dropped the hand he'd been fending me off with—and thrust it out to shake—"No offense then, nigger...?"

It kind of made me start. Then I laughed. "No offense, you fart-faced old toothless piss-drippin' scumbag honky!"

He grabbed my hand as I raised it, and pumped it hard laughing too, and, with his other hand, grasped my bare shoulder. "That's more like it, boy! Hey, I don't give a fuck if I *am* late. I'll give you a ride up to wherever you live anyway—four hours late now, five ain't gonna kill me! You just gotta point me in the right direction. When we get to the truck I'll even pop my teeth and suck your dick for you—you can blow your big black load right down my throat. You sucked my dick; I done pissed in your mouth—twice! And I'll suck your fuckin' dick, nigger—without my teeth, too. How you gonna think I'm fuckin' prejudiced after that, *huh*? Come on, now. We'll—"

"That's okay," I said. "You have to get on. And so do I."

"Now, come on! I'd be *right* obliged to suck your dick. You gave me a real good suck—two of 'em. And you don't find a toothless cocksucker like me everyday—I can make that meat of yours feel real good, nigger!"

I laughed. Because there was nothing else to do. "Thanks. But, maybe when you come through the next time. Okay?"

"Well—I guess if you gotta go. And, well, yeah—I should be gettin' along, too, I suppose. Okay. Maybe I'll see you next time I'm through." He ducked his white-haired head. "G'night! Hey—and thanks again for my birthday blowjob! That was real nice!" He turned down the nighttime city sidewalk heading—shirtless and bowlegged—toward the corner.

I turned and walked the other way.

How does a black guy wearing a pair of urine-soaked jeans and no shirt, I wondered, get a cab two blocks from the waterfront at four in the morning?

But on the corner, I saw the Number 11 bus that runs right up Amsterdam Avenue.

I had some change in my pocket. I hurried across the street, made for the bus's open door, wondering if the driver would say anything.

I climbed up and funneled ninety-five cents off my fingers into the change box.

The driver frowned up at me from under his visor and said, "Jesus, nigger—a rough night, huh?" But he was another black guy.

I smiled, nodded. "Yeah—rough night." That was the good feeling speaking. I wonder if the driver heard any of it. Or, really, if Tex had.

"It looks like it." Then he shook his head and went back to looking out the windshield.

But maybe when you're feeling that good—and looking that bad—it has to be a private thing.

I walked to the back of the bus, sat, and leaned on my knees—I was the only passenger.

After waiting another thirty seconds, the driver leaned forward to take the wheel, pushed the pedal that yanked the doors closed and, hauling the wheel around, pulled from the curb to start the whining bus uptown.

Photographic Memory

William S. Doan

My posse of perverts is in jail, again, and likely to be caged for several years. Curtis urged me to dump them, and, because I love him, and because I have become indifferent to their criminal careers, I have done as he asked. My personal poverty has also been a major factor in this decision. It is easy to distance myself from their problems when I cannot afford them, although they are very low-rent. Vice can be taxed to death. Call it "virtue by other means."

The members of the posse are not taking separation well. In their heart of hearts they are exhibitionists; they made use of me as the recording angel of our mutual fantasies. They have lost the artist-voyeur who created the virtual stages on which they performed for their own satisfaction and the audience of horny men who found release in their displays. On paper, they will always be young, virile, and unmarked by the sharp edges of time; they fuck and jack with earnest simplicity, apparently self-absorbed, but always ready for their close-ups. Eternally hard, eyes closed to focus the other senses on their drooling dicks and spasms ahead, their photo images are a treasury of sex remembered.

Curtis says he thinks I am addicted to roughnecks who have done time. He smirks knowingly at my small stack of R. Kelly CDs. His neck is smooth and professionally shaved. Curtis is proud that he has never braided a single strand of his carefully cut hair. I like the way he looks, but, if he decided to imitate Sprewell, I wouldn't object.

I have pointed out to my lover that, when I met them, the posse members did not have adult criminal records. In fact, I have watched their long slow falls into the tight embrace of the felony courts for almost two decades. Their problems were magnified by the effects of alcohol and drugs they used to dull their pain, but they were all trapped by the inability to acknowledge their strong sexual urges toward other men and their failures with the opposite sex. Their adventures on the down low were no more fulfilling than their heterosexual philandering, although they did avoid no-contact orders, child support demands, and charges of sexual battery from male sex partners.

I have a letter from J.A., reminding me how, years ago, he allowed me to believe I was seducing him at the edge of a secluded farm pond in the style of a proletarian novel. (In fact, he was the most experienced and daring of the posse.) He has written to curse me for not accepting his jailhouse phone calls. He declares he is going back to religion, a threat so idle that I laughed out loud when I read it. In the unlikely event his jailers would allow him to visit Salem Baptist, he would be met by at least two of the five women he impregnated and abandoned, not to mention the children and grand-babies who hold no kindly thoughts for their long-absent parent. He would fare as badly at the Methodist and Spiritual parishes.

The videos J.A. made with me, twenty years ago, are still hot. (Curtis has never seen them.) His skin is perfect, his body is very muscular and well-defined, and he turns himself on the moment the tape begins to roll. Slowly and gently, he covers his body with oil poured from a green and gold Venetian glass bottle. The background behind him is red and gold silk. Studio lights catch the rippling abs, full chest, and strong arms of a young athlete in love with his own physique. He begins to massage his tumescent dick with both hands, maintaining a slow, steady rhythm until a minute before thick, white streamers pour over his fingers and then shoot upwards toward his heaving, muscular stomach and chest. The second video is similar, except that the background is black velvet. The beautiful young brother in those tapes has become a crackhead, about to be sentenced for attempted rape; his victim is a female addict who is astonishingly ugly and utterly unforgiving. J.A. demanded a DNA test. The results were "positive," and his fate was sealed.

I disconnected from J.D. by telling him that I had deposited all his worldly goods in the parking lot next to an adult book store, near a hetero strip club. When he searched for the two large soft-sides crammed with clothes and assorted toiletries, he found nothing. I will miss his big, bad, dildo-sucking ass; however, I do have video and audiotapes to remind me that he was an anal pig who loved toys. He also had a fund of prison sex stories, mostly about a couple he called "Amtrak" and "Red," insatiable lovers who spent hours fucking in the prison shower room, while J.D. "shot jiggas" for them. Watching for stray guards, he was also able to observe their sexual antics, which he described to me with enthusiasm and many details.

J.D. and Amtrak met in the prison weight room. (Each time J.D. did time, he returned to the free world with a better body that promptly turned to undisciplined fat. I learned to photograph him within two weeks of his release, before his abs sank in a lake of blubber.) I have always suspected that, when Red was not available, J.D. serviced his training partner, but he denied it strenuously. On the other hand, he seemed to be able to recall every vein in Amtrak's stunningly big dick—eighteen inches!—and I knew from personal experience that J.D.'s ass could handle large equipment. When he finally introduced me to Amtrak, briefly free on parole, I was disappointed to find that this giant sex god was a doper in denial who turned hostile when I mentioned Red. J.D. was also pissed, because Amtrak knew that he had published their private business on the street. I never got to see the fabulous Amtrak dick, but I did notice a sizeable bulge in his too-tight denims.

J.D. never lived with me, but he did store his bags at my house. He used that occasion to steal money from me, while I was putting his luggage in a closet. When he called to say that I could deliver his things to his new address, the next evening, I told him where to look for them. His parole officer, a lipstick lesbian who was more macho than J.D., revoked his parole and a judge returned him to the joint. I suppose he is cruising the weight room, waiting for the next Amtrak.

Curtis has seen one of the books I published and most of the prints that have found homes in more than a dozen art museums in this country, Europe and Canada. He also owns copies of cards and calendars that feature my photographs. I have even taken images of Curtis for our private pleasure. Much as I love him and lust for his body, neither one of us has ever spoken of Curtis as a model for the kind of pictures I made of the posse. He says that I have "gone beyond" the erotic imagery that made my name, but not my fortune, decades ago. (I think he is wrong; I have changed far less than the posse, although fate has not been kind to me.) The last of my models disappeared into the maw of justice only recently, shortly before my sixtieth birthday.

The departure of A.H. was the least dramatic of the three. Although I had told him that Curtis and I were determined to be faithful to each other, he called, late one night, and asked me to meet him in a nearby convenience store, where he begged me to buy a worthless, secondhand camera that was probably stolen; I refused his offer. I suspected that the tiny amount he asked for the camera was the going rate for a very small piece of crack cocaine. Of course, he claimed that he was clean; in fact, I knew he spent the previous month in a drug rehab center. He tried to get to me by reminding me of our most recent sexual encounter, months ago, when he appeared at my house with a blazing erection and was soon buck naked, feet up, moaning and shouting, while I went after his ass without mercy.

Ever the virgin, his favorite role, A.H. always claimed that, whatever we did, it was the first time he allowed himself to be used in that way; we both knew better. His calendar bondage images are still popular with leathermen all over the world. Most muscular of all the posse, his ass mounds, round as terrestrial globes, are a national standard for the male butt. I asked him why he didn't accept some of the offers to dance he said he got from strip clubs, gay and straight. He told me that was "too much work." He was waiting for a male patron to pay his bills, so he could return to the girlfriend and children he had abandoned, ten years ago. This illusion resisted the best efforts of rehab psychologists and his own parents, who took him in, from time to time, trying to keep him out of jail. When they finally figured out that he was living on the down low, they reproached him, but they still kept him under their impoverished roof. He repaid them with small thefts.

The night A.H. wanted to sell the camera to me, I tried to explain my promise to Curtis, but he, who could be faithful to no one, did not understand what I was telling him. A few days later, the news of his arrest on multiple drug charges appeared in the police reports. Adrift on his "straight" fantasy, he was headed toward the whirlpool one more time.

A curious thing has happened since I cut loose the posse. Each time I see their pictures, I find it hard to remember who they are (or were) and how we met. I have even lost interest in the tapes, which used to be a sure turn-on for me. (That is why I made them!) They are not strangers to me, but the excitement they once provoked has faded. Curtis says this is because they are getting old. This statement is oddly flattering to me, because I am at least ten years older than the oldest posse member, J.A., and much older than Curtis.

I have become absorbed in my relationship with Curtis to an extent I find surprising. Handsome as he is, I am more interested in his thoughts and feelings than the size of his erection. I also find that I fear losing him, a feeling I never experienced with any member of the posse, because I could sense that they would always come back for my attention. (Curtis says they were merely hustling me.) The stock market disaster has made me an unlikely target for gold diggers.

If it were not for Curtis, I would probably have lost my home. Yesterday, another letter with a jail address arrived. Curtis gave it to me, but I made a show of tossing it in the trash. Curtis embraced me from behind and kissed my neck.

I don't think he knows how easy it was for me to throw away the letter. I won't tell him anytime soon.

Some People Wear Green

Jonathan Ivy Kidd

> It was borne in on me: *But Joey is a boy...* The power and the promise and the mystery of that body made me suddenly afraid. That body suddenly seemed the black opening of a cavern in which I would be tortured till madness came, in which I would lose my manhood.
>
> —James Baldwin, *Giovanni's Room*

In an era when people spend most of their childhood afraid of death and most of their adulthood afraid of life, Benny lived quite well at the intersection. Benny's father beat his mother, and his mother in turn beat Benny. Benny used to kick the dog, but over the course of time, he forgot how. And the kicking stopped while the beatings continued. Benny would always be able to tell when the storms were coming; his father would call him "son." "Get me my beer, son" or "Where is the newspaper, son?" The tirades would eventually be unleashed, usually in the small of his mother's back. The same portion that Benny's father so admired for its curvaceous nature, sloping slightly from her buttocks and into her elegant posture, the build of a queen. The wounds would heal there silently, with no one able to discern the disorder beneath heavy cloth. That would be until Benny's mother's kidneys began to fail, and she started to menstruate via her bladder, rather than her uterus. She died slow, and left Benny alone, while his father's guilt assumed the duties of husband and dad, a storm turned inward. Showing in the simple flecks across Benny's face usually, sometimes with marks on his ass. Because by this point, Papa Joe did not care. He was already a murderer, so what if he beat the shit out of his son?

Benny began selling his ass in order to raise money to get away from Papa Joe. In actuality, Benny only sold his dick for sucking and caressing, never his ass. Usually Benny would change his persona for each customer, sometimes ramming them hard twice in the throat before coming and selfishly demanding his money from "the dirty faggot cocksucker" or on other occasions pretending that he had never had his dick sucked by a man before and begging them to let him come as they went slow, long, and deep. But they never knew him. A repeat customer, Vic came up with Benny's hustling pseudonym, "Cherry," because on their first night together Vic offered Benny twelve hundred dollars to let him have at it. Benny refused and Vic laughed at Benny's fear of "giving up his cherry ass." Benny started wearing the name as a badge of honor, as it meant higher wages from the johns who hoped to be the first or thought Benny was just gay for pay and his masculinity communicable.

After making decent money and growing complacent to the dangers of his craft, Benny found himself in an alleyway with a john who could tie cherry stems into knots with his tongue and did. When Benny declined the john's invitation Benny was hit across the face with a two by four. From there Benny became his father's son and left the john in the alley to die. Papa Joe was drunk when Benny returned en route to skipping town. He asked his son where he thought he was going and Benny randomly said, "France," at which his father's eyes for the first time turned glassy as he stumbled off to bed.

Getting off the plane at Orly, Benny heard people complain about the dirty bathrooms, frustrated at there being no paper towels to use on crusty door handles. Outside he noticed tourists agreeing to take pictures of homeless teens for a fee, but they sought to do it with the teens' cameras so as not to have to give them anything. The teens had no cameras and got no money. Benny pretended to have the shakes for heroin, but it was just a nicotine fit; he wanted to appear cool to the snapshot vagrants. Looking to the ensemble, Benny found himself attracted by wont to Lola; she conjured for him his recent days of the street life, brutal in her balance between truth and reality. Initially, Benny thought it was her obvious attempt to pass as French when she was an Algerian by trade. Later he decided on the belief that it was Lola's more pressing routine of living her life as a transsexual without means for surgical relief that pulled him into her vortex.

Lola's surrounding cast was composed of biological females who sniffed out Benny's desire to disrupt their space, make Lola a man again; they ignored him when he wandered over and asked them for a smoke. Benny waited as Lola asked Gwen, asked Faslyn for a cigarette. No one wanted to share; eventually Lola gave Benny one of her cigarettes and her lit one to ignite it. After lighting, Benny dropped them both on the ground with clumsiness. He thought that he returned the correct one; hers was nearly new, partly crumpled at the filter because of his fingers' manic attack. Lola did not seem to mind and asked Benny if he was related to any famous Negroes. Benny smiled his reply, "*Oui.*"

Lola brought Benny back to her apartment and immediately

fell to her knees. Benny leaned back against the door of Lola's apartment as she fumbled with his belt and zipper, involuntarily tensing when Lola unsheathed his pulsating manhood from his dirty jockeys and drew it to the back of her throat. Benny enjoyed the synchronistic movements of Lola's lips and throat, a push-pull of tension and release that Benny matched breath for breath before flashing to ten-dollar blow jobs given to him in parking lots, back rooms, and alleyways. Driven by a need to separate his recent career from true love, Benny lifted Lola up and demanded that she kiss him. Lola refused, saying she only kissed men that she loved. Benny replied that he only loved those men whom he had kissed. Lola relented and breathed in the last drag from Benny's third cigarette. Benny lifted Lola and carried her upstairs to the bedroom.

Upon entering her bedroom, Benny asked Lola softly, "Will you kiss me?" Lola nodded yes, knowing Benny's every intention. She kissed Benny strongly, pulling his bottom lip into a playful nibble before pushing Benny backward onto her bed. Benny, suddenly fearful, told Lola that he wanted to take a shower. Lola released him, staring at her chipped fingernail polish while Benny ran the hottest waters over his body. When he emerged Lola grabbed him again and pushed him back onto her bed. Benny ran his hand up Lola's green skirt and squeezed between her thighs. He felt envious. In an instant, he had her cock in his mouth. Lola asked, *"Nous baisons?"* and Benny, fluent in the language of trade, blinked yes. Lola pushed off from Benny and began to rub his shoulders, then his lower back, and finally his ass. Benny rolled over as Lola embedded her teeth into his asscheeks, shaking each one like a rabid dog who has caught some pussy; he felt goose bumps rise all over his body as Lola parted the hair that covered his asshole and began to lick, gently as a kitten new to milk from the bowl. Lola wrapped her arms around Benny and felt his stomach quiver as she entered him. She read by his expression in her nightstand mirror that she gave him both the pleasure and the pain that accompanies a first poke in the ass. At first Benny begged her to stop, but Lola kept pushing deeper, knowing that the burning would stop this time or the next. Benny tried to get up but Lola pushed his face into the bed and growled, *"Nous baison,"* before biting the side of his neck and caressing his nipples. Benny, satisfied to have found one strong enough to conquer him, clinched his teeth and began to murmur, "I love you." Then Lola began to press harder into him and Benny knew that the end was near. As he watched his life as a hustler flash before his eyes he whispered a "goodbye, Cherry"—Lola, losing control of her rhythm ejaculated into Benny while exhaling, *"Amour."* After they healed their troubled souls in a way that can only be done by individuals who share a common craft, Benny drifted off to sleep and did not rise from his dreamlike state until the next morning.

Lola had relocated to the kitchen downstairs as Benny sat near her crumpled bed, his clothes upon the floor, the putrid smell of sex sticking to his skin like sweat. He hadn't showered after they'd had sex last night. And she did the usual amount of probing and caressing with various body parts. He did not warn her, having felt it time to end the street politeness equivalent to manners in their transactions. So he let her find his musk and pretend that she enjoyed it. Perhaps she had. What if her fingers smelled of his shit while she cooked their eggs? It was Benny's shit beneath her fingernails after all, so he could risk it along with the chance of salmonella.

Down to the kitchen Benny would have to venture sooner or later. He knew it, but was afraid that today he might have to make a decision that would end his life or hers. He loved Lola. And she beat him. It was fucked up; he allowed her to beat him. Both wished to find a nostalgic way homeward through cyclical infliction or absorption of pain. His shitty eggs might end up in his face or perhaps this time she might even put rat poison in them. Benny found that he didn't care. Let them read about it in his journal, what kind of man he really wished to be. The world would discover his brilliance via some act of martyrdom on the altar of relational neurosis and violence. That might be how he made his name or at least it was a suggestion to be followed, perhaps after some eggs and a few drinks.

Benny had one hour to drain his beer and find Arnaud. The attempt at a rendezvous would occur somewhere in that great area located by word as Bastille. After walking for hours in a bid to stave off signs of impatience, Benny felt good to sit, crunching on stale popcorn, drinking his tepid beer within a shaded locale. He had intentionally avoided the bars that seemed to hold artistic types. Benny wanted no part of their creative franchise. He had not come to Bastille, Rue de la Roquette, in order to forge artistic bonds. He came to drink and think of Arnaud. Across the street stood one of those cafés, populated with artists gazing nonchalantly in his direction. They could do without Benny today—perhaps not tomorrow, but today Benny was a commodity most unnecessary. The French took their smoking so seriously. Benny smoked upon his initial arrival in Paris. He had gone dancing, met Arnaud, and scorched an entire pack of Lucky Strikes in the span of a few hours. Benny never really inhaled, and the bottom of his tongue suffered. Benny had found the women in that club that night most irritating, but he played the part of fisherman in order to catch the bigger fish.

Arnaud, having already spent two months in Paris studying, had secured the talents of two different lovers, Faline and Nyeupe. Faline served as Arnaud's initial taste of French love. She was North African by way of Kush and Arnaud spared no expense in proving to himself and to her that she was his Nubian Princess, his pride and happiness. Faline's black skin was the color of night over the ocean when moonlight is lacking. One may look to heaven or to the sea and observe nothing but the blackness of Faline. Her ability to encase her lover's entire ecology made Arnaud decidedly anxious. She was a Negro in the classic sense, "black as the night is black, black like the depths of...Africa." Arnaud lacked security in attempting to colonize this being—body, soul—with hands unfit for imperial enterprise.

It was when he paraded through the streets of Paris—openly drunk with his guilt—that he met Nyeupe. Nyeupe—white in Swahili—had a way of presenting herself as an unimportant feature grazing the world. She moved through its realm like a simple pair of pearl earrings. Nyeupe was an accessory that did not draw gaudy attention to herself, but her elegant frame and divine posture exuded class, whatever that term could really mean. Arnaud had shared with Benny that Nyeupe walked as if she had a string pulled taut coming from the epicenter of her crown. He felt blissful walking with a woman of such exterior pride and secretly believed that her white name gave her an advantage in the world, a feeling of invincibility.

Benny used beer to rinse his teeth of bits of popcorn and the thoughts of foreign women. His cheap watch told him that fifteen minutes remained before he himself would test Arnaud. Hunger and alcohol were getting the best of him. He had not eaten for the entire day, save Lola's eggs. Consequently, the beer made his eyes glassy. It also permitted the precipitation of a more intrinsic hunger. One that Benny knew he could never fully satisfy with Arnaud. Waving a flag of friendship, Arnaud would not allow such activities.

Benny's clock read ten minutes remaining. All he had left was a two-hundred-franc bill. He wanted to use credit, but the waiter would not allow it. So Benny broke his twenty-six-dollar badge of survival and the waiter turned on him. Benny was not a starving artist just yet, but one of the landed aristocracy, the leisure class who wrote for pleasure. But Benny had not the opportunity to correct such a careless mistake regarding fictive notions of class responsibility. The beer and the time provided a taste for flesh.

Benny did not see it, until he allowed himself to see—what Arnaud gave to the world. Denial. Arnaud denied the world an existence, and within the aftermath of such activities, Benny found himself wishing he were nude and alone with his friend.

When Benny happened upon Arnaud again, another meeting, although it seemed by chance, Arnaud stood wearing a green T-shirt in front of a record store. They decided to wander to a nearby pub and drink beer, with olives and peanuts serving a necessary purpose. They took pictures and laughed and made fun of those Americans who wore their exile so flagrantly. Benny shifted his stack of journal poems and found three that he would give verbal utterance in the presence of Arnaud. Arnaud gave a solemn nod as his sign of acceptance, but Benny knew that Arnaud could only give denial. Having had four beers before splitting a few with his pal, Benny was in the midst of a most dangerous landscape, for the roles of friend and foe become difficult to decipher when placed into a context of an inebriated savanna. Benny spoke his pigeon French, claiming, *"Je suis de la ghetto,"* whenever Arnaud moved to correct his adopted tongue. This sequence of repeated exchange provided Benny with great pleasure and subjected Arnaud to a great irritation. The dance had been set, and Benny knew it'd only be a matter of time before the floodgates seeped, then broke open—washing away what had come to exist as his Parisian reality.

Returning to the park of St. Sulpice, Benny sensed from Arnaud something not of France, but in total, American. Fear. As Arnaud passed a few Lucky Strikes his way Benny pondered, when did Arnaud cease existing as a friend and begin to live as prey? In New York City, one would fear gun blasts, in France, it was merely fireworks celebrating Bastille. But Benny felt as if Arnaud clutched his true feelings like old white women clutched their purses as Benny passed by. Arnaud had read Benny clearly while they drank, so he placed himself beside a femme who sat on the park fountain, making life suddenly unnecessary for them or so it seemed. Then Michel and Stefan passed by, and Arnaud rushed to meet them as if expecting them, but their visit was unforeseen. Stefan had the more erogenous name, but Michel had the eyes and body of one that a man would desire, if he desired men. Michel projected an aesthetic of fulfillment, which perennially attracted those who lacked. Benny knew lack once; the taste remained in his throat, but he was not in need of Michel. Perhaps if Arnaud had not run to them.

Beneath Benny's disinterest lurked great disdain. Benny at once felt arrogant in his dealings with Arnaud. Arnaud had shown his fear, and like a wild dog of the Parisian streets, Benny sensed that recapitulation of emotion. The hunt was unintended, but fear always made hunting absolute. It was the lone way things could be. Arnaud claimed to be free of Benny and it was this element of escape that moved Arnaud to consider new strategies. It was the unresolved agitation that Arnaud exhibited which served as a sign, baiting Benny to do—to say more. Sex ceased to be an issue of sharing and became one of control. If Benny could not fuck Arnaud's body, then surely he would fuck his mind. Simply because that process was available to him. A European couple next to Benny gave him looks. Benny brushed back his hair and flirted with them just to make Arnaud wonder, wonder—about what Benny did not know, all that he knew was that here within the ville of Paris he was in Arnaud's thoughts. And that, at this moment, was the safest place for him to be.

In a bar surrounded by men, Benny sought disconnection

from his world. Shots of rum seemed to accomplish the feat desired. Arnaud had gone out with Faline, a woman for whom Arnaud's detestation floated with the words he spoke to her like flakes of bile. Benny's realization about Arnaud made situations difficult. Would Arnaud's own doubts prevent Benny from having faith in this latest conversion? Arnaud had whispered on the Metro with a faint smile, "I realize that I am not queer." Benny responded only with, "I have never been." The dialogue ended there as Arnaud realized that Benny knew what Arnaud was doing. In a world devoid of form, attempts at the creation of order inevitably fail. And that is what Benny cavalierly pointed out to his friend. That the world Arnaud himself created was in the end inescapable because there were no borders, no definitions.

Benny wondered momentarily if this game would lead to violence. That is usually what happened when a man had laid all his cards down to fold, just to be told by the dealer that the hand continued. Ante up. Most put in this position would find the strength to flip over the table.

But with Arnaud, man of letters, Benny figured that the tool of choice would not be violence, but rather ignorance. Arnaud would place himself into the position of forgetting everything that had occurred in Paris with Benny. Their mild flirtation would cease to exist, exploding the reality in which the two men lived. Benny had felt a prelude sharply on *Bastille la fete*. He had sought out Arnaud for the company of French women and Arnaud had refused. The presence of a question mark personified was not what Arnaud wanted when he was attempting to make love headway with *les femmes*. And Benny, through his sheer existence, made vectored narratives of sex and sexuality most tedious, if not impossible. The inability to resolve this tension only proved to Benny that Arnaud was not as free as he thought he may have been. Arnaud was trapped and Benny was the lynchpin within the schema. So rather than suffocate, Arnaud would just pretend that the situation he was in did not exist. And he would breathe deeply, repeating to himself, *"J'ai beaucoup de space, c'est beaucoup de la temps."*

Benny sat and waited outside Faline's apartment. Arnaud did not come. Benny's joints betrayed him with the coming of damp nightfall, his skin turned to ash in juxtaposition to chilly wind. Benny realized what he never was to Arnaud, a friend. Their interactions would consequently take on more than what friendship would allow. They were marked by overdetermined emotions, transforming every missed appointment, change of schedule into grand dramatics, living theatre. Benny wondered if he were born to act.

The Pain Seeker

Giovanni

The heat from the strong hands smoothed the slick skin back and forth like the skillful kneading of dough by the hands of a master chef. The friction between the hands and the body that gyrated under its guidance made the receiver of this delightful treat moan with the deep sounds of pleasure. Marcus tossed and turned through the frantic desire of the strokes, pulls, flicks, and squeezes of his dick. He didn't care that the oil-based lubricant dripped from his slippery hands and shiny hard dick onto the white sheets of his full-size bed in his mother's house. He didn't care that it would stain the fresh, new linen that Dorothy Johnson had picked out during the Macy's One Day Sale and had proudly displayed on his bed that evening after her long day of shopping. The deep, oily stains spotted the linen like the spots of a Dalmatian, and his butt prints spread over the sheets like the snow angels kids made in the wintertime. His hot grip tightened just a little as the beginning of a nut-busting climax announced itself through the tingling in his ass. The tremors that claimed his body made Marcus vibrate like the powerful massager that he often used to manhandle his ass on more adventurous nights. It was coming, and his hands worked feverishly to get him to the point of no return, to the place in his mind where the sounds of Parliament and the Funkadelics exploded among the firecrackers and roller coasters. His climaxes were always full of noise, excitement, and rides that brought out the most thrills. The hands moved faster and faster and his butt bounced up and down off of the sheets, and saliva dripped from the corners of his mouth, as the climax sped closer and closer to the surface. It felt so damn good, and Marcus couldn't wait for the final explosion, but as the knocks on the door and the sounds of his mother's worried voice came crashing into his hot, sweaty playground, Marcus's climax was muffled by the thick pillows on his bed.

"Pumpkin, are you in there? I need your help with the trash... Marcus, do you hear me?"

Marcus knew his mother well. She wasn't going to go away without acknowledgment from him. So he quickly grabbed his Joe Boxers from the end of the bed, and pulled on his T-shirt while he hopped to the door before she tried to enter. She would complain about the locked door, and make an attempt to search the room for that *stuff,* as she referred to marijuana. She always assumed that if Marcus or his brother, Sam, were closed off in their room that they were sniffing or smoking on that *stuff* and she wasn't having it in her house. She had threatened to kick them out in the streets if she found it. Marcus smiled devilishly to himself at the thought of what she might do if she found out what he was really hiding in his bedroom.

Marcus quietly unlocked the door and opened it just a crack to his mother's cocoa-brown face. The lines of worry that formed on her face didn't dampen the forty-year-old woman's attractiveness. Her premature salt-and-pepper hair lay neatly in the latest coif her hairstylist, Keesay, had given her. The wisp of gray hair that fell into her face only accentuated the sweet, dark brown eyes that peered into Marcus's room.

"Baby, is everything all right?"

"Yeah, Mama. I'm fine. What's up?"

"I need your help with the garbage. Your brother and his *posse* have cleaned out my refrigerator and left the remnants all over the kitchen floor."

Marcus sighed under his breath as he retreated to his bed to pick up his Nike flip-flops to join his mother in the kitchen. His mother knew that he wasn't pleased by the responsibility of cleaning up behind his brother, but she knew she could always count on Marcus to help her make things right. Even though Marcus, a senior at Grady High School, was the youngest, Sam had never given her as much support around the house as Marcus had. Sam was a junior at Morehouse College and was supposed to be the man of the house, but spent more time chasing cheerleaders around the football field and sexing them in the back of his Jeep than he did helping his mother with the bills and chores around the house. Marcus had threatened to go to college outside of Georgia, and his mother feared that he would live up to that threat, but she prayed every night that he wouldn't leave her. She really didn't know what she would do without her quiet, gentle son, who always made good grades in school, never hung out with rough boys, worked a part-time job at Kinko's to help out with the finances at home, and made the best fried turkey and Cajun dressing on Thanksgiving a cook could ever make. He was her perfect little man, and she knew she relied on him too much, but couldn't help herself.

Marcus silently grabbed the two large bags of trash and headed toward the front door, while his mother continued to sweep the floor. Sam and his crew were busy playing the latest Sega game on the living room big screen TV. They were oblivious to his entry into the room—except for the tall, muscle-bound airhead, Derek Woods. Derek's cold black eyes zoomed in on Marcus as soon as he entered the room. His sly grin increased in size as he watched Marcus struggle with the two large bags of trash. Marcus tried not to acknowledge his stare because he knew it would only lead to fifteen minutes of stinging remarks from the asshole...but it didn't matter whether Marcus acknowledged him or not, Derek was waiting for an opportunity to slam the young boy.

"Hey Punk-in, you got that?" Derek screamed over the shouts and laughter of his friends.

All eyes turned on Marcus as the others realized he was walking through the room. He tried to make a mad dash for the door, but the bags felt like tons of bricks instead of the beer cans, pizza boxes, and other trash that the guys and his mother had dumped in the garbage can.

"You hear me talking to you Punk-in! Whatcha doing, trying to wrestle with the trash? Man, what's up with your puny little brotha?"

Sam shrugged and kept on hitting the buttons on the controller. "He's a growing boy. You know we were all like that at one time."

"Hell naw! I wasn't nowhere near his skinny little ass. He's built like a little girl. He should be called Barbie instead of Pumpkin!" Derek continued.

The other two guys, Brent and Steven, burst out with laughter as their chips flew into the air and landed in the crevices of the carpet. The jokes and chips seemed to go unnoticed by Sam. Marcus always wondered why his brother allowed his friends to come over to the house and disrespect his family, but he never got enough courage to ask the question. Sam was either one of two ways when he was around: hungover from a drunken binge, or in the process of getting drunk. Either way, he was not to be messed with. He may not have stung Marcus with nasty little remarks, but his fist had come across

Marcus's face a time or two, and that was enough for Marcus to remember to stay out of his way as much as possible.

Marcus crept out of the house without a word to Derek, and dumped the garbage in the larger trash can. The garbage man would pick up tomorrow, so the sour smells of leftover food would not attract the stray dogs and cats around the neighborhood before it was removed. Slowly he crept back into the house, silently praying that the boys would be back into their game and would leave him to go back to his own private game.

He let out a sigh of relief as he noticed Derek was no longer present in the group, and the others were engrossed in their game. He hurried to the kitchen and checked on his mother before retreating to his room. As he entered the threshold of the bedroom door, a strong hand grabbed him around the neck and pushed him inside the dark room. The thick fingers squeezed his larynx and he felt his throat tightened as he gasped for air.

"Be quiet, Barbie!"

Marcus recognized Derek's voice and tried to remain calm, but felt his body tremble at the thought of what Derek might do to him. The boy always harassed him verbally and had threatened to make a man out of him on several occasions, but he had never actually harmed him physically. Marcus wished that his mother would interrupt him this time, but she was nowhere in sight or earshot. Derek removed his hands from around Marcus's neck and pushed the boy onto the bed. Marcus fell into the thick pillows face-first, with his butt raised in the air. Derek came charging behind him, and grabbed him around the waist.

"I know you're a little punk. You know that, don't you, Punk...in?" Derek teased him with the name his mother often called him. Marcus tried to struggle from Derek's grasp, but the bigger and stronger boy merely tightened his hold. He pulled Marcus's body into his own pelvis repeatedly as he snarled into the boy's ear, "You want to get fucked don't you, Marcus? You're just a little ole faggot aren't you? Closed up here in the dark, jerking off to your dirty little fantasies. Don't you, faggot?"

Marcus fought harder as he resisted the images that Derek was creating in his mind. Try as he might to remain in fear of his attacker, Marcus felt his dick get harder with anticipation of being raped by Derek. He didn't want to admit it, but the roughness of Derek's hands, the thickness of his thighs, and his attacker's hot, wet breath were playing a devilish game with his libido. Derek was right, Marcus did want him to fuck him, and probably always had. Even though he hated the teasing, Marcus couldn't help lusting over the taut, muscular body of the running back, especially his tight ass when he bounced around on the field or on the basketball court outside of their house.

Derek pressed Marcus into the bed and stretched his legs open. He grabbed at the waistband of his boxers, and began pulling them down. He could hear Marcus's muffled pleas from the pillow, but he only laughed at the futile struggle, and became even rougher with the boy's soft behind. He pinched it and smacked it a couple of times before ripping the boxers off of him. "You ready to become a man, Punk?"

The feeling of a hot, painful rod shot within Marcus's ass like the prodding of the largest dildo he had ever taken. The burning sensation of the penetration as Derek's dick stretched his ass shook Marcus's entire body. The thick hands held tight around his waist, and the thighs pounded against his smaller ones as the dick pummeled him into the bed. Tears stung his eyes and dried up on the corners of his face, as the fucking continued at lightning speed. Derek moaned and groaned in his ear, and pulled sharply on his earlobe with his teeth, as he came inside of Marcus's ass like a tidal wave.

"Ooooh shiiiitt!!!"

With his last scream, Derek's heavy body fell onto Marcus's back while his semi-hard penis stayed inside his ass. Marcus waited for Derek to remove himself, but that didn't come as quickly as he thought. Instead the very thing that he would never have imagined happened. Derek rolled over on his side and pulled Marcus with him. His hands moved to Marcus's still erect dick and with the slowness and seduction of an expert rocked Marcus's dick into the land of Parliament and the Funkadelics. As Marcus felt his body tense with the excitement of a climax, he also felt Derek's dick harden again and begin to fuck his ass with a slower, gentler, determination. Derek rocked Marcus into oblivion with his dick and his hands. Without further notice, Marcus's dick shot cum all over the new linen, and his shouts of pleasure were muffled by Derek's other hand. As he lay in the silence of the room and waited for his heartbeat to return to normal, Marcus felt the weight of the bed change, as Derek got up and pulled on his pants. Without giving Marcus another glance, he dropped a card on the bed, and before leaving the room, commanded, "Be there at midnight tomorrow. No excuses, no cancellation. Be there."

Six A.M. Thursday morning. Marcus's alarm clock woke him to the smell of his mother's bacon and eggs, and the noise from the trash collectors outside. His eyes opened to the sunrise that was slowly appearing in his bedroom window and he briefly wondered had he dreamt the rape from last night...but then the pains in his ass reminded him it had been no dream. After Derek left, Marcus had drifted into a deep sleep that was not to be disturbed. Normally he woke up a few times throughout the night to take a leak, and to masturbate, but this night, he slept straight through. As he dragged himself out of bed and into the shower, thoughts of Derek's big dick slamming into his ass, and his rough hands giving him a hand job, made Marcus's dick throb for a repeat. Even though Derek was long gone, the memory was sufficient for a shower jerk off. Marcus replayed the fuck over and over in his head as he stroked his own dick until cum shot all over the shower stall and mingled with the cool jets of the water. He would be late for school, but he didn't care. The masturbation session for the morning was worth the jog he'd have to do to make it before the homeroom bell rang. When he had finished his third hand job, showered, shitted, and shaved, he rushed downstairs to grab his breakfast and lunch before rushing off to school.

During his English Lit class that morning, Marcus daydreamed about Derek's dick. He couldn't believe that he wasn't pissed off at the boy, but every time he tried to be mad, he kept thinking about the feeling of Derek's hands around his dick, and the way Derek's dick fucked him the second time. Even the first time with force was good, he had to admit it. As he turned his notebook to the next page, the card that Derek left fell onto his desk. Marcus had forgotten that he had thrown it into his backpack to look at during lunch. The card was completely black except for the gray lettering that read LION'S DEN – 404-123-1212. Marcus remembered Derek commanding him to be there at midnight, but he didn't know where this place was.

On his way to his part-time job after school, Marcus debated whether or not he would search for the place. Then he remembered Derek's threat, and knew that if he didn't go, the boy would come and get him. At 7:15 P.M., during his break at Kinko's, he called the number and got the directions to the club from a woman that sounded like someone's little old grandmother. When his shift was over at nine, Marcus took the bus home and waited for eleven-thirty to slowly creep its way to the present. He ate a quick dinner, watched some TV, read his homework assignment, and tried desperately not to think too much about what the Lion's Den would be like.

THE LION'S DEN. Marcus took the northbound train to the Lenox Square stop then took the Number 12 bus to Briscoe Avenue. The bus ride was only ten minutes, but it saved him the hike through the busy party district of Atlanta. He hadn't really known what to wear to the place, so he chose his favorite pair of black Sean John jeans and matching shirt, with a pair of black Tim's. His normal school wear or Kinko's uniform usually consisted of khakis, button-downs, and loafers. On the rare chances that he got to sneak into one of the local hip-hop clubs, or if he were really daring, the Warehouse on a gay night, he would dress in the latest B-boy gear like the popular kids at his high school wore. Sam often chided him about looking like a little nerd, and offered to pay for a new wardrobe with his extra money from his financial aid, but Marcus would always decline. His brother and mother had no idea about the secret wardrobe that he kept hidden in the roof of his bedroom closet. He didn't want his mother to worry that he was turning into one of the roughriders at his school or a younger version of Sam, so he kept his love of the latest street wear a secret from her.

Marcus only had to walk a few more blocks before he saw the neon-blue sign reading LION'S DEN from the alleyway on Briscoe and Trinity. His steps slowed down a little as he neared the small brick building at the end of the alley. A tall, big black man that reminded him of Mr. T without the mohawk stood quietly at the entrance, as still as a statue. His eyes were covered with shades and his arms were planted firmly across his chest. Marcus briefly wondered if the man were a lifelike figurine of the '80s actor, like the ones in the wax museums, but as he grew closer, the man reached out his hand. "Card."

Marcus pulled the card nervously from his back pants

pocket and handed it to him. Marcus couldn't imagine that the man could really see anything on the card through his shades in the middle of the dark alley, but the man smiled a gold-toothed grin, and then directed Marcus toward Room 8. When Marcus approached the entrance to the Lion's Den, the heavy, gold doors opened automatically, and the loudest roar he had ever heard greeted him as he stepped into a world like none other.

The dark, smoky club smelled of that *stuff* his mother threatened to discover. Sounds of music intermingled with loud, guttural moans and the cracking of whips, the clinking of glasses and smacking and pumping noises. Marcus wondered briefly where the noises were coming from and soon received his answer as he passed the threshold of the club. Flashes of nude male bodies lined each side of the walkway as he passed down the hall toward Room 8. Mouths wrapped around small and large dicks licked and sucked like they were afraid all the meat and juices were going to melt away before their hungers were quenched. Dark hands feverishly pumped other dicks into a frenzy of cum explosions that flew across the room like popped champagne. Other sweaty bodies pumped and rocked their dicks into eager asses that were hunched on the floor, straddling chairs, hanging from ceiling straps, or hidden behind a wall with only small openings for the dicks to stick into. Marcus noticed that none of the men were surprised by his presence, and many smiled at him and beckoned him to come join them. The heat from the bodies and his own increasing desire soaked his shirt and his Joe Boxers that tightened around his throbbing dick. Hands reached out to him and grabbed his hardened nipples, pinching them and twirling them into an even more painful/pleasurable erection. "Mmmmm, let me suck your dick," one of his attackers pleaded.

Marcus nervously brushed the hands away and proceeded

with a quicker gait toward the rows of rooms at the end of the hallway, but he wasn't fast enough. Other hands grabbed his behind and rubbed him up and down, and others grabbed his dick and rubbed it into a stiff erection. A tongue shot out and lashed the back of his neck with hard passion marks, and another tongue sucked on his right nipple through the shirt, while someone else's fingers twisted and teased the left nipple. Marcus was trapped in the frenzy of the gang bang, and was liking every minute of it. Someone pushed him down to kneel before one of his attackers, and the largest dick he had ever seen pushed its head right into his mouth and pumped against his face. The anonymous body rocked back and forth over Marcus's face, and the smells of the man's spicy cologne intermingled with the scent of sweat from his hairy balls. The dick pumped faster and faster, and hands grabbed the back of Marcus's head and pushed him tighter onto its throbbing manhood. Marcus felt his throat tighten a little and feared that the dick would choke him, but before the feelings overtook him, the man's dick filled his throat with its salty climax.

Marcus sucked and lapped at the juices as if drinking a cool glass of water. He was hot and thirsty in more ways than one. He needed to be cooled off and relieved of this tension, but that was not to happen anytime soon. The hands were stroking him in all of the right places, and his body moved against them with encouragement. Then just as he felt his own climax threatening to explode, a door at the end of the hallway opened. What was uttered by the man standing there was incomprehensible to him through his soaring desire, but whatever he said, the hands fondling him ceased and returned to their previous fuckbuddies.

Marcus looked up from his kneeling position, and saw Derek's tall muscular body standing before him. Derek's large hand reached out with a dark, circular object that he snapped around Marcus's neck. When Derek pulled on the silver chain, Marcus realized that the object was a dog collar. Derek walked him like any good dog handler would toward Room 8. At first the feeling of walking on his knees was uncomfortable, but Marcus soon learned to allow his master to guide him after being choked a couple of times by the collar. He trotted as best he could like a show dog, and waited for his master's cue to stop. When they entered the room, Derek slammed the door loudly behind him, and tied Marcus's leash to a pole.

"My, my, my, Barbie showed up," Derek said, as he clapped his hands in approval of Marcus's presence.

Marcus looked nervously around the room at the various chains, straps, leather accoutrements, paddles, and other objects that he had never seen before. In the candlelight of the room he noticed Derek's clothing for the first time. He was sinisterly dressed in leather pants that were cut out in the back to expose his tight, muscular, hairy ass to Marcus's hungry eyes. A leather belt crisscrossed over his broad hairy chest, and leather boots adorned his size fourteen feet. His bald head was shaved and his bright white-toothed grin promised Marcus more than just a good time. In all of the fantasies that Marcus had dreamt of Derek, he had never thought that this would be the older boy's hidden identity. He had always wondered if there was more to Derek than his snide remarks, but never had he imagined him in a gay boys' bondage club.

"Surprised, aren't you Barbie?" Derek asked as if reading Marcus's mind.

Marcus didn't utter a word, only shook his head in acknowledgment. Although he had never had the painful pleasure of an S/M experience, he had read and seen enough movies about them to know what his role was. He was the passive one that would be dominated, and Derek was the master who would dominate him.

But as Marcus prepared to be even more submissive, Derek switched their roles. Derek walked slowly towards

Marcus, letting the heels of his black boots pound against the hardwood floor with a loud determination. Each step pounded in Marcus's heart, as he felt the beating of his life force pulse within his chest. Derek roughly untied his leash from the pole. He pulled Marcus up to his full five feet nine inches and removed the collar completely from his neck.

"Time to be a man, Barbie."

At first Marcus didn't understand what Derek meant, until the older boy placed the collar around his own neck, and knelt down before Marcus. Without warning, the master had become the slave, and the hands of the former slave were freed to do whatever he willed.

The excitement of this reward made Marcus's heart beat even harder. *What was he to do with such power?* Derek could sense Marcus's lack of comfort with the role.

"You gonna be a punk the rest of your life? Come on Punk-in, there's gotta be more to you than your vibrating dildo! Do you even want to know how to be a man, or are you content cleaning up behind your brother, and reassuring your mother that you won't leave her?"

Derek's taunt had done the trick. Marcus knew what he had to do...what he wanted to do. He was tired of Derek's constant teasing and threats to control him. He would show him just how much of a man he was.

"Come on pu*nkkkkkk!*" Derek choked on his last words, as Marcus's strong hands grabbed the leash and pulled on the collar, closing off Derek's airway.

"Shut the fuck up, pussy!" Marcus commanded.

He tightened his grip on the leash and dragged Derek across the floor to a bench in the center of the room. Two circular clamps lay waiting for Derek's wrists, and Marcus swiftly secured them to his slave. His eyes caught a glimpse of a shiny, silver object that hung on the wall, and Marcus smiled at the thought of using the knife. He pulled it from its sheath, and tugged once on Derek's leather pants to get a good grip, before completely opening them with the sharp edge.

"What the fuck!" Derek shouted.

Marcus pulled on the collar again, choking Derek into silence. "Shut the fuck up, pussy! See your problem, Derek, is that you've been impersonating a man, and all along you're just a big, fat, pussy! A cunt, a bitch, a muff with no balls, and I'm about to show you just how much of a woman you are."

Marcus couldn't believe the sound of his own voice. The nervousness and softness of his former self was replaced with a deep growl. He stuck the knife into the bench where Derek could see it, and without notice, took one of the large paddles from the wall and began pounding Derek's ass with it. At first the other boy kept the pain of the beating to himself. But as Marcus's swings became more and more forceful, the pain began to show in the redness of the boy's skin, the sweat that rolled freely from his forehead, and the tremble in his lower lip.

"Didn't think I had it in me, did ya pussy? I work out too, you know. You'd be amazed at how much of a workout your wrist, triceps, and biceps get jerking off five times a day." Marcus laughed at his own revelation.

Truth be told, he had never gotten more of a workout than tonight, swinging the heavy wood on Derek's tight ass. The redness of his brown skin glistened with each whack. The shininess reminded Marcus of how hard and shiny his dick would get every time he fantasized about the boy. In fact, he could feel his dick rising to that point at that very moment. The head poked at his pants, begging to be unleashed from its jean-clad prison. Marcus never missed a beat with the beating, while his other hand unzipped his jeans, and removed his dick from the Joe Boxers. The thickness of the head pulsated with pre-cum and tempted him to release the fluid.

"Aiight, damn it! You made your point. Stop this shit!" Derek screamed.

Marcus continued the beating and laughed at his slave's pleas. He was enjoying the shades of red, black, and blue marks that covered Derek's ass. It felt good to release all of the anger and pent up frustration he had over the boy's constant ridicule. He was in control now, and the only thing that would please him more would be to have this moment on videotape to show the world that the Big Dick on Campus was nothing more than a Big Pussy.

"Shut the fuck up, Derek. It'll end when I say it's over."

Marcus continued the beating for what seemed like another hour, but was really only a few more minutes. By the time the beating ended, Derek was slumped over on the bench soaked in sweat. Even though his face appeared to be contorted with pain, his long, massive dick seemed to be filled with glee as it stood proudly waiting for its release.

But Marcus had other plans for his slave that would not allow Derek to be released anytime soon. He walked toward the door, and left it open as he entered the hallway full of fuckbuddies. He could hear Derek's pleas for him to come back as he walked through the rows and rows of boys. He was looking for someone in particular, someone that was sure to please him and make Derek go absolutely crazy. He knew that Derek had brought him to the Lion's Den to allow Marcus to control him to some degree, but his ultimate goal was to have a night when the two of them could fuck any way, any how, as long as they wanted to. What he surely had not expected Marcus to do was to invite a third party. Marcus knew that Derek wanted him to himself, but he would not allow the boy to control the events of the night even from the slave's role.

As he was about to turn around and search the row again, he came across the perfect specimen. The tall, muscular burnt-chocolate boy was just entering the den of men, and was checking out each one to make his selection for the night, but Marcus chose him instead. With the confidence of a regular Lion's Den member, Marcus grabbed the man's hand and pulled him toward Room 8. He thought for a moment that the guy would resist, but the glint of laughter in the guy's dark brown eyes told him he was game. He led him into the room where Derek knelt on the bench beckoning his return. Marcus walked the guy to the front of the bench so that Derek had a full view of their guest, and quickly removed the guy's clothing.

"What the fuck are you doing, Marcus!" Derek shouted.

"Shut up pussy! I got a real man to do what obviously you can't do. So keep your mouth shut or I'll beat your ass again and give you something to shout about! Just sit there and watch like a good little pussy while I show you how to really fuck a man."

Derek's eyes grew darker at the insult, and the vein that appeared in his neck threatened to explode from beneath the glistening skin. He motioned to say something else, but Marcus eyed the thick wooden paddle to remind him of his predicament. The new guy stood quietly as he took in the scene between the two, and allowed Marcus to expertly suck his dick to attention. Marcus's thick, wet lips pumped the fleshy meat of the guy's dick, his head moving like a piston. The moans fell instantly from the guy's lips as his hands moved instinctively around Marcus's neck. He pushed Marcus closer to his dick and guided him in a rhythmic suck that took them both to the land of Parliament and the Funkadelics. Derek was forced to watch the entire scene, and he moved his body in writhing motion, longing to be released in the same manner. The pain of Derek's horniness wrapped itself around his stomach, tingled in the depths of his ass, and covered his entire body with sweat. He bit his lip so hard that blood began to trickle down his chin, intermingling with the sweat droplets that fell freely onto the bench.

Marcus and the guy continued to move enjoyably in their rhythmic samba to their own private music. The bumping and grinding against his face filled Marcus with a heat that could only be extinguished by the same dick fucking the shit out of his ass. He wanted this guy's dick all up in his ass, and he couldn't wait any longer to feel the thick, long, black dick pummeling him into an adventure ride.

Marcus pushed the guy back from his face, stood up, and walked toward Derek. His own dick was stiff and ready to be serviced by Derek's waiting lips. With his right hand he led the guy behind him, and with his left hand he pulled Derek's waiting face onto his dick. The guy didn't need any further prodding, grabbing his waist roughly and pushing his dick without grace into Marcus's already slippery, hungry ass. As Derek's large mouth opened and engulfed his dick, Marcus's ass opened as wide as that mouth and engulfed the guy's dick. They continued a dance that was definitely meant for three. The guy beat Marcus's ass with his dick like he was beating a drum, and strummed his erect nipples like the strings of a guitar. Derek sucked and blew on his dick like he was playing a trumpet. Marcus was their instrument and the music that came from his mouth could be heard by all in the Lion's Den. Marcus's climax shot through him like a thunderbolt, like the rush of a roller coaster, like the *stuff* that his mother forbade, like the icing on a cake, like the best damn fuck he had ever had!

"Aiiiiiiiiggggggtttt Dammmmmnnnniiiiittttt!" Marcus screamed.

Marcus's cum filled Derek's mouth with the thirst quencher he had been longing for. Derek licked and sucked, and lapped it up like a man lost on a desert island. The guy climaxed shortly after Marcus, and sprayed his juices all up Marcus's ass.

The only person that remained unsatisfied was Derek. His throbbing dick still poked out in clear frustration. The redness of his erection indicated its readiness to explode. His dark eyes softened and pleaded with Marcus to relieve him. His dark Hershey's Kiss nipples stood erect, longing to be suckled. He was a Pop Tart ready to be had, but Marcus wasn't through punishing his slave. No, it wouldn't end that easily for Derek. He ushered the guy out of the room, and left Derek waiting again for his return. This time he took a little bit longer because he had many more guests to invite into Room 8. When he returned, Marcus had eight boys with him.

"What the fuck are you doing, Marcus!" Derek screamed, completely out of control with frustration.

"Making you the woman you've always been," Marcus responded with laughter.

For the next hour, he forced Derek to give each boy a blow job, while Marcus whacked his ass with the paddle, or fucked his ass roughly with a dildo. He affixed nipple clamps to his taut nipples, and pulled on them sharply when Derek tired or fussed about servicing the other men. Marcus refused to relent, and continued the torture with teasing using some of the same words that Derek had used on him for many years. After the final blow job, Derek was reduced to tears. He begged Marcus for relief, and trembled with the desire that was long overdue to be released. "Plllllleeeease, Marrrrcus!"

"What? What do you want Derek?"

"You...to make...it better," he said looking down at his throbbing dick.

Marcus smiled at him, then knelt down near Derek's ear. "Just say the words and it'll be done."

Derek turned toward Marcus, and frowned at the request. He hadn't a clue what Marcus was referring to. "Whhhaatt words?"

"Say, you're my pussy, and that I've made you a woman tonight," Marcus explained with laughter.

Gone was his bravado and resistance. Derek wanted to be relieved and would have said whatever Marcus wanted to hear. "I'm your pussy, Marcus.... You made me a...woman tonight," he pleaded.

Without further ado, Marcus removed the clamps, and Derek dropped to the floor with exhaustion. Marcus removed the collar from his neck, and then turned him onto his back. Derek winced as his bruised ass touched the coldness of the hardwood floor, but Marcus showed no mercy. He lifted the boy's legs up into the air to rest on his shoulders, and without warning pushed his hardened dick into Derek's ass. Derek screamed with half pain and half pleasure. Marcus grabbed Derek's throbbing dick and stroked it as his own dick stroked Derek's ass. The simultaneous climax of the two came quicker than either expected, but within the darkness of their roller coaster ride, the two heard Parliament and the Funkadelics together as they came crashing to the end.

"Aiiiiiigggggght dammmmmmmnnnitttt!" they screamed in unison.

No one really noticed that things were different around the Johnsons' house except for Marcus and Derek. The guys still came over and hung out in front of the big screen TV eating pizza, playing Sega, and trashing the place. His mother still cleaned up behind them and expected Marcus to help out. Derek even still teased him with his usual banter. But the connection between the two when their eyes would meet during the taunts spoke volumes that no words could ever say...and in the middle of the night, they joined each other among the other pain seekers at the Lion's Den.

Riding the Tiger

Blaine Teamer

I checked my machine when I got home from the support group. I had four messages, three of which were from Shauna.

> **Message #1:** *Lee-Lee, call me as soon as you get in—this is Shauna. I got something to tell you. I can't tell you over the phone. You are not ready for this.*
> **Message #2:** *Girl where are you? Bye!*
> **Message #3:** *Girl, I'm two seconds away from telling you over this machine. Call me as soon as you get in!*
> **Message #4:** *Hello, Lee-Lee. This is Nia. I wanted to invite you to be my date for the Black & White Ball. I hope you would do me the honor.*

Nia Davis was a forty-five-year-old professor of African Studies at the University of Pennsylvania. She was quite a catch, a tall distinguished looking sister with salt-and-pepper hair that she wore in a natural. She would do quite fine. She was also a good choice because she was older than my past pieces and had a white-collar job; she was mature, she seemed settled. It was time I started moving in a new direction. UP!

As I reached to dial the seven digits, the phone rang. It was Shauna. "Girl, I've been calling you all night."

I said, "I just walked in the door. Child, guess who asked me to the B & W. Nia!"

"Girl, that's nice but I got something to tell you—wait, Nia that drives the Lexus and is a professor at Penn?"

"Yes."

"Go on with your bad self."

"What did you want to tell me?"

"Girl, I'm on my way over. I can't tell it to you over the phone. You'd never believe me."

"Okay. Bye."

While I waited, I called Nia and left a message on her voice mail asking her to call me, if she was still interested. I took a shower, heated up some soup and put on some Nina Simone.

Shauna was at the door. She had her uniform on, so I figured she was going to go to work after she left me. She drives an ambulance for Hahnemann Hospital. She rushed in with her backpack. "Girl, sit down." She ran to the kitchen to see what I had and came back empty-handed. "Okay, remember that story you told me about when you and Jerry were dating and you two got into this big argument? He called you a cheap, sleazy no-good whore and a high yella' bitch?"

"I think he just called me a whore, but go on."

"My bad... Remember how you said you were on the train, and he called you that, and you two ended up having sex on the train."

"Yeah...sorta."

"Do you remember what you had on?"

"Vaguely. A red micromini dress with spaghetti straps, matching open toe pumps, and matching panties—French panties—real ones, from France."

"Okay, whatever. I was over at my brother's crib. You know he's moving."

"Yeah, to DC."

"Yeah, so I was helping him pack and such. So I'm throwing out shit, and I come across his porno mags, and he's got *Penthouse* and *Playboy* and *Players.* So I'm looking through *Players,* checking out the chocolate honeys, and I start reading this article. Oh—I heard about your reading child it's the talk of the town. I heard people were about to tear the place down."

"See how shit gets turned and twisted. It was not that serious. Go on with this story. You're reading this article..."

"Yes. Yes. I'm looking through the magazine and something caught my eye. I almost had a heartafuckingtack!"

"OH MY GOD." I remembered those pictures that I let him take of me on my kitchen table. He said that the pictures didn't come out, but I never really believed him. I would beat his ass. I'd slit his throat.

Shauna slowly pulled out a *Players* magazine (as if it was the Ten Commandments) and passed it to me, saying, "Page sixty-four."

Well, I took the magazine. It was old and brittle and several of the pages were stuck together. I flicked through the sisters with their legs spread wide open letting in the sunshine. I thought, *My God, they look cheesy and they had professional photographers.* What was I going to look like? Had I shaved past the knee? I couldn't remember. It was so long ago. I came to page sixty-four and there were no photos there, just some article. I said, "What?"

She said, "Read it."

Child I breathed a sigh of relief that you would not believe.

I read the title out loud. "*The Nonstop Love Train.*" And then I silently read the piece.

I work as a subway train conductor in Philadelphia. I'm a twenty-nine-year-old black male, and I am an amateur body-builder. As a conductor on the graveyard shift, I've seen a lot of freaky shit, but I never imagined in my wildest fantasies that I would have a story that was nasty enough to make it into your magazine.

I was running the nonstop express train from Olney to Patterson, which is about a thirty-minute ride. It was 12:00 A.M. *and I was at Olney. I didn't see anyone at the station, and I was about to pull off when I heard a man yelling for me to wait. He got on with a beautiful young woman. She was about five foot three and had a body like a dancer, and it was poured into a skintight tiger print Lycra minidress. I couldn't figure out what a hot bitch like her was doing with such a pretty boy. I was about to start the train up when I heard them arguing. "You look like whore," he yelled.*

He was pissed that his woman had worn a dress that made her look like a slut. He probably couldn't take the heat that she was getting from real men like me. I started the train up, and set it up for automatic. When I looked back at them through my security window they were making out. I turned around to get a good voyeur's view of their action.

They must have made up because they were kissing long and hard. Her lipstick smeared both of their faces. She ran her fingers through his wavy black hair and untied the knot that held his long ponytail together. He then grabbed her by her long mane of red hair and pulled it off her head to reveal a cleanly shaved head. My fat ten-inch dick threatened to bust my zipper wide open. I've always had a fetish for women with no hair, and this horny bitch was a true fucking fantasy.

I watched as he pulled her two firm tits out of her red

dress, forcing her red bra to push her ripe melons up in the air. He then mashed her tits together and manipulated her already rock hard nipples. He then took turns biting one nipple, then the other. I could tell this was driving her crazy as she pulled his head deeper into her tits. She fed him her juicy fruit and he ate them like he'd never had a piece of food in his entire life. He lathered her breasts with his hot saliva making her juicy mounds of flesh glimmer in the light of the subway train. The train rocked their bodies together even harder.

I watched as he unhooked a strand of pearls from her neck. He wrapped the strand around his fist. Her eyes grew big as he began to rub her hot pussy with the pearls. I then watched as he began to stuff the strand of pearls into her hungry snatch. Her eyes rolled into her head, and she began squirming like she was about to lose her mind. She opened her eyes and looked like a wild tiger, as he pulled the pearls out of her wet cunt. I looked down at my rock hard dick and saw the precum seeping through my uniform, dripping down into my belly button. I grabbed my balls and tried to relieve some of the pressure.

When I looked up he was standing up holding on to the handrail. She unbuttoned his jeans and pulled out his dick. She let the semihard piece of meat hang from his jeans. She pulled out a tube of lipstick from her purse and as she coated her lips they turned a hot pink, making them look like pussy. The more she painted her lips the harder his dick got. He lunged his hips forward, straining to stuff her hot pink lips with his dick. As she opened her lips, I began tugging the fat head of my cock with one hand and stopping the train with the other. Right before her lips were about to wet his throbbing dick the automatic doors flew open and she ran to the doorway, jumped off, and said, "Tee-Tee is a whore that's just got off."

She pulled up the top of her dress and ran up the steps. She stayed on that incredible train ride just long enough to get off and then she got off. That was a smart bitch. The train station was empty and the man stood with his dick out in the empty train station. When he realized where he was he hurriedly pulled his jeans back up and stuffed his dick back into them.

I couldn't believe that the hot wench had cheated us both out of satisfaction. My dick was aching, one wrong move and I would have dumped a hot load of jism up to my chest. I needed to get off though. The man sat back down and looked half embarrassed and half angry, his long hair cascading over his shoulders. I prepared to head back to Olney. I shut the doors. He seemed surprised that the train was turning around so quick, but the biggest surprise was about to come and so was he. *(Continued on page 105.)*

"I'm going to sue this...this...magazine, Shauna! Clearly this is me!"

"Clearly, girl."

"I am mortified. I can't believe this."

"I couldn't believe it either girl, it's a dirty shame, but when you have sex in a public..."

"Can you believe they spelled my name wrong?"

"Is that the only thing you have a problem with? Finish reading the article."

I was still fuming that they misspelled my name. "Who the hell is 'Tee-Tee'?"

(Continued from page 65.)

I put the train on automatic. When I stepped out of the compartment he nearly jumped out of his skin. I walked up to him and my fat dick was right in his view. I had readjusted it so it ran down my khakis making them stick out like a pup tent. I told him that I had the whole scene with the prostitute on videotape, and that he was under arrest for lewd and las-

civious behavior. I told him that the police would be waiting for him at the end of the line. He knew he was busted but he had no idea how much he was going to be. I pulled the punk up and slammed a pair of handcuffs on him, pinning his hands behind his back. I had them in my gym bag to use on one of my sexy girlfriends who is an aerobics instructor at my gym. She loves for me to tie her up and then nail her hot pussy to the mattress.

He begged me not to turn him in, but I paid him no attention. I pulled him toward my compartment and pushed him up against the wall. I then proceeded to frisk him. Starting at his calves, I roughly worked my way up to his tight little ass and around to his crotch. I squeezed his bulge and groped for his dick, then his balls. He was starting to sweat, and I loved it. I then pulled his shirt out of his pants and put my hands up his shirt. As I roughhoused him I constantly pulled his butt toward my rock hard dick. He moaned as I mashed his nipples and squeezed his pecs. I hadn't fucked a bitch like this since I was in prison, and I didn't want to admit it, but it was clear by my dick's reaction that I had missed it. I loved the power: I had no authority to arrest this man, but he didn't know it.

I then pushed him into the compartment and slowed the speed of the train. It was going to be a long, slow ride. I made him sit on my stool in the cramped compartment. My raging hard-on was once again nearly in his mouth. He was scared, but he knew what I was up to and what he had to do to get out of the situation. I told him to unbuckle my belt and pull my zipper down. He did what I told him to do, and when he tried to pull out my billy club from my pants I scolded him. "What are you some kind of faggot? Did I say that you could touch my dick, bitch!?" Hot in my hand, I pulled it out myself, and began slapping his face with ten inches of fat licorice-colored manmeat. He opened up his mouth, trying to get a taste of it. That's when I grabbed him by his long silky hair and stuffed my fat sausage down his throat. His mouth was boiling hot like a juicy cunt. I could hear him choking on it, and I saw the saliva dripping down his stretched pink lips. I rose up on top of him and started a slow hump into his eager hot mouth. I felt his hands grabbing my sweaty asscheeks as he pulled me deeper into his mouth. The air of the compartment was filled with the smell of my pungent man-funk that emanates from my crotch, and it made me grind into his mouth even deeper. I knew he couldn't breathe out of his mouth that was filled to the brim with my brick-hard dick, and I could feel him inhaling and exhaling into my wiry pubic hair, so I knew he was getting a good fucking whiff.

As I was pounding my hips into his mouth, I thought about my girlfriend. I thought about how gentle I had to be when I had fucked her. I knew I didn't have to be this way with another man. I was ready to get busy. I pulled out and spun him around. I unbuckled his pants and dropped them to the floor. He had on a pair of long johns and I ripped them open where his sweaty buttcrack waited. I first wet my middle finger and then pressed it against his sphincter. It was tight and puckered like a pecan. It was so tight I thought it was going to break my finger off at the knuckle. He whimpered like a puppy, and I worked it loose like the big dog I was. He was about five-six and I'm six-three, so I had to kneel down to place my dick up against his pulsating asshole. I took my leather glove off and stuffed it into his mouth and covered his mouth with my hand. I took my free hand and grabbed his dick. Then I began to force the fat, meaty head of my dick into his butt. His back arched and he rose up on the balls of his feet. I had about five inches of my dick in his butt, and I waited for him to relax his ass muscles on my dick. When he relaxed, I stood straight up, impaling his ass with the rest of my monster dick. I could hear him scream and moan and I felt the sweat dripping from his face. He was there hang-

ing on my dick with his feet dangling off the floor. When his ass began to relax again, I pulled my dick out and rammed it back in. Eventually his screams turned into moans. I fucked him so hard I thought my dick was going to come out of his throat. The closer we got to the station the harder I pounded his greasy wet ass. I pulled the glove out of his mouth only to hear his screams of "More, feed my hungry hole, more!"

I gave him exactly what he wanted. Finally, I pulled out and spun him around, and he fell to his knees and stuck out his tongue to reach for my dirty greasy dick. When his tongue made contact, I exploded a gallon of piping hot creamy cum all over his pretty boy face, just like I used to do to the new boys in prison. Big loads of cum dripped down his face like creamy gravy. I pulled my pants up and brought the train into the station. I told the pretty boy he was free to go and not to pull any more shit like this on my train. I opened the doors and laughed as he limped off.

After I read this I felt like a boulder had been dropped on my head. I was mortified. I felt so...violated. *More, feed my hungry hole, more?* How *could* he? That was my line! Jerry stole that from *me!*

from *Rude Boys*

Jay Russell

Meanwhile, the music pounded and the sex got hotter and wilder. Don slipped behind Malcolm, not wanting a confrontation until he was ready for it, and disappeared into one of the partitioned-off parts of the room. As it happened, he found himself in the one where a line of thick-cocked guys were linked up, stroking their hard-ons casually, all waiting to fuck the ragga star up the ass. The handsome and rough-looking star, who had short aerial dreads, had been bent forward over a pommel horse, and then his wrists and ankles had been tied to metal loops on the feet of the horse. His muscular butt was up and in position and as each man, one after the other, plugged the ragga star's well-used asshole with a thick hard prick, he growled, "Oh, yeah, *fuck* my battyhole, man! Fuck it! Plug me like a bitch!" Turned-on by the singer's dedication to anal ecstasy—there was no way he could touch his own long, stiff, and dripping cock; all his pleasure was being taken anally—Don joined the line of determined butt-fuckers.

When Don got to the head of the line—Stixie having taken

six stiff dicks up his juicy battyhole while Don was waiting—he wanted to give the randy Jamaican something more. Reaching between the brown-skinned guy's spread thighs, Don gripped his cock and roughly twisted it round and back between his legs. The ragga star moaned and inhaled sharply at the rough attention suddenly being paid to his pulsing tool.

"What you doing, man?" he called out hoarsely, trying to look round at Don from where he was tied, facedown, over the pommel horse.

"I'm gonna stick your own cock up your ass and stick mine in alongside it," Don informed him brutally. "Then I'm gonna fuck you and you're going to be fucking yourself at the same time, man. Maybe you're even going to shoot your load up your own asshole. That get you off, man?"

"Shit, bredren," the star said breathlessly. "Me couldn't stop you now, could I? Me strapped down, man. Me can't stop you a go do anything you want to. If you a want force my own dick up me battyhole then me must take it and like it."

"Yeah, man," Don said, getting the measure of how the ragga star wanted to be treated. "And if I just wanna fuck you up the ass so rough and hard your bunghole bursts, you just have to take it like a bitch, yeah."

"Yeah," Stixie said. "So what you waiting for, man? Make me your bitch! Oh, Jesus—" he gasped sharply as Don brutally twisted his stiffly curving cock back and yanked it up hard between his beefy buttocks, before pushing its slick head into the ragga star's slack, slippery asshole. The singer's balls hung down heavily either side of his inverted shaft and he groaned as Don kept firm hold of his twisted dick and roughly and rapidly rammed its head and the first inch or two in and out of Stixie's already well-fucked battyhole.

"Oh, yeah!" he shouted out as Don started to push his own thick hard-on into the ragga man's upturned asshole alongside his own bent-round cock. The two cocks filled the star's asshole, stretching it, and Don's long, thick erection held the ragga man's twisted one in place up his own ass. As Don began to pump his dick in and out of the ragga star's anal sphincter, the singer groaned and gasped and tossed his head, his short dreads flicking back as he did so, ecstatic at receiving the ultimate pleasure from Don. A long, hard cock poling his ass and filling it with deep, muscular strokes and, at the same time, the extra stretching he was getting from his own dick being up there too, and the slippery, juicy excitement he was getting from the feeling of Don's rigid manhood sliding slickly back and forth along his own swollen cock, the precome from the two men's dicks providing the lubricant for a smooth wet ride.

Don fucked Stixie until he came up the muscular black man's upturned ass with violent thrusts of his hips; the ragga star gasped high and shrill as he was butt-fucked poundingly hard with two cocks at the same time. When Don pulled out, he carefully held the star's dick in place up his own asshole. Turning to the next guy in the line, Joe, Don said, "Keep this cock up his ass when you fuck him or he's too slack to satisfy you. He won't be complaining. You won't need lube; the load I shot up there'll keep his passage slick."

Then, his dick at half-mast, Don slipped out of the partitioned-off area and went in search of a beer. *Maybe I'll get myself rimmed,* he thought idly; he stepped over Kam, who was lying spread-eagled and facedown on a rug, having a shiny black dildo slithered rapidly in and out of his dilated asshole by a squatting Asian boy. *I could do with an eager tongue up my butt and a pair of hot lips on my asshole.* Glancing back, Don noticed that the brown-skinned boy was sitting his own shapely butt down on another dildo, a rubber cone that was a near-impossible seven inches across at the base. Don stroked his semierect dick idly, and watched for a while as the young man lowered his narrow hips further and further down onto the black rubber cone, dilating his elastic anal ring wider and wider until, finally, his buttocks were brushing the rug and his asshole had been stretched open to such a width, Don was surprised that his pelvic bone hadn't cracked. As he opened himself up, the handsome Asian youth made sure he kept the thick rubber dildo moving rapidly in and out of Kam's slack asshole. Kam wriggled his hips, grinding his slickened cock-head excitedly into the rug beneath him.

Up on stage, Prince Fela was casually fisting Marlon the bartender, the pretty black youth bent over his lap as Fela sat on his ornately carved stool. Marlon lay there limply, with his legs open and his ass up, enjoying the back-and-forth movement of Fela's impeccably manicured hand inside his anal passage. Camara stood alongside Fela, watching the spectacle engrossedly; the butt plug was still up his ass, and the steel cock ring round his hard-on and heavy ball-sac. Catching sight of Camara's swollen, bobbing cock-head out of the corner of his eye, Fela turned his head and started to suck on Camara's throbbing dick. As Fela moved his mouth back and forth on the now softly moaning Camara's rigid erection, the African Prince also moved his hand inside Marlon's asshole in time with it.

While all this was going on, Bertil clambered up onto the stage to join them, and slid round in front of Marlon on all fours, then pushed his muscular brown ass up into Marlon's face for the young man to rim and eat out. Fela's fist was still thrusting back and forth in his asshole; Marlon struggled to focus enough to get his soft tongue between Bertil's buttocks and push it past the black soldier's sphincter and into his rectum. Bertil opened with the easiness of a guy who's just taken it up the ass—which he had, from two well-hung guys, in quick succession—and Marlon could taste the hot fresh spunk in the soldier's open asshole.

Meanwhile, Bobbi had dropped his shorts and was eagerly taking on all comers. Oba had recognized him from the taxi ride earlier that evening, and had demanded a fuck, and Bobbi had been delighted to oblige him. Oba lay back on the floor and kept his foot-long pole held upright with both hands. Bobbi squatted down on it and, after an initial moan of how Oba's massive dick was just too big for him, had given Oba a thrill by sitting right the way down on it all at once, sucking all twelve stiff inches straight up into his back passage with only a soft gasp as he pushed his buttocks firmly into Oba's crotch, eager to make sure he had got every last inch of Oba's monster cock up inside his ass. Bobbi bounced his asshole up and down on Oba's lovemuscle, sliding his anal ring up and down its shaft, and finally—now he was here at Fela's party—free to work a hand on his own cock as he rode Oba's rigid muscle like a pro.

At the same time as he was taking it so enthusiastically up the ass, Bobbi licked his pouty lips and gestured for any hard-on that bobbed past him to come over for a complimentary blow job. While he rammed his asshole up and down on Oba's throbbing pole, Bobbi quickly sucked off the young white punk with the green mohawk and the Asian muscleman with the gold Prince Albert, around which pre-come flooded as he pushed it into Bobbi's willing mouth. Bobbi gripped the men's muscular buttocks to brace himself so that while he eagerly gave head he could slam his juicy butthole up and down on Oba's massive cock as hard as possible; the African man groaned beneath him and stretched his arms out above his head as Bobbi's anal love-muscle gripped his cock-shaft and slid rapidly and firmly up and down its rigid length. Bobbi pumped both his holes hard, moving like a pro, eager to taste hot spunk being shot into his mouth, and feeling that nothing would satisfy him except a flood of hot jism up his well-fucked ass.

By this time, Malcolm had the tousle-headed Pierre bent over the bar, had pulled his hot pants down to his ankles, and was fucking him hard while he watched Bobbi squatting on Oba's outsize weapon. As Malcolm fucked Pierre's accommodating asshole, the lean black boxer with the exceptionally-ridged stomach and the elaborate patterns shaven into his scalp, now naked except for his boxer-boots, came over to him. To Malcolm's surprise, the boxer sprang up onto the bar and stood up on it, straddling Pierre. The boxer's rigid dick bobbed temptingly in front of Malcolm's mouth. While he continued fucking the horny barboy bent over in front of him, Malcolm kissed the pulsing brown head of the boxer's smooth dick. The glistening pre-come tasted good on Malcolm's soft lips. He slid his mouth further down the boxer's shaft; the boxer moaned in pleasure and let his head fall back as Malcolm began to suck him off.

"Man, you know how to suck a cock," the boxer said throatily, as Malcolm started to move his mouth hungrily backward and forward on the bobbing hard-on, swallowing its sweet length to the back of his throat and pressing his lips firmly against the cropped stubble at the base of the boxer's shaft. His balls hung smooth and heavy against Malcolm's chin as Malcolm swallowed the boxer's cock-head right down his throat, gagging excitedly as he did so; he was gratified to force a groan out of the young black man standing above him, looking so hard and so fine and sweaty and wild, while still sliding his dick rapidly in and out of the asshole of the white boy bent over before him.

Behind Malcolm, and as yet unseen by him, Don had sprawled back on a pile of cushions, getting his ass up in the air. He moved a gold-ringed fist on his long dick as a succession of guys came over to rim him, licking and tonguing his immaculately hairless chocolate star. The cute would-be tough skinhead, who had been fucked by the afroed guy earlier, had licked Don's ass with hungry thoroughness, as had the moustachioed black muscleman who liked having dildos rammed up his ass. But the best rimmer was Camara, who had come down off stage after shooting his load into Prince Fela's greedy mouth. His long, muscular tongue opened up Don's wet hole more than Don ever thought possible; his compulsive top-man assertiveness normally prevented him from getting his ass up in the air, in any circumstances, even to be rimmed.

Don's star was so wet and slippery with saliva and anal juice that he wasn't aware of Camara slipping the head of the enema tube into his asshole until the strong red wine began to flow into his rectum. Like Malcolm, Don had been powerless to resist it, the attentive rimming relaxing him and making him open to possibilities. The alcohol soaked straight through the lining of his ass and intoxicated him; the exciting stretching of his rectum as a bottle and a half of strong red wine was pumped into his upturned asshole was irresistible. Don shivered and shuddered and gasped as the wine poured in; he threw his quivering legs wide open.

"Jesus, man—"

Camara stopped his mouth with a full, passionate kiss. He pulled the tube out of Don's puckered asshole, put down the enema bulb and, still tonguing Don's now wide-open mouth, Camara reached between Don's legs and folded his long cool fingers around Don's thick, throbbing cock and began to move his fist slowly up and down on Don's hot, rigid pole.

"Oh, Jesus, that's good, man," Don moaned. "Oh, man, keep that hand moving on my hot hard lovemuscle. Oh, yeah..."

On stage Prince Fela, gleaming like a muscular ebony god, was fucking the muscular black punk with the low mohawk while Kam knelt behind Fela in tight golden briefs, his skin glowing, his shining black hair tumbled over his face, and buried his hand up to the wrist between Fela's dark smooth buttocks, his fist well up the Prince's accommodating asshole. Kam rammed his closed hand backward and forward in Fela vigorously as Fela slammed his cock in and out of the juicy asshole of the horny black punk who was sticking his ass back and out for Fela to fuck it hard. And Bertil was kneeling on one side of the stage, waiting for the Prince to shoot his load up the black punk's juicy bunghole, so that Bertil would have another asshole to eat come from. As he knelt there, waiting hungrily, combat trousers around his ankles, Bertil allowed the blond-dreadlocked black DJ to fondle his ass possessively, and eventually stick two fingers up it and work them in Bertil's butthole vigorously, in between changing records.

Meanwhile, the boxer's chest began to tighten as he pumped his saliva-slickened prick in and out of Malcolm's eager mouth, while Malcolm continued to fuck Pierre up the ass.

"Oh, man, I'm gonna come," the boxer called out throatily, gripping Malcolm's head with steely fingers as he held Malcolm's mouth in place on his throbbing cock, making sure that Malcolm would swallow his load when he climaxed. "I'm gonna come, I'm gonna come, oh—" Jerking his hips upward, the boxer pushed his dick to the back of Malcolm's throat and ejaculated violently; the hot jism filled Malcolm's mouth and spilt down his throat. Malcolm swallowed the boxer's come, keeping his hips pumping against Pierre's upturned and now bright-pink ass as he did so.

Now that Oba had come up his ass, Bobbi had lured Bertil down from off the stage to felch him, and was squatting over the black squaddie's face, pressing against Bertil's lips, letting Bertil eat him out; he enjoyed the sensation of Bertil's eager tongue in his well-fucked asshole.

"Eat me out, man," Bobbi instructed Bertil throatily as he sat down more fully on the soldier's flushed face. "Eat the good African spunk that twelve-inch cock shot up my open butthole."

After Camara had given him the red wine enema, Don had become so hot and turned-on and dizzy he thought that there was nothing he wouldn't try, but in the meantime he had quickly had to go and find a toilet. Coming out of the cubicle, after emptying out, he had found himself sucking face with the bleach-blond, dreadlocked white surfer-guy, leaning against the sink to steady himself. Now Don was fucking the passive surfer-guy in the middle of the main room on a vast Persian rug, the surfer was spread-eagled facedown on the floor. Don held the horny blond down and poled his juicy, stretched pink asshole; the surfer grunted excitedly into the pillows his goateed face was half-buried in, with each thrust of Don's cock up his eagerly-offered backside. The blond man's willingness to be fucked turned Don on heavily, and yet—most unexpectedly—Don found himself feeling that his own asshole needed filling, that he needed to be satisfied as he was satisfying the dreadlocked white guy.

Don reached back and began to finger-fuck his own asshole with the index finger of one hand as he fucked the surfer beneath him. Malcolm, still thoroughly poling Pierre, had first noticed Don's presence when Don came out of the toilet with his hand on the ass of the blond-dreadlocked guy. By this time, Malcolm had guessed that Bobbi had managed to trick Don into coming to Prince Fela's party, too, to get him and Don to sort out their differences; Malcolm was happy, because he wanted to make it up with Don. And now here was Don, Mister Top Man, fingering his own asshole like he wanted something good and hot and stiff up it. It was just too tempting, Malcolm couldn't resist...

Malcolm slid his dick out of Pierre's asshole. Pierre gasped loudly, in mingled relief and disappointment that Malcolm wasn't going to give Pierre his load. Malcolm slapped Pierre on the ass, to signify the fucking was over, and turned away; his thick cock bobbed and glistened above his heavy ball-sac. Then he went over to Don and touched him on the shoulder.

"Peace, man," Malcolm said as Don looked round at him, his narrow hips grinding against the blond surfer's upturned butt as he swiveled his cock around inside the slack rectum, his forefinger stuck up his own ass now to the knuckle.

"Peace and love, man," Don replied hoarsely. Malcolm knelt, bent forward and kissed him on the cheek. Don squeezed his eyes shut. "Fuck me, man," Don whispered unexpectedly. "Go up in me."

"What, man?" Malcolm said, surprised, but immediately intensely turned-on at the idea of fucking Don's unploughed top-man bunghole.

"Please, man," Don begged him. "Do me. Do me good. Fuck me wicked. I need it, man. And only you can do it. Only you can be my man. I couldn't give it up for no one else, man. So please fuck me, yeah?"

"Get your cock out of this bitch and I will," Malcolm said breathlessly, indicating the surfer with a nod of his head. "I want all the concentration going on in your ass."

"Yes, man," Don said, pulling his dick out of the handsome surfer's asshole. "Sorry, guy," he mumbled to the dreadlocked blond as he struggled to his feet. "I just got to go and get fucked myself, yeah."

The white guy shrugged. "Whatever, man," he said, leaning over and picking up a shiny black dildo, then reaching back and starting to work its thick rubber head in his slack hole, pleasuring himself thoroughly with the sex toy until the next top man wanted to give him a real dick up there, keeping himself loose and ready for action.

Don and Malcolm slowly got to their feet. Malcolm gripped Don's hand and led him like a virgin bride to one of the partitioned-off parts of the room, his dick harder and heavier than it had ever been at the prospect of fucking Don's shaven hole.

As they disappeared behind an embroidered screen, Kam lay sprawled on his back with his legs up in the air and held open by the Asian bodybuilder with the pierced tit and the gold Prince Albert. He was enthusiastically pumping his lean hips against Kam's upturned butt, sliding his pierced erection in and out of Kam s exceptionally slack and well-fucked asshole. Kam grunted with excitement as the Asian guy rammed his throbbing cock deep into Kam's stretched rectum, his breathing impaired by the fact that another man—a good-looking white bodybuilder with slicked-back dark blond hair—was now straddling the pretty Japanese youth's face and fucking his throat with his dick, making Kam feel totally and utterly used. He lay back, surrendering deliriously to the hard fucking he was receiving in both orifices. He suddenly realized that the feeling of fullness and surrender as both hard cocks pushed into his body, down his throat, and up his asshole, was what he had always needed. Kam could never be satisfied by a single man, he could never have been happy with Malcolm or anyone else. He needed a cock in his mouth and one in his ass at the same time, to really shoot a truly satisfactory load, to really be satisfied. Liberated by this awareness, he reached back and pulled his asscheeks open as wide as be could, to ensure that the Asian man's gold-pierced cock would be slammed up him as far as humanly possible, and tilted his head back as far as he could, so that the blond bodybuilder could get his cock-head in as deeply as possible.

Meanwhile Bobbi's attention had been caught by a handsome, mixed-race guy with a tight physique and boyish features; his circumcised cock stood out from his crotch like a projectile. It was must-suck dick for Bobbi. He went over to the guy, who looked to be in his early twenties, and was about to sink to his knees in front of him, when the clean-cut young man said, "It's Bobbi, ain't it?"

"Yeah," Bobbi said, looking at the handsome black guy intently; he was puzzled, sensing some familiarity but not quite making the connection. "I never forget a cock," Bobbi continued. "If I'd sucked you off, I know I'd remember your smooth chocolate pole. And why wouldn't I have got my lips round such a tasty looking weapon, man? It looks like a perfect fit for my mouth and throat." Bobbi stared at the good-looking black man's flawless face and wrinkled his brow.

"I'm Ashton," the black guy said.

"Oh, my God!" Bobbi squealed, remembering his adolescent crush on the college's top sprinter, remembering licking out the used condoms that Ashton regularly presented to him to give him a taste of his load. He remembered the time he had licked one out in front of Ashton, trying to drop to his knees and nuzzle Ashton's bulging crotch, get Ashton's beautiful cock out of his pants and give him the thorough oral pleasuring that only one man can give another. Bobbi's stiff dick bucked and he almost came just from the memory—and from being confronted with Ashton's beautiful big dick so unexpectedly, right now, long and thick and stiff and inviting.

"All these years, I've wished I'd asked you to suck me off, back then," Ashton said, nervous and excited, his dick rigid and throbbing, pre-come beading his slit. "I've fantasized about your pretty lips on my cock, your eager mouth moving up and down on my rock-hard shaft. And now here you are, man, like a dream, like a fantasy. Would you still like to suck me off, man? 'Cause I sure could use a killer blow job."

Wordlessly, Bobbi sank to his knees in front of Ashton's beautiful hard-on and kissed its head. The taste of Ashton's pre-come sent shivers of pleasure running through Bobbi's chest and his own heavy erection twitched and bobbed painfully, excitedly, in response. Bobbi slid his lips firmly over the smooth hard-on he had fantasized having in his mouth for the last few years. As it filled his mouth, Bobbi became so excited that he realized he was about to come without touching his cock, just from the total, utter turn-on of having Ashton's cock finally where it belonged, filling his mouth and sliding down his throat. Bobbi's pulsing dick bucked between his legs and his hot load exploded in thick, violent spurts, spattering onto Ashton's feet and ankles and the rug Bobbi was kneeling on. But Bobbi gripped Ashton's buttocks in both hands and kept right on sucking. This was the load he'd waited years to taste.

Behind one of the many folding screens in the large rug and cushion-strewn living room, Don and Malcolm were kissing passionately; Don's well-defined lips were hot and soft and yielding, electrically charged against Malcolm's larger café-au-lait ones. Malcolm ran his hands over the shorter, aubergine-dark-skinned man before him, while Don explored Malcolm's light brown body gently, running his hands over the fanlike spread of Malcolm's back as they ground their stiff dicks together, their heavy ball-sacs fusing softly beneath their throbbing erections. Don's hands ran down to Malcolm's newly depilated buttocks; a current crackled up through the palms of his hands at feeling such extreme and utter smoothness.

"Man, you shaved your ass," Don whispered breathlessly, choking on his words. "And your legs," he added, working his hands down Malcolm's curving thighs. "Man, your skin's just so fucking—smooth, man. So beautiful."

"I did it for you," Malcolm replied, his light hazel-green eyes on Don's dark-brown ones. "Because when you're like that, you look so cool, all shaven and waxed smooth. So hot. And I wanted a bit of that, like on me, 'cause I never thought I'd ever be able to get any of the real thing. Any of your real thing."

Now Malcolm breathlessly explored Don's totally smooth ass, moaning softly as they ground their crotches together. "I want to give you the real thing, Malcolm, man," Don groaned, before kissing Malcolm hotly. Malcolm slid his tongue into Don's receptive mouth, exploring it, feeling Don's heart hammering through his pumped chest as he did so. Don and Malcolm's built-up chests pushed together, tingling mocha nipples brushing against electrically charged mid-brown ones; the thrill of excitement from their contact almost tipped over into pain, it was so extreme. Both felt as if their skins had suddenly come totally alive, as if they had stepped from a sauna into the snow and every nerve in every square inch of their skin were crackling with static. Passion was pulling their breath away. Don reached for Malcolm's hand, brought it to his lips and kissed it, then sucked on Malcolm's fingers.

"I need you inside me, man," Don said hoarsely to Malcolm. "I need you to make me feel complete. Shit, man, it looks like that's what I always needed. Maybe that's why I did Kam. To make you jealous. To make you see the sex in me and push him out. 'Cause I wanted you, man. Only you."

Malcolm lifted Don's gold-ringed hands to his lips, kissed Don's gold-covered knuckles reverently; he was so moved he was unable to reply. All Malcolm knew was that he had to plug this beautiful black brother, had to give him what he needed. And more than that, Malcolm wanted to be inside Don: not to punish him by topping him, but to give him the utter ecstasy and relief that he was begging for, that he could only accept from Malcolm.

"C'mon, man," Malcolm said gently after hugging Don for a long minute, leading Don to a low couch spread with a soft zebra-patterned rug at the back of the partitioned-off area. As if by some psychic awareness, the other revelers sensed that Don and Malcolm didn't want an audience, and did no more than peep inside the shadowy space before passing on in search of more ready exhibitionists.

Don lay back on the couch and sprawled out on his back, arching to display his magnificent physique. Malcolm slid on top of him and they kissed hotly on the mouth, sucking on each other's tongues, probing each other for what felt like hours as they writhed their bodies sensually together: bodies that felt molten, that felt as if they were fusing, muscle into muscle, hot throbbing cock into hot throbbing cock, vein and sinew meshing together in pulsing heat. Eventually Don looked up at Malcolm with intense and needing eyes.

"Make love to me, man," he begged hoarsely. "I ain't never taken a cock before. But I want to take yours. I want it bad, man. But don't be rough with me, yeah? 'Cause I never done this before."

Don's eyes were frightened. Malcolm, moved, nodded. "I'll be gentle, man. I'd never do anything to hurt you. I just wanna make you feel good. 'Cause you're a gentleman, Don. And a beautiful man."

And Don opened his firm, muscular legs for Malcolm, spreading them wide and raising them to offer up his chocolate star to the handsome black man standing before him with bright hazel-green eyes, full lips, and tightly coiled plaits. Don's cock arched stiffly above his totally-shaven crotch and pressed its shining head against his belly, dripping and throbbing. His tingling balls hung down heavily above his gleaming asshole. Malcolm's rigid pole extended heavily from his trimmed crotch towards Don's waiting hole, bobbing and pulsing as he looked down on Don opening himself beneath him, and his heart hammered in his chest.

Don yielding to him so unexpectedly turned Malcolm on more than anything he could have ever imagined, and he almost came, just looking down at him lying there and spreading himself open so eagerly. Malcolm took hold of Don's ankles lightly and opened Don's thighs, until Don could grip his own ankles and hold his legs totally spread and get his ass up and available. Then Malcolm reached for one of the nearby bowls of lube and smeared the thick length of his dick until it was slick and shiny and, pulling his own foreskin back, positioned his smooth cock-head against Don's unfucked sphincter. Then Malcolm pushed his cock slowly and smoothly into Don's virgin asshole. Don gave a moan of pure pleasure at being finally taken up the bunghole, and by a man as handsome and as loving as Malcolm, and taken by a cock as thick and satisfying as Malcolm's. In his sudden ecstasy, Don opened more easily and more smoothly than either of them had expected, and sucked the whole length of Malcolm's rigid pole right the way up his asshole, to the root.

"Ah, shit, you're up me, Malcolm, man," Don groaned loudly. "You're right the way up me and it feels so fuckin' good, man."

Malcolm began to pump his dick in and out of Don's asshole: a tighter, more exciting, and more satisfying asshole than any Malcolm had ever fucked before. His movements were slow and easy at first, as he slid in and out of Don's butthole, then built in rhythm, in depth, and intensity as Don—now gasping and writhing as Malcolm impaled him on his sweet hard-on—showed he could take a serious butt-fucking.

"Use my ass, man," Don ordered throatily as he lay back, heart hammering, ass up, legs thrown wide open, now totally into it; the cock filling his rectum filled his chest with a soaring ecstasy that he could never have imagined, and that made him have to shout out, "Fuck my hot, tight ass with your hot pole! Make that asshole yours, man! My butthole is yours! Fill me with dick! Pound me! Fill me with your come, man! Fuck me! 'Cause I'm yours, man! I'm totally, utterly yours! Give it to me, man! Fuck me up the ass!"

Malcolm leaned forward as he poled Don's tight smooth hole and kissed Don so hard on the mouth it hurt; he swallowed Don's panting breaths as he bruised his lips with his passionate hunger for Don's kisses, Don's tongue, Don's glittering saliva.

Don wrapped his arms around Malcolm's broad shoulders as he felt Malcolm's hot erection slither in and out of his open backside—the first cock he'd ever had up him, in his rectum, inside his body—gasping and groaning from being so fully and passionately anally filled. They kept their mouths pressed hotly together for the whole time they fucked, all their anger with each other understood now, and transmuted as Don finally gave it up for Malcolm, surrendered to Malcolm utterly and completely. And found an ecstasy Don had never believed was possible as he yielded to the beautiful, thick, and rigid brown cock sliding in and out of his juicy, dilated asshole with increasing weight and speed, pushing Don uncontrollably up to his own climax as it rammed against his pulsing prostate with greater and greater firmness.

"Oh, Jesus, man!" Don yelled. "Fuck me, man! Fuck my motherfucking brains out! I love you, man! Give me that big brown lovemuscle till I can't take no more! Oh, Malcolm, oh, God!—"

And later, with a load of Malcolm's hot come up his thoroughly-fucked asshole, Don called Gregory up on his mobile and told him to get his slack ass over to Prince Fela's, along with their gear. Gregory drove over with Thom, and the Boot Sex Massive performed their first ever live gig for the freaky revelers at Prince Fela's place in Notting Hill Gate.

Afterwards, as dawn was crawling up above the skyline, Don turned to Bobbi. "You were right, man," he said, rubbing his bleary eyes.

" 'Course I was, man," Bobbi said, yawning sleepily. "Uh, what about?" he asked.

"The party, man," Don said. "No one leaves without they've done something they never did before."

"In so many ways, man," Bobbi said thoughtfully. His lips ached, his throat ached, his stomach was queasy from swallowing so much spunk, his thighs and arms ached, his still semi-stiff dick ached, and his asshole ached so much it was pulsing warmly.

It had been one of the best nights Bobbi could remember.

About the Authors

SHANE ALLISON, born and raised in Florida, has had poems, stories, and reviews in *New Delta Review, Mississippi Review, Mind Caviar, Van Gogh's Ear, Suspect Thoughts,* and *Velvet Mafia*. His poems have appeared in anthologies such as *Coloring Book: An Eclectic Anthology of Fiction and Poetry by Multicultural Writers, Fantasy Made Flesh, Wild and Willing*, and he has work forthcoming in *Gents, Badboys and Barbarians 2:This New Breed,* and *I Do/I Don't: Queers on Marriage*. His book of poems, *Black Fag,* is out from Future Tense Press. He is thirty-one, single, and loves Kung Fu movies. Shout-outs to Darieck Scott and the Gods and Goddesses at Cleis Press for giving his work a home.

RED JORDAN AROBATEAU is the author of forty books of gay, lesbian, bisexual, and trans fiction, poetry, and plays. He sells his work on his website at redjordanarobateau.com and through his mail order address at 484 Lake Park Ave., PMB228, Oakland, CA 94610 USA.

BELASCO's work has been collected in *The Brothers of New Essex*, and has been featured in *Best Gay Erotica*, *GBM*, *Whazzup!*, and *Meatmen*. His chapbooks include *Lust for Sale, Confessions, Enter Lewd*, and *Nasssssty*, and the collections *What Gran'maw Saw, Nuthin' But Feet & Azz, Li'l Big Dick in Midnight B-Ballin'*, and *Boo: Down 'n Dirty*. He lives in Los Angeles.

CHRISTOPHER DAVID, a passionate spirit with much to say, was born to write...but not just to write...but to sing, speak, nurture, and motivate. Born and raised in the heart of Bedford-Stuyvesant in the borough of Brooklyn, Christopher David is geared up and ready to revolutionize the way the world views him, homosexuality, and the black experience. To find out more visit him at www.christopherscypher.com.

SAMUEL R. DELANY is a novelist and critic. His fiction includes *Dhalgren*, the *Return to Neveryon* series, and *Atlantis: Three Tales*. His nonfiction writing includes *The Motion of Light in Water*, *Village Voice* best-seller *Times Square Red, Times Square Blue*, and *1984: Selected Letters*. Winner of the William Whitehead Memorial Award for a Lifetime's Contribution to Lesbian and Gay Literature, he currently teaches at Temple University in Philadelphia.

WILLIAM S. DOAN (b. 1940) is a writer, photographer, and political activist. His previous books include the cult classic *Photoflexion: 100 years of Bodybuilding Photographs* and *Al Urban*, a monograph about the late pioneer on male photography. His photographs have been acquired by a dozen American museums, including the Art Institute of Chicago and the Historic New Orleans Collection, as well as the Tom of Finland Foundation. Since 1981, he has been the secretary of the Doan Family Foundation. He is an associate member of ONYX. Washington, DC, multimedia artist Brian S. Baker has been William Doan's muse since 1999. All the characters in "Photographic Memory" are fictional.

GIOVANNI is a thirty-year-old professional weight trainer by day and an aspiring writer by night, born in Atlanta, Georgia, and raised by a mother who dedicated thirty-four years of her life to teaching English in the public school system, and a grandfather who spent the last thirty years of his life instilling good values in his grandson. He spent two years of college working toward a degree in journalism before developing an interest in bodybuilding and leaving school to pursue a career as a personal trainer.

THOMAS GLAVE is the author of *Whose Song? and Other Stories*, the forthcoming *Toward Nobilities of the Imagination: Essays*, and editor of the forthcoming anthology *A Fi We Time: Contemporary Caribbean Lesbian and Gay Writing*. He has recently completed *The Torturer's Wife and Other Not-Fictions*. He is an assistant professor of English and Africana Studies at the State University of New York at Binghamton.

JAMES EARL HARDY is the author of the best-selling *B-Boy Blues* series, which chronicles the relationship between a journalist-turned-creative-writing teacher and a bike messenger-turned-supermodel/actor. The titles include: *B-Boy Blues: A Seriously Sexy, Fiercely Funny, Black-on-Black Love Story; 2nd Time Around; If Only for One Nite; The Day Eazy-E Died;* and *Love the One You're With*. The sixth and final novel, *A House Is Not a Home*, will be released in spring 2005. A 1993 honors graduate of the Columbia University School of Journalism, his byline as a feature writer and cultural critic has appeared in *Entertainment Weekly*, *Essence*,

Newsweek, *OUT*, *VIBE*, *The Source*, and *The Washington Post*. He lives in Atlanta.

REGINALD HARRIS's *Ten Tongues: Poems* was a finalist for the 2003 Lambda Literary Award. Head of the Information Technology Support Department for the Enoch Pratt Free Library, he has received Individual Artist Awards for both poetry and fiction from the Maryland State Arts Council. His work has appeared in numerous venues, including *5AM*, *African-American Review*, *Harvard Gay and Lesbian Review*, *Sou'wester*, and the anthologies *Black Silk*; *Chocolate Flava*; *Intimacy: Erotic Stories of Love, Lust, and Marriage by Black Men*; and *Brown Sugar I, II*, and *IV*. Born in Annapolis, Maryland, he lives with his partner in Baltimore.

JONATHAN IVY KIDD earned both his 1997 BA from the University of Michigan and 2004 PhD from Yale University in the fields of African-American Studies and English Literature. His work has been previously published by *Velvet Mafia* and *Clamor* magazine. A proponent of drama, Kidd currently resides in New York City where he runs Adam, Eve, & Steve Productions, a theater/film company which he cofounded in 2001.

TIP LANGLEY is an actor, singer, writer, and longtime connoisseur of erotica who lives in Oakland, California.

CANAAN PARKER is the author of two novels, *The Color of Trees* and *Sky Daddy*. A songwriter and graphic artist, Canaan is a native New Yorker.

ROBERT F. REID-PHARR is professor of English in the PhD Program in English at the Graduate Center of the City University of New York. He is the author of two books of criticism: *Conjugal Union: The Body, the House and the Black American* and *Black Gay Man: Essays*. He lives in Brooklyn.

DOMINGO RHODES was born in north Louisiana, and lives and works north of Los Angeles. He is enamored of all things Tyson Beckford and has spent most of his thirty-six years day-dreaming.

JAY RUSSELL is the author of *Booty Boys* and *Voodoo Man*, both published by Idol Books. He is in his thirties, lives in London, and works at a library.

BLAINE TEAMER was born and raised in Pennsylvania. A Penn State graduate who earned his degree in English in 1991, he moved to Los Angeles and began work at The National Black Gay and Lesbian Leadership Forum. A former member of the Los Angeles Theater Center's WORDSMITH program, his theatrical works are *Momma's Boys*, *Black Coffee*, *Delicate Flowers*, and *Pandora's Trunk*, which was invited to be performed at the renowned biannual National Black Theater Festival in 2003. His published work includes *Maya: Diasporic Juks* and *Shady: A Novel.*

About the Editor

DARIECK SCOTT lives in San Francisco, and is the author of *Traitor to the Race* (1995). His fiction has appeared in the anthologies *Black Like Us, Shade, Giant Steps, Flesh and the Word 4,* and *Ancestral House*. He has published nonfiction essays in *Callaloo*, *GLQ*, *The Americas Review*, and the collection *Gay Travels*. He is assistant professor of English at the University of California at Santa Barbara, where he teaches African American literature and creative writing. He has recently finished a sci-fi manuscript, *The Missing*, and is at work on a book of criticism entitled *Black Bottom: Male Rape and the Body of History in the African American Literary Imagination*.